THE ONE WHERE THEY FALL IN LOVE

ALSO BY CRISTINA WOLF

How to Write a Rom-Com

THE ONE WHERE THEY FALL IN LOVE

CRISTINA WOLF

HEAD of ZEUS

An Aria Book

First published in the UK in 2026 by Head of Zeus,
part of Bloomsbury Publishing Plc

9 7 5 3 1 2 4 6 8

A catalogue record for this book is available from the British Library.

ISBN (PB): 9781035915392
ISBN (eBook): 9781035915361

Cover design: Jessie Price
Cover illustration: Debs Lim
Typeset by Lumina Datamatics Ltd

Printed and bound in Great Britain by Clays Ltd, Elcograf S.p.A.

MIX
Paper | Supporting responsible forestry
FSC® C018072
www.fsc.org

Bloomsbury Publishing Plc
50 Bedford Square, London, WC1B 3DP, UK
Bloomsbury Publishing Ireland Limited,
29 Earlsfort Terrace, Dublin 2, D02 AY28, Ireland

HEAD OF ZEUS LTD
5–8 Hardwick Street
London, EC1R 4RG

To find out more about our authors and books visit www.headofzeus.com
For product safety related questions contact productsafety@bloomsbury.com

For anyone who feels like the hype girl.

You're the main character of your own story.

"The minute I heard my first love story, I started looking for you, not knowing how blind that was. Lovers don't finally meet somewhere. They're in each other all along."

— Rumi

NOTE TO READERS

While my books are romantic comedies, there may be topics in this book that might be triggering for some readers. If you consider content warnings to be spoilers, you may want to skip this page.

This book contains a main character with obsessive compulsive disorder and panic attacks. I acknowledge that everyone's experience with this illness is different, and the experience of this character is not intended to depict the universal experience of OCD, because it does not exist. Having OCD myself, I hope that this story feels relatable to some readers, while helping others to understand the day to day lives of those affected.

The book also contains mention of divorce, explicit language, a sibling with a disability, and descriptive sexual scenes.

Please take note of these warnings if you need them, and always do what is best for you and your mental health.

xx Cristina

PROLOGUE

Elle

"I'm just saying that if I die a tragic death, don't go on *Dateline* and lie about me."

Lucy stuffs another book on my already full shelf and it bangs against the wall with a *thud*.

"You're reading way too much into it, Luce," I say, shaking my head at her.

"No," Lucy stops me. "There is no way that literally every victim on these shows '*made the room brighter when they walked through the door*.' I mean I don't know them, but *statistically*, there's no way," she rants.

"Okay, sure," I reply, placating her. If I don't stop her now, we'll never finish unpacking. "If I ever have to go on *Dateline* and talk about you, which I really hope I *don't*, I'll say you were a sassy bitch who never returned her shopping cart."

"That's all I'm asking!" Satisfied that she's proven her point, she swivels around on the wood floor to grab another box of books. I roll my eyes at my best friend. Lucy's helping me move into my new studio apartment, and she's been on this tirade about *Dateline* for at least ten minutes.

Technically it isn't my *new* apartment anymore—I've lived here for almost two months, ever since Lucy moved in with her fiancé, but I haven't had the chance to fully unpack all of my boxes that I drove—*horribly*—uptown in a rented U-Haul from the apartment Lucy and I used to share.

We spent most of the morning putting together a bookcase from Ikea, and we only mixed up the screws once. Lucy is now filling said bookshelf with the hundreds of books I own, and I think there's a real chance the whole thing might come crashing down under the weight of it all. That would be just my luck.

"Can I suggest that you just stop watching crime shows? I don't think it's good for you," I say, flopping down onto my bed. I look up to admire the pictures I hung above it. From this angle, they're mostly straight.

"Liam likes them, which might be a bit of a red flag, but I'm trying to make an effort to like what he likes. Apparently, mature people in relationships do that." She shrugs at the last statement, implying that she is not used to being said mature person in any relationship.

"Well, it's good to know that he at least has *some* red flags. It's creepy how perfect he is."

"Perfect? Where is he while we're doing all of this manual labor?" Lucy scoffs.

"You're the one that told me he has a business to run," I state, using her own words against her. Lucy smiles. I know she misses him, but this is the first weekend we've had alone together since she met Liam, and I am not going to let it be derailed by boy-talk.

"Ugh, my fiancé is *so dreamy*," I say in a high-pitched voice. "I miss him *soooooo* much when I'm away from him." I laugh as she throws a pillow at me.

A loud bang shakes the floor above us and both Lucy and I jump. My eyes roll to the ceiling, half expecting it to fall down on me. This building is at least a hundred years old, and my apartment is in the basement. I'm not fully confident in its structural soundness.

Lucy looks concerned. "I think the girl upstairs is moving out," I say, turning my attention to another box of pictures. "I've seen her carrying boxes down the stairs a couple times."

"Have you ever spoken to her?" Lucy asks, walking into the minuscule kitchen to get a drink. No girls weekend is complete without pre-mixed margaritas. I make grabby-hands at her and she pours me one, too.

"No, I don't think she's home much. I rarely hear any noise coming from up there."

Lucy makes a face that reads *yikes*. "You're so screwed for the next neighbor then. They'll probably be the loudest person you've ever met."

"Thanks for speaking that into existence, Luce," I huff, glaring at her. Lucy shrugs, downs her drink, and rips the tape off the next box.

ONE

Elle

This cannot be said enough: Living in New York City in your twenties is nothing like *Friends* makes it out to be.

Really, nothing about being in your twenties is how *Friends* made it out to be. I'm thirty years old, and I have not had an all-consuming romance like Ross and Rachel. I haven't found my Chandler. I don't have a close-knit group of friends who would drop everything if they heard my apartment was on fire. Or who would go to see a terrible play just because I'm in it. I don't have a two-bedroom apartment and a roommate who I can share clothes with. I don't even have a one-bedroom apartment. Heck, even when I *had* a roommate, *we* didn't even have a one-bedroom apartment.

Man, I'm feeling cynical tonight.

I blame the episode of *Friends* that was on TV when I got home from work. It was "The One Where No One is Ready." Ross makes a speech at the museum, and the whole gang has to dress up to go support him. Chandler steals

Joey's underwear, Joey wears all of Chandler's clothes and does lunges, Phoebe has "the hummus." It's a classic. Damn, I'd kill for that kind of support— renting a tux just to watch another friend make a boring speech, someone doing the little things just to make my day better.

I reach across the bed for my phone, thinking about Lucy. My best friend and former roommate moved away to live her happily ever after with a hunky mountain man she met upstate. I miss Lucy, but I'm happy for her. Or at least, I *want* to be happy for her. Given that I'll be her maid of honor in three months, I should really work on my "happy for you" face. But, how does Rachel put it? I'm about 80 percent happy and 20 percent jealous.

I want to call Lucy. I want to tell her that at my annual review last week, I was promoted to editor.

Editor.

I've worked my ass off for five years at Heartwarming Romance. I made copies and got coffee as an assistant, continued to make copies and fought tooth-and-nail to acquire books as an Assistant Editor, and then Associate, and now, I am an editor. I did it. My hard work paid off.

Maybe I'll just text her instead, in case I interrupt her cooking or watching TV with Liam, or whatever else it is couples do. I don't want to bother her.

SLAM!

My hesitation is interrupted by a huge crash from the apartment above me. Of all the things I've tried to actually manifest in my life—a boyfriend, a thousand dollars, a friend that didn't move away—Lucy's one statement about a noisy neighbor just *had* to be the one to come true. That's another example of how unrealistic *Friends* is: the gang all live in the same building, and don't have problems with their neighbors. Well, except for Mr. Heckles, but he only lasted a few episodes.

I can already tell that my new neighbor and I are *not* going to be friends. He is a self-centered ogre sent from the sixth layer of hell to torture me. Granted, I haven't met him yet to confirm this, but I haven't gotten a wink of sleep since he moved in two days ago.

It is almost 9 p.m., and the jerk has already done a thirty-minute session on his treadmill, dropped what I presume to be everything in his shower, and slammed the door so violently I swear dust started falling from my ceiling. I only saw the girl who used to live there a couple times, but I really miss her right now.

For the past two nights, the guy has left the apartment around eight o'clock, and I've heard weird noises above me for hours afterward. The floor is so thin that I can't tune whatever it is out. I'm really hoping this is not a regular thing, because I *love* sleep. I live for my sleep. If I don't sleep, I'm the most bitter, nasty version of myself. I know New York is the city that never sleeps, but that rule doesn't apply to me.

I haven't met him, but so far I know this guy stays out all night and seems to love heart-pumping workouts. I don't think we'll get along.

I close my eyes again, trying to focus on my meditation practice. It's not long before I hear scratching above me. Seriously, *what the hell*?

Scratch. Scratch. Whine. I wonder if the guy has a very needy cat. I put my pillow over my head, and focus on the sounds of the nightlife outside to try and distract myself.

It's the crying that finally propels me out of the bed.

My apartment building is an old brownstone, so each floor is split up into either two or three apartments. When Lucy moved out, I had to move to a smaller apartment a few blocks from our old studio, because renting in New York is *absurdly* expensive. I'm in the basement where there are two other studios, so I have to walk upstairs to the entrance level to get to New Guy's door.

I'm not really sure what my plan is as I climb the stairs to the first floor. Maybe he has a roommate whose humanity I could appeal to? A knot of nerves builds in my stomach, and I wrap my sweatshirt tighter around my torso and look behind me for the tenth time as I round the railing of the stairs. I doubt any resident of the building is a serial killer. We have to consent to a background check when applying for the apartment, so hopefully this expedition won't end in me getting murdered. Something a lot of people don't realize about New York is yes, we do all live on top of each other, but we never really see our neighbors. So I could be living next to Ted Bundy and not even know it.

I swallow hard as I approach the door to 2A. The anxious voice in my head makes me pause. *What are you doing, Elle?*

Avenging my lost sleep, I answer myself. *I love my sleep.*

I turn back around. This is ridiculous. I can't investigate a noise if no one is home.

And then I hear the crying again.

I take a deep breath as my shaking fist knocks against the door.

It's met with a small, yappy bark, and I jump back in surprise. Okay, definitely not a cat.

I see a shadow of the dog moving back and forth in the crack under the door. His sad little barks are clearer with just the door between us. Mystery solved. I start to back up to make my way back to the stairs when I hear the barks morph into a muffled snorting sound.

I look down and see a small black nose trying to squeeze under the inch-wide space under the door. The poor dog is squishing his nose so much that he makes himself sneeze.

"Oh, puppy," I whine, crouching down at the door. This poor thing must have separation anxiety. My annoyance towards my new neighbor immediately turns to rage and disdain. Who leaves a dog alone all night? When will he be back? What is *wrong* with this guy?

I boop the dog's nose with my pointer finger and he sneezes again. "It's okay, buddy. You're okay," I coo. I give the door a once over, wondering what the chances are that he locked the deadbolt before he left, and then scoff at myself. I would need three of me to break that door down.

"But I'd do it for you, bud," I say softly to my new friend.

The dog sticks his tongue under the door. I can picture him in downward-facing dog, butt in the air, head turned to the side to be able to get his snout under the door. I giggle as he licks my finger. What am I going to do? I can't in good conscience leave him here alone. And it's not like I would be able to get to sleep with all the whining anyway.

God, I hate this schmuck and I haven't even met him.

The black nose returns to the door crack. He's snorting like a horse. I can't suppress the smile that spreads across my face.

When I was eight, I convinced my mom that my brother Nicky needed a dog. As sad as it sounds, I knew my only chance of getting one was if I made it about Nicky. I did all kinds of research on our dated desktop about the benefits of dogs for kids with Down's syndrome. Finally, we got Meatball. Nicky chose the name. I wasn't mad about it because Meatball was a bulldog with an eating problem—that is, he *never stopped* eating. Food, treats, trees, grass, dirt, anything. He once found a box of candies that he individually unwrapped before eating them. That incident was only topped by the time he jumped up (*jumped* being a strong word) onto the kitchen table and ate an entire plate of bacon. I loved that dog so much.

I remember how he used to stick his nose in the corner of the back door and snort, trying to smell anything he could. My heart hurts watching this poor guy do the same.

"Wait here, I'll be right back," I say, presumably losing my damn mind. No, losing my mind would have been breaking the door down. This is one step below that.

When I get back down to my apartment, I quickly grab some peanut butter, a spoon, and my yoga notebook off of the counter. Yes, I'm going to sit in that damn hallway and keep the dog company, because that's the kind of crazy I am.

I run back up the stairs with gleeful excitement, a stark contrast to my first trek up this flight earlier. Of course participating in a stakeout with a dog I can't even see is the first thing that would make me happy since Lucy's fleeting visit.

"Hey, bud," I say, sitting on the floor outside of my heartless neighbor's door. "Look what I got." I take a spoonful of the peanut butter and squeeze the spoon under the door.

I smile when I feel a tongue pushing against the other side of the spoon.

This, my mother would say, *is why you're single.*

Damn straight, Mom.

TWO

Oliver

There's a woman sitting outside my door.

Actually, there's a woman *sleeping* outside my door.

I stand there, frozen at the top of the stairs, really unsure of my next move. It's almost 6:30a.m. I don't have time for this.

I swear New York wasn't this crazy when I left.

I take a step closer, careful to be quiet in case I wake her before I figure out how to deal with this. The woman has her back up against the wall adjacent to my door, a notebook in her lap, and a pen falling from her limp hand. I notice a tattoo on the inside of her wrist—the outline of a crescent moon and three stars. I stare at her face, side-stepping the fact that she is *stunning*, and gauge how likely it is that she is insane. I mean, her sleeping outside of a stranger's door gives me some indication, but I'd like to know how likely she is to jump up and shank me when I try to wake her.

Her hair is tossed in a messy bun at the top of her head, but some untamed blonde curls seem to have escaped confinement. They frame her face, where plump lips sit just barely parted, a shallow breath passing through them every few moments.

I wonder what color her eyes are.

Get it together, Cole. Her eye color has nothing to do with whether she poses a threat at this moment.

Fuck, I'm tired.

I just finished my third night shift in a row, and the ER was especially insane tonight. I'm pretty sure I have pee on my shoe from a catheter that leaked in one patient's room, and I cannot wait to shower. Three night shifts combined with sleeping on my sister Sophia's tiny mattress *and* taking care of her exceptionally needy dog that she adopted before jetting off to a gap year in Italy, has me a bit on edge. And now… *this*.

My gaze drifts to the floor next to the woman, where I spy an open jar of peanut butter and a spoon wedged under my door.

Final answer: Definitely crazy. Probably not a threat.

I clear my throat and she jumps. Not in ready-to-attack mode, but definitely with a why-the-fuck-are-you-disturbing-my-sleep attitude.

Brown. Her eyes are brown. And big, and staring at me like I'm dead meat.

"Can I help you?" I ask, my eyebrows raised.

She studies me, *really* studies me, from top to bottom, before responding. "That depends. Do you live here?" she asks, her voice gravelly from sleep. Her tone implies that *I'm* the one inconveniencing *her*, as if she's not blocking the way into my apartment. She stretches out her neck, turning it side to side.

"Is there a problem?" I reply, crossing my arms.

She stands up abruptly and opens her mouth as if she's about to cuss me out, but a whine from the other side of the door catches both our attention.

"That!" she groans. "Is the fucking problem."

Oh, man. What could he have done? Guilt settles in my stomach for leaving Thor alone for so long, but I didn't have much of a choice. He didn't destroy anything the other night. I could tell that he was scratching on the carpet, but I figured that was the extent of it.

"I'm sorry. Was he barking?"

"*Barking*?" she says in disbelief. "The poor thing was *crying*. Scratching at the door, whining. You've been gone all night! How could you do that to him?"

I'm not really sure how to respond to that. Of course, I'm not happy about leaving him, but the multiple night shifts are making this whole situation difficult to process. Surely this woman could have simply left a note if she was concerned—sleeping outside my door all night feels *wildly* out of proportion. Maybe this is just a very bizarre dream about having a hot neighbor. Although, I think if she *was* a dream-induced hot neighbor, she would be a little nicer.

"Let me get this straight, just so there's no confusion. You're angry with me on *behalf* of the dog, not *because* of the dog?" I say slowly.

"I'm upset, *buddy*, because a dog does not deserve to be left alone in an apartment by himself all night! I can't sleep knowing he's distressed upstairs, and I *need* my sleep." Her gestures get more animated as she gets louder. "Have you never left him alone before?"

"It's my sister's dog, and my sister's apartment. She got him a few weeks ago and then went away, so I moved in and—" I run my hand across the stubble on my jaw. "It's a long story. He must be having a hard time settling in."

"You think?" she huffs, crossing her arms across her chest. I take the brief moment that the berating has ceased to observe her. She's small, about a head shorter than me, with a petite frame and a curvy stature. Her face is round, centered by doe-eyes that pull me in like a magnet. In any other situation, I'd be enraptured by her. Right now, I'm just irritated.

I shake my head. I already feel bad about having to leave the dog, and maybe that's why I didn't want the responsibility of watching a damn dog in the first place. *No offense, Thor*. But I don't need this girl adding to my guilt—she literally doesn't know anything about me. She's already disrupting my schedule by making me stand out here in this hallway, and I'm sure one of the other neighbors is going to come angrily bursting out at any moment.

"Ma'am—" She looks at me funny when I say that. "I'm very sorry if my dog disturbed you, but can we table this discussion for another time? It's pretty late… or early," I amend, seeing the sun start to peek through the shades of a nearby window.

"Ma'am? Did you just *ma'am* me?" Her eyes narrow.

Okay, she definitely looks like she is going to murder me now. Maybe I was wrong about her being a threat. She's small, but I bet she's scrappy.

I take a deep breath and exhale loudly. "I think we got off on the wrong foot. Let's try this again. I'm Oliver." I hold out my hand, which she looks at like it's holding a vial of a fatal disease. After a few moments, I let it awkwardly fall back to my side.

"I'm Elle, and I don't think we can start over after this, *sir*."

"I'm sorry. After *this*?" I question, not sure what she means.

"You upset a dog. That is a capital offense in my book," she says matter-of-factly. She purses her lips and raises an eyebrow at me.

"It's *my* dog!" I say, throwing my hands up.

"And that makes it *better*?"

I blow out a harsh breath. "Okay, I'm going inside now. Please move away from my door."

"Move away from your door?" She scoffs, like *I'm* the crazy one here. "What do you think I'm going to do, follow you in?"

"Honestly, I'm not really sure what you're capable of. You're sitting outside of a stranger's apartment at the ass-crack of dawn with a jar of peanut butter," I say, pushing the key into the lock.

She gives me a hard stare before moving to walk away, but turns back at the top of the stairwell.

"At least tell me the dog's name," she says, her bun flopping as she tilts her head to the side. My annoyance is giving way to pure exhaustion, and I hate to admit it, but I can't help find her hallway-bedhead endearing.

I stop short with one foot in the door. "Why?"

"Because I've been calling him *Buddy*, and I don't want to assume gender. And I have a feeling that he or she and I will become good friends, given that you are clearly as nice to live with as the *Beast*."

I shake my head, so perplexed by every sentence that comes out of this woman's mouth. I would usually be better with comebacks, but I've been trying to keep people alive for ten hours, and my senses are a little dulled. "Thor," I say quickly, cringing. Leave it to my sister to give her dog the most ridiculous name possible. "And please stay away from my apartment—and my dog," I add, tonelessly.

Elle doesn't seem to notice the absurdity of the name. She barely takes a beat before she responds, "Only if you promise not to do a full-blown cardio workout at some ungodly hour today."

"Wha—" I start to say, thinking back to last night, when I couldn't sleep and ran on the treadmill until I couldn't breathe. "What I do in my apartment is none of your business."

"Maybe a run outside would be better for you. Thor might enjoy it," she says, eyeing me knowingly. Why is this woman talking to me like she knows me? It's very unsettling. "And it would be less disruptive to your neighbors," she adds, raising her brows.

"It's freezing outside," I say. Plus, the last time I tried running outside, I wore a black hoodie and hat, and at least three people thought I was going to mug them as I rounded a corner. But I don't tell her that part.

"I hear that's good for your stamina," she says.

"Is that so?" I say, condescendingly. "Do you run?"

"Only when someone is chasing me," she quips back, casually.

I take one more look at her, trying not to get distracted by the hitch of her hip that she has her hand placed on. I look her dead in the eyes, step into my apartment, and slam the door shut.

THREE

Elle

"He is the *worst* human I've ever met!"

"So he's nice, then?" Lucy says, mocking me from the other end of the FaceTime.

"He *is* like the Beast. I was right. He is like a big, hairy beast that stomps around the castle roaring at innocent furniture that—"

"What do you mean *you were right*? Did you call this man a *beast*?" Lucy asks, interrupting me with a concerned tone.

"I called him *the* Beast, as in *Beauty and the Beast*," I explain.

"Yeah, I know what Beast you mean, that doesn't make it any better." Lucy smacks her forehead and shakes her head in disbelief, like I've somehow stressed her out.

"Can I use this opportunity to chime in and request that you please not fall asleep in the hallway of your building in the middle of the night? You know, for like… *safety* reasons?" comes Liam's voice from the background. It's

Saturday morning, which means Liam, being the perfect man that he is, is in the kitchen of their house using his degree from the Culinary Institute to make some kind of delicious breakfast for Lucy.

Lucy is seated on the couch, and I can see the bar top behind her and beautiful wooden ceiling beams above her. Lucy lives in a lake house in upstate New York, in a small town called Hudson Hollow. Having been to the house several times, I know that she is positioned facing the wall-to-wall windows that overlook a gorgeous blue lake, which is probably covered in ice and snow right now.

"Liam, don't take this moment to get all alpha hero on me, okay? Stay over there with your French toast," I tease.

"They're actually lemon ricotta pancakes," he calls back.

"Lemon ricotta?" Lucy says, slightly turning her head toward the kitchen. She has an uneasy look on her face. "What happened to chocolate chip?"

"Lucy, I'm a chef. I can't make chocolate chip pancakes every day. I need some creative liberty," he replies in an exasperated voice.

"You own a restaurant. Be creative there. Your fiancé needs chocolate. It's literally a requirement for marrying me." Her voice is stern, but when she turns her attention back to the phone, she sticks her tongue between her teeth, silently laughing.

I own him, she mouths.

"Oh yeah, real alpha hero," I say with a chuckle.

"I heard that and I know what it means!" Liam calls from the kitchen. "I am marrying a romance novelist, I've been brushing up on my terminology."

Lucy met Liam when she was sent to Hudson Hollow for a work project. She moved in with him a few months ago. Lucy was not only my roommate, but my coworker at Heartwarming. She quit to become a writer. Her first book comes out in a few months.

"Then accept your beta hero status with pride and add some chocolate into that batter!" Lucy yells back, unable to hide the smile that forms on her face. She turns around, and I can tell she wants to make sure that our banter hasn't actually offended Liam. He knows what he signed up for when he stole Lucy from me (as I frequently like to remind him). We come with baggage, and weekly FaceTime calls. "Love you, babe," she coos.

"Love you, babe!" I shout around a mouthful of English muffin. I look down at my depressing breakfast. I would accept pancakes even if there was no chocolate right now.

"You two are weird," Liam mumbles in the background.

"So, Liam, pop quiz. Elle's got a jerk for an upstairs neighbor. What trope are we looking at?" Lucy asks, walking over to the bar in their kitchen. Liam's frame comes into view, and I can't help but chuckle when I see him in an apron that says "Property of a romance author." Liam's dog, Blue, is splayed out across pretty much the entire kitchen floor, so Liam doesn't have much room to maneuver. Liam tosses him a blueberry before turning his attention to Lucy.

"Well," he says, pretending to ponder the question by scratching his jaw. He flips a few locks of his blonde hair out of his face. "I would say neighbors-to-lovers, and from what it sounds like, some enemies-to-lovers as well." Lucy gives him a high five.

"No! *No* lovers. *Just* enemies," I grunt back.

The image of Oliver standing over me last night flashes through my mind. I can't deny that for a moment when I opened my eyes last night, I was mildly terrified. It took me a moment to get my bearings, given that I didn't intend to fall asleep in the hallway and leave myself exposed to, well, *anything*. But when I saw Oliver standing over me, the only thing I could think was "*Oh shit.*" Because the man is *huge*. And it wasn't just because I was sitting down. He is a full head taller than me, and in the middle of arguing with him, I couldn't help but notice the solid muscles on either side of his neck. Yes, I was standing there, fighting with a stranger, wondering how the hell this guy turns his head. He is literally the definition of tall, dark, and handsome—however much I hate to admit it. His brown hair looked like it had been cut short and was starting to grow back in waves. Dark stubble lined his face, and he looked about as tired as I feel now.

"You are very sassy today," Lucy notes, sitting on a barstool and pulling her knee into her chest. She's wearing one of Liam's sweatshirts, and it drapes halfway off her shoulder in the effortlessly chic way that only men's clothes do. I try to remember the last time I wore a guy's sweatshirt, and a wave of sadness comes over me and settles in my chest when I realize I can't. These calls with Lucy used to be a solace for me, but lately my brain likes to use them as an opportunity to point out everything Lucy has that I *don't*.

"I'm just tired," I reply automatically.

"Well maybe you shouldn't be staking out strangers' apartments all night," Lucy says, raising her eyebrows as if to say, "*Duh!*"

"Well, a normal human would think: *Huh, this woman has been keeping my dog company all night, and she said she can hear me through the floorboards, maybe I should be quiet.*" I deepen my voice, imitating Oliver. "But no, not him. This jerk gets on a freaking treadmill at 7 a.m. after being out all night. Who lives like that?"

"You may be thinking about this stranger's sleep habits a bit too much," Lucy says, a wary look on her face.

"Only because his sleep habits are affecting mine. And you *know* how I feel about sleep."

"I know, I know," Lucy replies quickly, nodding. A beat passes between us, and although I'm fully ready to continue ranting about the inconsiderate oaf that lives upstairs, Lucy changes the subject. "Hey, what happened with that guy? James? You haven't mentioned him lately."

"Oh, he's been gone for weeks. Keep up," Liam says. Lucy narrows her eyes at him.

"It's true," I say.

"Why? I liked him," Lucy whines.

"You never met him," Liam deadpans.

"Hey you, be quiet over there!" Lucy scolds.

"I kept forgetting he existed, so I figured it was best to let him go." I shrug. It's the truth, and I genuinely feel nothing about it.

"Aw, Elle—"

"Don't *aww* me," I reply with an eye roll. "I'm not torn up about it. He was just so *blah*. All of them are." Lucy grimaces, but she doesn't press the issue. After all these years, she's learned not to argue with me about my love life.

"Well, I have another bone to pick with you."

"I never understood that expression. Why would anyone pick bones?" I make a mental note to Google it later.

"Don't try and deflect," Lucy says, eyeing me.

"What?" I ask, trying to remain innocent.

"Oh, I don't know… Maybe you forgot that even though I live in Bumblefuck, Nowhere—"

"Rude," Liam interjects.

"I still check my email," Lucy continues. "And I still receive weekly PubLunch newsletters that update me on the goings on of the publishing industry."

Busted.

"I was going to tell you. It just happened the other day," I start, but Lucy raises her brows at me. "I've had a lot going on."

"Assaulting people in hallways and such," Liam mumbles.

Lucy and I ignore him. "Elle, I'm so happy for you," she says, and the genuine pride in her voice makes me inwardly cringe.

"Thanks," I say, feigning a smile.

"You're… happy about this, right?" Lucy asks warily.

"Of course. I'm excited. Moving up the ladder." Lucy doesn't say anything, just watches me, and I can tell she's not convinced. I speak before she has a chance to, practically stumbling over my words in my haste to get them out. "I need to plan tonight's class. I'll talk to you tomorrow, 'kay?"

"Okay," Lucy agrees, clearly noting that I don't want to talk about my promotion and respecting it. I love her for that. "And oh, before I forget, I'm coming to the city next week for a meeting in the office—and Ruby's new book launch."

"Ruby's book launch? You think that's a good idea?" I say with a skeptical look. Lucy and Heartwarming's most popular author aren't on the best of terms after Lucy's stint in Hudson Hollow resulted in *Lucy* writing a book for

Heartwarming, not Ruby, as intended. Even though it all worked out and Ruby started another series for the imprint, they haven't been in a room together since.

"Anne wants me to go to try to smooth things over so maybe Ruby will write a blurb for my book."

"Wow, a wedding and a book. When did you get so busy?" I say, shaking my head.

"I know, right? My plans used to solely consist of sweatpants and staying home," she says with a goofy smile. "Anyway, can't wait to see you and talk wedding planning!"

"Absolutely," I reply. "Can't wait."

After we hang up, I don't move right away. I drop my phone and put my head in my hands. If Lucy were still here, everything would be different. *I* would be different. Lucy was a self-described shut-in and I made it my mission to help her "get out there," even when I didn't really want to either. But I've found that when I'm focused on other people—my family, Lucy, my boss—I have less time to be stuck with my own thoughts. When I was being Lucy's hype girl, pushing her to go after her now fiancé, I poured all my energy into being there for her. When I lived at home, I was always aware of what my family needed. If Mom was taking Nicky to the doctor, that meant she wouldn't have time to fold the towels or take something out for dinner. I acted before I was told. I anticipated people's needs. That's what I'm good at.

But now, I don't have to force Lucy to go out for dinner, so I usually get take-out. I feel less and less motivated to fight the "sweatpants and stay home" lifestyle that Lucy embraced, so that is what I do.

After I finish my breakfast, I pull out my yoga notebook and start to plan tonight's class. I started teaching at a studio on Columbus Avenue last year, after years of trying to find a studio that worked for me.

Before trying yoga for the first time in college, I was one of those people who thought it wasn't that hard. I took my first class in my sophomore year. Ten minutes into the class, I wanted to crawl into a hole and hide. I was a flailing mess of arms and legs and bumped into the girl next to me three times. She was understanding the first two times. By the third, she looked like she wanted to kill me.

But the next week, I went back. And again the week after that. Even though I made an absolute fool out of myself, I loved it. I loved how the instructor's words moved in rhythm with the movements. I loved the structure—warm up, sun salutations, flow, savasana. It was comforting.

I'm still not the best yogi I've ever seen. But the mat has become a place where I can commit to failure. I can fall over and laugh at myself. I can make mistakes in my instruction, confuse my right and left, and feel completely comfortable. I mainly teach beginner classes. Instructing a group of people who don't expect me to be perfect feels a lot like talking to my brother. I can be my most authentic self, and have fun. Which I don't do all that often.

I break my paper up into three sections and plan out my sun salutations and flow. I've found that yoga can get monotonous after a while—plank, upward-facing dog, downward-facing dog, repeat, repeat—so I do some funky sun sals that people don't expect. I like to get the heart rate up, but also allow for moments of moving meditation. Those are my favorite parts of yoga, when everyone's eyes are closed, and we're breathing in tandem. It's powerful.

I put my pen down and put one hand on my heart and one on my belly. I take a deep breath and close my eyes. I focus on taking a long, slow inhale, feeling my lungs expand. I fall into meditation mode, as if I was teaching. I picture myself in front of the class and try to imagine what moves would make the most sense to end the practice.

And then I jump nearly two feet off of my chair at the sound of screaming music.

My gaze travels upward, anger rising in me. The jerk is blasting Metallica at full volume. I don't know what this guy's problem is, but I intend to find out.

My yoga students find me lying flat on my back when they enter the studio. Before I teach a class, I need that moment to ground myself. To have a moment of peace where I'm not worrying about a million and one things I have to do. I'm simply still.

I never really understood what the word "grounded" meant until I started studying yoga. As a kid, I was always obsessed with the sky. I loved being the one to take Meatball out at night, because I wanted to be able to stand and stare at the sky for as long as I wanted without any judgment. It made me feel small, but I loved being reminded that there was a whole universe out there. In the grand scheme of things, I was insignificant, so why should I care what anyone else thought about me?

As I got older, though, I learned how much I loved to be on the ground. I would always lay on the floor in our living room, and I figured it was because I wanted to be close to Meatball—which was true—but there was a comfort in being low, close to the earth. As I studied more yoga practices and learned the importance of savasana—the practice of being still, like a corpse, at the end of a practice—I realized that even though I loved the stars, it was just as important to connect to the ground beneath me as well.

I have some soft rock music playing in the background of the studio as the students come in. The owner, Tanya, likes us to call the people taking the class "students," and also says we should address them as "friends" to "make the space seem more welcoming." I try, I really do. But I always end up reverting back to "people" or "you guys." I think it's a Jersey thing.

"Welcome, friends," I say, trying not to visibly cringe. I straighten my mic on my ear and fiddle with the knot I've made on the back of my shirt. "Take a seat on the mat and we'll meet in hero's pose or easy seat to start."

I see the last spots fill in and I signal to Tanya to start my playlist on the speakers. The music I play during class usually surprises people. I'm not into the meditative, chanting vibe. I play contemporary songs. I like the mood of the music to be rhythmic and sexy. That's the kind of class I would like to take. And I figure if I structure the class how I would like it, maybe other people like me would like it too.

The group is all women across a range of different ages, and many of them are frequent members. I hear a lot from my students that they like my classes because I am funny and make yoga easy to understand, so I guess that's why they keep coming back. I own that, because for the next thirty minutes, the mat is my sanctuary, and I want to make it theirs, too.

I run the class through a series of sun salutations—downward-facing dog to plank, chaturanga, back up to plank, child's pose to upward-facing dog. I only fall twice, both times on half-moon pose because balance is not my strong suit. The crowd laughs just as they did when I forgot a *vinyasa*, and because they were falling with me.

I leave feeling refreshed, ready to have a nice evening to myself—or do battle with my new neighbor, whichever happens to come first.

FOUR

Oliver

There should be a support group for first year residents.

Because it's pretty irrational to say to people, "*Here, after eight years of school, your reward is working absurdly long shifts at all hours of the day until you can't feel your feet anymore. And by the way, don't kill anyone,*" and expect them not to freak out.

I worked three night shifts this weekend, so I finally have some solid time off. It's Monday, and my next shift isn't until Wednesday night. After getting some much-needed sleep, I spend the afternoon transforming Sophia's apartment into a place I can actually live for the next year. I have OCD, and while I wish people knew that it consists of *more* than just wanting things neat and orderly, that is still a big part of it. So a deep cleaning was necessary to help settle my mind a bit in this new space. Maybe now I'll be able to sleep more soundly.

While I was cleaning, I was also trying to wrap my brain around the fact that I'm really doing this. To my family, "this" is matching for an internal medicine residency at

Mount Sinai to live out my parents' lifelong dream of me becoming a doctor.

To me, "this" is just barely surviving having moved back to a coast that I never planned to live on again.

It's not that I don't *want* to be a doctor. It's that I'm *tired*. I busted my ass for four years in undergrad at Stanford and then another four in med school. I was told I'd make a great doctor from the moment I could pronounce "chemistry," and I'm tired of it. I'm tired of the pressure from my family. I'm tired of the weight that my family puts on said expectation. And I'm tired of doing something that is supposed to be my passion, but isn't something I really *love*. I'm tired of having no one to share the burden with.

Sophia always tells me that I like to avoid things. And it's true. I thrive in avoidance. I butted heads with my father for my entire childhood before I finally had the opportunity to avoid him in the best way possible: moving to the literal opposite side of the country. A six-hour flight separated me from my family in Long Island, and I finally felt *free*. But it didn't last for long. My father was furious when I didn't match with a surgery residency. At that point, I didn't think I would match at all, and it felt like a relief of sorts. So when I finally matched with one residency—at Mount Sinai in New York City, where my father's Stanford roommate just *happens* to be Chief of the Medical Staff—I found myself on a plane back to the state I escaped eight years ago.

Needless to say, I've been having second thoughts about moving back to New York for months. But after I just spent the last eight years of my life dedicated to becoming a doctor, what choice did I have?

None, according to my father.

So yeah, a support group would be nice. I don't have any friends at my residency, and my messed-up schedule and near-constant exhaustion makes it pretty hard to meet people out in the world. The only person I know in New York is my friend Henry, who I've only seen a handful of times since we graduated college. The one pro to living in Sophia's apartment is that it is close to Henry, who is a much-needed comfort right now. That, and the fact that I get a free membership to the gym he owns.

After a particularly brutal session with the punching bag that didn't distract me from ruminating on my life choices as much as I'd hoped, Henry and I start to head back to my apartment for pizza and beer. My hand is halfway to the door when I see a wisp of blonde hair out of the corner of my eye, and I spin so that my back is blocking the door.

"What are you doing?" Henry asks, just stopping short of chest-bumping me. He's shorter than me by a few inches, but I'm positive he would crush me in an arm wrestle—not that I would ever sign myself up for that. The guy's arms are so wide, I'm not sure how he fits through most doorways.

I ignore him and block the door, peeking over my shoulder to see Elle walk in the other direction. She has on a puffy winter coat and black leggings so tight they should be illegal. Her hair is up in a ponytail, but it still reaches down to the middle of her back and swishes side-to-side with every step. She has a yoga mat strapped around her back like a bag, and she stuffs her hands in her pockets as she walks in the direction of our building. I get a weird feeling in my chest when I think about her walking home in the dark by herself, and I try to shake it off. We only live a block away, she'll be fine.

"Sorry," I say to Henry as he smacks my arm. "Thought I saw something." Once I see that Elle has rounded the corner, I open the door and step out into the more than brisk night. You never forget how cold New York winters are, but it's definitely a shock to the system after living in California for so long.

While Henry locks the door, I take a moment to look at the building. It's a three-story walkup with an industrial exterior, easy to walk by and not think anything of, like most buildings in the city.

"What's above you?" I ask, looking up at the makeshift sign under one of the small windows.

"There's a yoga studio on the second floor—owner is *super* snippy—and storage on the third," Henry explains. He pulls his collar up to his ears and stuffs his nose into his jacket. "Let's go, dude, it's freezing out here." I roll my eyes at him.

He starts walking, and I look back at the second floor of the building again, still in disbelief that now I'll have two places where I might run into my pretty, yet questionably sane, new neighbor. I shake my head, wondering whether she'll be waiting to give me a hard time after my next overnight shift.

I walk slow enough that there's almost no chance we run into Elle on our way into the building. The entrance is actually a few steps down from the street, so it's easy to see that the light in Elle's basement apartment is on. I don't want to act like a creep, but I can't resist peeking over the line of trash cans to see into her window. It's not that I'm interested in her or what she's doing, it's just... when you find a girl sleeping outside of your apartment door in the middle of the night, it's natural to be a bit curious about her. Right?

"So how are you liking the place?" Henry asks, looking around my newly clean apartment as we enter.

"It needs some work," I mumble, handing Henry a beer. I try not to focus on the mess of my things flooding the apartment. I'm a minimalist, so even the small amount of stuff in this tiny space has given me a permanent twitch in my eye.

I have to admit, if I was any taller, I'm not sure I would fit in this apartment. It's narrow, to say the least, especially with the treadmill. One could argue a treadmill has no place in such a small apartment, but when I made this arrangement with my sister, I told her the only way I would pay her rent for a year is if she got me a treadmill before leaving. Another stipulation should have been that I will not take care of the dog that she adopted three weeks before spontaneously moving to Italy, but I have to admit that the little guy is growing on me.

Thor has black eyes and a round snout, a wet black nose, and a black patch of fur over his right eye that makes him look like the dog from *The Little Rascals*. He's mostly white, with spots of black skin showing through his thin fur like freckles. He's cute, there's no denying it. It's not that I don't like dogs, I've just never had one myself. I don't know what to do with him.

And then there's the name.

Knowing my sister, she chose the name assuming that he would grow, but this dog is never going to be taller than my shin at the rate he is going. His legs are short and stunted, and his head is small, with ears that stand up and flop over.

He's currently about ten pounds, and doesn't seem to be getting any bigger.

So I'm going to be the six-three guy walking down the street with a tiny dog called Thor. Great.

Thor curls up in Henry's lap as I fetch us drinks. At least I can open the fridge with ease now that the eggs are in a carton on the right, the fruit is washed and put in plastic containers, and the drinks are lined up in size order on the left. I adjust the carton of milk and move it behind the peanut butter as I grab two beers.

"The dog suits you," Henry jokes, scratching behind Thor's ears.

I scoff. "The girl who lives below me would disagree."

"Not making nice with the neighbors?" Henry asks, raising his brows. He runs his other hand through the side of his short brown hair. In college, he had long, straight hair that went down to his shoulders. He rocked a man-bun for the whole four years, but he cut it before graduation and hasn't gone back. That doesn't stop me from whispering "Garnier" to him at random moments, though.

I rub my hand over my eyes, remembering the shit show that was my first encounter with my new neighbor. "This girl is unhinged. And trust me, I know crazy." I wave my hand in front of my face. "But this girl… she was sleeping in the hallway outside of my door when I got home from work the other night."

"*What?*" Henry says, putting his beer down. "That's definitely not what I thought you were going to say." I recount the whole thing to Henry, watching his face light up with glee at the insanity of it all. "I guess it's kind of nice that she was looking out for the dog. Was she hot?"

"Gorgeous," I reply immediately. "But I can already tell she's going to be a gigantic pain in my ass."

Henry chuckles, taking a long drink of his beer. After a beat, he says, "But are you happy? I mean... are you glad you're here? Glad you... did *this*?" he gestures to the apartment.

"I kind of didn't have a choice," I mutter, taking a sip from my bottle.

"Sure you did," Henry says. "You could have stayed in California and tried to match for residency somewhere else next year. Worked as a paramedic or a medical assistant there. Done a fellowship. You had a lot of options," he explains, making me feel small with every item he lists. His face is compassionate, his brows slightly raised, making me feel like I don't really have a choice but to be honest with him. Part of me forgot how intuitive Henry is. I haven't seen him for more than a day or two over the past few years, but he has a way of getting right to the point. When I called him six months ago and said I was moving back to New York, his immediate response was, "*Do I need to bring a shovel?*"

"*What are you talking about?*" I'd said, so confused by his initial reaction.

"*A shovel. To bury the body. We're using your car though because I'm not getting mine dirty.*"

"*Henry, what the fuck are you talking about?*" I'd snapped.

"*You literally said you'd never move back to New York unless you had to. So I have to assume that you're on the run from the law, or the mob, or something. And I'm just saying I'm here for you, man. But I'm not getting dirt in my car.*"

And that's Henry.

"Alright, you don't have to be so dead-on about it," I say, placing my beer on a coaster on the coffee table.

"Dude, coasters, really?" Henry accuses, changing the subject for a moment. "You're a thirty-year-old man, not a grandma with plastic on her couch."

"Oh fuck off," I grunt, pushing a coaster in his direction. "Don't make a ring on the coffee table. This shit is from Pottery Barn."

Henry rolls his eyes and puts his foot on the table. I'm about to yell at him, but then I see that he is laughing, trying to goad me. I give him the finger as he moves his foot. "Sorry," he says, laughing. "Go on, you were saying something about me being right."

I squint. "Not sure I said *that*..." I reply and he raises his brows. "But I guess I could have done other things. And maybe I would have, if—" My voice trails off, the unspoken words filling the silence.

If not for my father.

Henry knows all about my relationship with my father. For four years in undergrad he listened to the monotonous lectures blaring through my phone about my future, the expectations I had to live up to, the role I was meant to play in our family's legacy. I was the next Dr. Cole, and my father made no mistake of explaining the consequences of my not following through on that plan.

It's not as if I was a student who struggled with the academics required for what was asked of me. I wasn't the kid born with a desire to be an actor or some shit instead of a doctor. I love medicine. Although sometimes—*a lot* of the time—I wished that I didn't, just to spite my father. But

I was good at it, and for the amount that my sister calls me a curmudgeon, I *do* like helping people. I sailed through a lot of undergrad, but the difficulty of medical school hit me hard. And residency interviews even harder. Because the fact is, I *am* a curmudgeon. I generally don't work well with others, and I don't make friends easily. Which is exactly what I had to do to match for residency—make people like me.

"Yeah, I guess you couldn't avoid him and the Cole name in New York forever," Henry says with a sigh. I nod, defeated. *The Cole name.* The name that will follow me every step of the way through residency. The name with a weight that I've been trying to escape for eight years. The expectation to be the exceptional son of Dr. Andrew Cole.

"It hurts me to not see you happy, though, man," Henry adds.

"It's not that I'm not happy. I'm just—"

"Surviving," Henry finishes.

I drum my lips. "Yeah, I guess." I take another drink.

"What would you do—if you didn't match for residency at all?" Henry asks, a genuinely curious look on his face.

"Dude, I *didn't* match. My father is the reason I'm in a residency program right now."

"You really think so?" I nod. Henry lets out a breath, trying to wrap his head around the insane level of nepotism. It's hard to believe shit like that actually happens, but I'm the proof of how far my father is willing to go to protect his name. I push away the intrusive thought about being unworthy of being in the program at all.

"But what if?" Henry adds.

I shake my head. I wish I could tell Henry the truth, that I would choose a career that didn't come with such anxiety, so much risk of something going wrong, and so much of a chance to indulge my obsessive tendencies. I wish I could tell him that my compulsions rule my days in the hospital. I wish I could tell him that even though there are some parts of medicine that I love, I would take the chance to escape from the path my father has laid out for me in an instant.

But those thoughts are still there, the ones that tell me if I share too much, if I tell people what I'm really thinking, they'll judge me, and that feeling of unworthiness will come back.

Not everything I think is true, I say to myself.

But still, I stay quiet.

FIVE

Elle

The Heartwarming Romance offices are one of my favorite places to be.

I acknowledge that not many people can say that about their workplace, but the reason I have survived in this industry is because I genuinely love what I do. Publishing is hard. There's high turnover and so much burnout. I'm not saying I've never experienced frustration at my job, because I've had my fair share of it, but for the most part, I truly love it.

There are pros and cons to our open floor plan office setup. One of the cons is that there are many distractions, which is why I can usually be found with my earbuds in, blissfully ignorant to the world around me. More so now that Lucy is gone—I've never really made small talk with any of my other colleagues.

It's nearing the end of the day on a dreary Wednesday. Anne, my boss, is working from home and I'm one of four members from our team that are in the office—Nadine and Terri, two of the more senior editors, and Callie, our publicist.

I have an hour to kill before I can go home for the day, so I open up my submission inbox and scour through some agent emails that I need to respond to. The second one I open is from an agent I've worked with several times. She knows my taste. She pitches the book as one of a duet—two books that center around the same characters and same central conflict. The heroine comes from a broken home and falls in love with an inner-city bad-boy who challenges her to open her mindset. But she is wary of trusting anyone because of the trauma she has experienced in her past.

I have always loved to read about heroines who were guarded. Leading women who had an angsty, troubled past, with some kind of "dark" secret that made them put their walls up and swear never to trust anyone again. I guess I found it relatable.

Growing up, I believed the fictional tales my mind got lost in. I believed if I hardened my heart, if I put those walls up, someone would come along and try to break them down, until I realized that they were who I had been waiting for my whole life. My walls would have been built for them to break. And I would find my person.

And yet, at thirty, I can't help but feel disappointed that no one has even attempted to climb them.

It's not that I'm not trying to find someone. I go on dates, but having identical getting to-know-you conversations has been painful lately. I want to find someone where that stage feels natural, where the conversation just flows, where I feel bubbly on the inside every time our hands touch. Someone who knows what will make me happy and will go out of their way to do it. Maybe I'm asking too much of the first few dates, but if I don't feel that, I can't keep seeing someone. It feels like a waste of time.

Who is that guy from Greek mythology that has to perpetually roll a boulder up a hill? Sassafras? No, that's not it…

Sisyphus. Zeus makes him roll a boulder up a hill for eternity. Every time he gets the boulder to the top of the hill, it rolls back down.

I'm starting to really feel that guy.

I spend the next hour reading the submission and ruminating on the lack of love in my own life. I'm so different from Lucy because before she met Liam, she didn't believe in happily ever after anymore. Me? I am a firm devotee of the HEA. I can't help but fall for every love story put in front of me. I eat up the romance every time, and I yearn for it for myself.

But no matter what I do—live on my own, stand up for myself, get promoted—I still feel this weight, this heaviness, that I can't shake. Lately, it's Lucy and wedding plans, the thought of actually having to go to her wedding and put my sidekick show on, all while trying to pretend I'm not that lonely. That I can handle being alone. Sometimes I wish I could have my own me: a hype girl, a sidekick, someone to lift some of the weight off for me.

And with every love story I read, I just hope that I haven't lost my chance.

When five-thirty rolls around and the office starts to empty, I shut down my computer and put my laptop in my backpack, so I can finish the submission at home. I already know I want to acquire this book. It's my own personal brand of click-bait. The angst is palpable through the pages, the sexual tension is fantastic, and I already think I know how the slow burn will come to a head. And of course, there's a perfect amount of family drama, which is always right up my alley.

I think about my own family drama—my childhood spent doing my brother's laundry or planning dinner for the week. Most kids got the chance to be kids, but that was my reality, and I dealt with it. From the time I was a child, I was the caretaker. It's ingrained in me. And sometimes I feel like I'm never going to escape it.

When I walk out onto the city street, a damp, cold chill in the air, something feels empty inside of me. I walk by a couple holding hands and try not to let it bother me, but I feel the sting in my chest anyway.

It's just so hard to feel hopeful about love when all I see scrolling through Instagram are people getting engaged, married, or posting pictures of their babies with adorable age-related signs from Etsy placed next to them. And then there's me—in this sort of limbo, waiting for someone to come and sweep me off of my feet. Even though I'm discouraged, I won't give up.

Because I know what I want: someone to take care of me for a change. Is that selfish? Maybe. But when I think about my life, what I want more than anything is a partner. Someone to go hiking with, to go out to dinner, go on vacations, go to one of those hatchet-throwing places. I want to enjoy my life with someone. Because it's my turn to.

When I get back to the apartment, I'm emotionally exhausted. Too tired to do anything else, I heat up a pre-made meal from Whole Foods and sink into my beloved green chair. My whole body relaxes like I haven't sat down in ages, when the reality is I sat down at work all day. But before I can even turn on the TV to really settle in, I'm jolted upright by a moan so pathetic my heart breaks.

That jerk left that poor dog alone again.

I might actually break down the door this time.

SIX

Oliver

No. No. No. No. "*No*!"

The final "no"—the one that I didn't realize I'd said out loud—wakes her up.

She jumps from the timbre of my voice, and the innocent look in those giant brown eyes makes her look like a startled deer. I almost feel bad for waking her up. She brought a full getup this time—blanket, pillow, the works. She's curled facing the bottom of my door, her fingers sneaking under the door itself.

I swear if she was trying to hold the damn dog's paw...

"*You*," she growls, and my guilt evaporates. Of course my mind also takes this moment to consider how absolutely filthy this floor probably is. Does she realize that people track germs on their shoes? And who knows what else? God, I hope she takes a shower when she gets back to her apartment...

"*Me*?" I say, actually pointing at my chest in disbelief. "No, no, *lady*, there is no universe in which I am the bad guy in this scenario," I say somewhat harshly. As soon as the word "lady" leaves my lips, her eyes widen like I've just slapped her across the face. In the back of my mind, I'm trying to discern if "lady" is better or worse than "ma'am."

She stands up, ready to pounce. "Are you kidding me?"

Worse. Definitely worse.

"Ma—" Damn, since when did I say "ma'am" so much? Maybe I'm just so used to trying to sound cordial at the hospital that it's just become a habit. "Elle—" She's taken aback when I say her name. "Please keep your voice down. I don't need any other tenants coming after me in the middle of the night."

"Are you afraid of them? You're as big as a fucking tree. Woman up, dude," she says, animated hand motions accompanying every word. I take this moment when she doesn't actively look like she's going to lunge for my throat to notice that she's wearing a thin t-shirt, which is a strange choice for an unheated hallway in March, but I guess it explains the blanket. Letting her tirade wash over me, my eyes track lower. She's wearing pajama pants with… dogs in pajamas on them. Her pants have *dogs with pajamas* on them. Pictures of cartoon dogs of varying shapes, sizes, and colors are spread across the fabric, each wearing a unique holiday sweater. I am *so* not equipped to handle this.

Then there's the fact that she's not wearing a bra.

Mother of hell. She has *dogs wearing pajamas* on *her* pajamas and I have a full view of her boobs through her shirt.

"Are you seriously looking at my chest right now?"

Aw, fuck.

I rub my fingers so deep into my eyes it hurts. I already feel the lack of sleep getting to me, even after one night shift. This new routine is *killing* me.

"I really do not have the energy for this," I mumble, taking a step toward my door. I look at my watch. 6:22. If I go inside now, I can walk Thor, do a quick twenty minutes on the treadmill and be showered and in bed by 7:30.

"Yeah, well, I don't have the energy for *anything* anymore because I never get any sleep!" she snaps back.

I take the calm approach, my training guiding me to talk softly and appear reasonable, just as if I was dealing with an unstable patient. Which clearly, I am.

"To be fair," I start, putting my hands up like I'm approaching with caution. "You are the one sleeping on the floor outside of a stranger's apartment. You could simply invest in some earplugs. Seems like a—"

"No, no," she interrupts, the bun on her head bobbing with every wave of her hand. "This is not a *me* problem. The problem is that you are the worst dog owner in the history of the planet. That poor thing is miserable when you're gone. Don't you feel bad at all?"

"Of course I do, but I have a job, and I think he'll get used to it. It's only been a few days," I say, trying to rationalize with her and with the pang of guilt building in my chest. I do feel bad for leaving Thor, but what can I do?

"Did you get him from a shelter?" she asks. I sidestep the fact that is the first not-vile thing she's said to me, and answer it plainly.

"My sister did, yeah," I mumble through a yawn.

"And what do you think happened when the people who worked at the shelter went home for the night?"

"What?"

"What do you think *he* thought?" she asks matter-of-factly.

"I don't—" What do I think *he* thought? *Thor*? She wants me to put myself in the dog's head? I don't even know how to respond to that.

"Do you think maybe he thought no one was going to come back in the morning?"

Oh, for fuck's sake.

"Look, I don't have to listen to this—" 6:26. This girl is messing with my schedule. I realize she doesn't know or understand how much my schedule means to me, but my brain does. And if my schedule is off, then my sleep will be off, and... I *like* my schedule.

"Yes, you do. And you have to let me meet him," she demands.

"Um, no?"

"Yes, because the poor thing has heard us talking and I'm not done yelling at you, so open the damn door."

"So I can listen to more yelling? Sign me up," I drawl.

"Oh, just do it!" she whines, stomping her foot. She takes a step closer to me and folds her arms across her chest. I try to ignore the way the hairs on my arms stand up once she moves in. I look at her and run my eyes up and down her body, sizing up if she's actually going to stay there. This girl is a real pain-in-the-ass, but she's determined. I'll give her that.

"Oh, oh, I'm convinced!" I mock, raising my hands in surrender before rolling my eyes. Still, she makes no move to step out of my personal space.

"Wow, isn't it *exhausting* being such an asshole all the time? I'm surprised you have to tire yourself out on the treadmill every night."

I shake my head in disbelief. I'm really trying to be the bigger man here, but she is making it hard. Part of me admires Elle. She is clearly someone who cares so deeply that she is willing to sleep outside my door to comfort a dog she's never met. But is she also a little crazy? Sure.

I watch her tighten her arms around her chest and rub one tricep with her palm. She's cold. She's laying outside my door in a freezing cold hallway because she feels bad for my dog. I never thought I'd have this particular problem in my life. But man, this girl makes it really hard to hate her.

I push past her, kicking her pillow and blanket to the side and jam the key into my door. I don't want her to think that she's won, but I also want to get her inside to warm up. Thor greets us both at the door, his tail wagging, butt-wiggling, and whining like a pig.

I decide not to comment on the fact that the little *traitor* completely sidesteps me to get to Elle. He is *definitely* not getting cream cheese off of my bagel tomorrow. Today? What is time anymore?

When the door closes behind her, Elle takes in my apartment before dropping to the floor and giving Thor all of her attention.

"Hello, my friend! How are you?" Her voice goes through varying levels of high pitch squeals as she rubs every inch of Thor, who soaks it up like he's never been given a minute of attention in his life. She sits down and Thor does a somersault into her lap, letting her scratch his chest and belly as his legs go limp. "Oh, did that mean man leave you alone again? He is the *worst*," Elle says, baby-talking Thor as he licks her nose.

"I hate to break up this love fest, but Thor does have to go outside and some of us would like to go to bed," I say, leaning against the counter, trying to save any energy I have to get this crazy lady out of my apartment. 6:29. Dammit.

Elle rolls her eyes at me but makes no move to leave. "Why did you name him Thor?"

"He's my sister's dog," I say, crossing my arms. "My sister—who does not think anything through—adopted him about a month before deciding to move to Italy for a year. The same sister probably thought he was going to be really big, hence, the name."

She looks up at me, pursing her lips—which are a bit mesmerizing. She really is beautiful. Shrill and a total nag, but beautiful. Part of me, maybe a big part, regrets that we got off on the wrong foot.

"What kind of work do you do?" she asks plainly.

I wish I had the balls to say, "It's none of your business," but I opt for the truth.

"I'm an internal medicine resident at Mount Sinai," I say. "And you?"

"I'm a book editor," she says with a wave of her hand, as if that could make her words less significant.

I try not to focus on the rise and fall of her chest as she takes a deep breath and gives Thor a final pat on the stomach. She looks like she's contemplating something. She opens her mouth to speak several times, until she finally stands up with a sense of determination. She takes a step toward me and I focus on maintaining eye contact with her, so my gaze doesn't drift downward. We're in close enough range that she could slap me now. She looks at me, almost like when she first opened her eyes and saw me the other night, and finally speaks. "Look, we can't go on like this," Elle starts.

"Like what, exactly?"

"You're probably *not* a horrible person, saving people and stuff as you do," she adds, shrugging her shoulders. "Thanks for that by the way." I nod my head, trying not to laugh at the way she says it so casually. "But unfortunately I have no other evidence to support that you aren't."

"A horrible person?" I confirm.

"Indeed," she says, interlacing her hands in front of her. "And the well-being of a dog is at stake, a matter which I do not take likely."

"A matter which is also none of your business," I add.

"If it affects my sleep, it's my business. I *love* sleep," she says, widening her eyes. "Plus, you have to—if you have any heart *at all*—admit that you feel bad about leaving this guy alone all night." She gestures to Thor who is sitting at her feet.

"Of course I do. I'm not a monster," I reply.

"So you say," she says passively. "Nevertheless, I'm left with no other choice. I have to intervene."

"Do you?" I wince. I squint and clench my teeth, like I'm bracing for impact. She rolls her eyes at me again. Man, that is either really starting to piss me off, or really turn me on. I can't decide which.

"So, here's my offer," she says, pulling back her shoulders and standing confidently. "I'll babysit Thor while you go to work."

"You want to watch my dog at night?"

"For free," she says, confidently. "*That* is how much I love my sleep."

"How do I know you won't just straight-up steal him? No offense, well, maybe *some* offense, but you seem like a little bit of a *squeeze-them-so-hard-you-choke-them* level of animal lover."

"No offense taken. But you know where I live. I'm not going anywhere with him." She folds her hands in front of her and rocks on her feet, clearly waiting for my answer.

I take a moment to admire her when she looks down to pet Thor again. I wish I could suggest a do-over with Elle. A version of our relationship that doesn't begin with her screaming at me, where I'm not the bad guy she thinks I am. Maybe even one where I show her what it does to me when she rolls those gorgeous eyes.

I'm not sure what to say to her ridiculous proposal. My initial answer is no, because Elle really is a stranger to me. I shouldn't leave my—well, Sophia's—dog with her. But she's right, she does live right downstairs. And as unreasonable as sleeping in the hallway is, it shows that she does care about animals. I don't think she'd hurt him. And I have to admit it would take a massive weight off my shoulders.

She must take my hesitancy as a form of agreement, because she speaks before I have a chance to.

"You can drop Thor off before your shift, bring any toys he likes and food if he doesn't eat," she says. I can tell she's trying to be serious, but there's a hint of a smile on her face.

She gives Thor a quick pat on the head, shoots me one more satisfied look, and walks out the door. Thor comes over and sits in front of me and wags his tail innocently. I'm sure the look of complete disbelief is still on my face long after she leaves.

SEVEN

Elle

The irony of an extremely attractive man living in the apartment upstairs is not lost on me. In another world, Lucy and Liam could've been right—the whole neighbors-to-lovers set up feels like the perfect opportunity for a meet-cute that sparks a storybook romance.

Except right now, I hate him.

And I'm pretty sure the feeling is mutual.

But last night—before or after I fell asleep on the hallway floor *again*—I realized that fighting with Oliver Cole was the first thing I've looked forward to in a long time. His arrogance makes my blood boil, but sparring with him was almost… *fun* in a way. It tapped into the kind of energy I've been missing since Lucy left.

Do I still loathe him for leaving his dog alone for hours on end? Yes. Do I think he shares some qualities with a beastly Disney prince? Also yes. But there was a moment, albeit fleeting, when I didn't want to fight with him. I mean, he's a doctor. A handsome, tall doctor. With nice eyes and muscular forearms.

He could be…

We could be…

But he is infuriating. And stubborn. And I can't imagine him being any other way.

When I open the door at exactly 5:59 p.m., Oliver stands there, taking up the whole damn frame. He's leaning one shoulder against the side of the opening, with his arm outstretched, holding the top of the molding. The aforementioned forearm muscles are on full display. But that's not the worst part.

He's wearing a black Henley.

Neither of us says anything for a few seconds. In my mind, I'm trying to reconcile that I'm still in real life and this guy is still the *worst*, even though he is wearing the kryptonite of romance readers everywhere.

And he—well, he seems to be checking me out.

I watch him take in my skin-tight yoga pants and white sports bra. His gaze feels hot on my skin, like his eyes can actually send heat rays to my body. I feel my cheeks flush. *Abort situation*, my brain screams. *Make an awkward comment or something!*

"Hey buddy!" I say excitedly to Thor, bending down to scratch behind his ears. Oliver clears his throat, seemingly trying to focus himself. The dog enters my apartment without hesitation, galloping in a cute way that makes it look like his paws are too big for his body. Which they kind of are.

I turn my attention back to Oliver as Thor tries to jump on his hind legs to see out my very small window. At first I'm smiling, but then I remember that I'm not supposed to be happy to see him. I raise my brows at the bag in his hand. He follows my gaze.

"Oh, these are some toys. He ate his dinner already, so I put a bone in there and some treats in case you want to give them to him."

"All the essentials. Are you secretly a helicopter parent?" I tease, taking the bag from him. I place it on my kitchen counter, implying that he could follow me into the room. He takes one step in and hovers awkwardly by the door.

"I would have had a baby monitor on him the last few nights if the shipping wasn't delayed," he deadpans. I know he's being sarcastic, but still, there's a subtext along the lines of "*See? I'm not a terrible dog owner.*"

"And before you ask, the bone in there is predigested rawhide, so it's okay for his intestines," he adds, gesturing to the bag.

"Someone's done their homework," I say snobbishly. I hate that he brings out this side of me. I'm not a stuck-up person. I'm not mean. I just feel like everything he says, I have to have a comeback for. I'm not usually very competitive, but Oliver makes me want to be.

I change the subject. "So I'll drop him back before I go to work tomorrow. About eight." Oliver nods.

"Give me your phone," he commands. I furrow my brows at him. "So you can call me if I don't answer the door right away. I'll probably be asleep."

"Oh." It occurs to me that I may not have thought this situation through. This seems like some kind of shenanigan I would involve Lucy in, and then I'd discreetly fade into the background while she figured out what to do. When she and Liam had their "dark moment," I threw her on a bus to Catskill and basically made her figure out the rest. Now I'm staking out hot guys' apartments and babysitting their dogs. How did I get here?

Oliver puts his number into my phone and calls himself. He hands the phone back to me and I try not to focus too much on the millisecond when our fingers touch.

"Thor," he says, in a stern voice that makes me jump. The dog waddles over to him, his tail still wagging so hard that the whole back half of his body is moving. Oliver kneels down and scratches Thor as the dog nuzzles into his chest. "Be a good boy. Don't let this lady take you into a white van or anything."

"Rude," I interject.

"I'll see you in the morning, bud." He puts his hands under the dog's scruff and touches his forehead to Thor's snout. Thor licks his nose and my heart melts just a bit. I give Oliver a sympathetic look when he rises.

"He'll be fine. I promise. So much better than being up there by himself," I say, placing my hand on the door handle.

"Okay. I still can't believe I'm doing this, but thanks. I guess," he adds, unsure.

I shuffle him out the door and keep Thor back with me.

"See ya!" I yell, slamming the door behind him. Payback.

The next few days go by pretty smoothly. I barely see Oliver except for the few minutes that it takes for me to drop Thor off in the morning and for him to do the same at night. Thor accompanies me to my yoga classes, and he is a hit with the students. Tanya is less thrilled about it, but she allows it, which is all I can ask for. And with a furry little buddy curled up next to me, I'm sleeping better than ever.

By Friday, the night of Ruby's book launch, Thor and I have fallen into a groove. I worked from home so that I could spend the day with Thor while I waited for Lucy to arrive. Oliver had to cover a day shift for another resident, so he'll be home around nine.

I truly don't understand how people in medicine have any kind of sleep schedule. Or how they function on so little sleep. While also keeping people alive. Kind of concerning. If his sister knew how crazy his schedule was going to be, she shouldn't have left the dog with him. How can you give a dog to someone who works twelve-hour shifts?

I'm hoping that Thor will be okay for the hour in between me leaving and Oliver getting home, since he's had company all day. With only a little coercion, Oliver and I even exchanged keys so he could get Thor from my place when he gets back from his shift. The conversation over text about exchanging keys with Oliver was one I never thought I'd have. I was running late from work and I had to pick up Thor from Oliver's apartment because he had to leave. We only missed each other by a few minutes.

Elle

Can you leave the key under the mat or something?

Oliver

People actually leave spare keys under their door? That is so unsafe.

Oliver

I'll put the key in an envelope and slip it under your apartment door before I leave. Keep it in case you need it another time.

Elle

Don't you think you should at least take me out to drinks first before giving me a key to your place?

Oliver

I think we skipped a few steps when we jumped right to co-parenting.

Elle

Can we back up to the part where you own envelopes? You like having them lying around your apartment? Do you send a lot of mail?

Oliver

Envelopes are a perfectly normal thing to own and keep in the house.

Elle

Only if you're a young homeowner turning into your parents.

Oliver

Are you comparing me to a car insurance commercial?

Elle

That depends, do you also watch documentaries about submarines?

Oliver

No comment.

"Can you explain this arrangement to me again?" Lucy asks, snapping me out of my thoughts. She's sitting on the carpet in front of my TV with Thor on her lap. Her thick mahogany hair is up in a curled ponytail, with long bangs framing her face. Her eyes are painted with an elegant gray eyeshadow and a sleek cat-eye. It's a stark contrast to the sweatpants and oversized t-shirt she's wearing, because she's procrastinating getting dressed.

"I'm babysitting his dog while he's at work. It's not that weird, is it?"

"I guess not, but it's just unusual for you," Lucy says with a shrug. "I'm happy about it—especially if he's as beautiful as you say he is."

"I didn't say he was beautiful!"

"No, maybe *gorgeous* was the word you used?" I can feel my cheeks turning red, and Lucy cackles with delight.

"Would you get dressed already? I'm waiting on you, babe," I say, trying to change the subject. Lucy groans, rising from the floor and slinking off to the bathroom as I evaluate myself in the floor length mirror propped against the wall next to my bed. It's a dressy night for both of us. Even though we're only going to Barnes and Noble in Union Square, there are going to be upwards of a hundred people there, and we're taking Ruby out for dinner afterwards.

I'm wearing a one-shoulder green sweater dress that is a bit more form-fitting than I'm used to. I'm used to wearing oversized clothes to downplay my boobs as much as I can, but they are pretty much front and center in this ensemble. I take a look at the clock and realize there's no changing now. Front and center it is.

Lucy emerges in a deep red satin dress with tights and knee-high boots. We look each other up and down and laugh.

"Shit, we look *good*!" Lucy exclaims. I shake my head at her and we take a few photos in front of the mirror, kiss Thor on the nose, and head out. He seems to be thrilled with the bone I give him before we leave, so hopefully he won't be too unsettled.

When we arrive at the store, crowds are already lining up in the lobby. Since it's so cold out, the managers must be letting fans wait there for the event instead of outside. Lucy and I show our I.D.s and head up the escalator to the third floor. Before I moved to New York, I thought my local library was the best place in the world. And then I learned there are bookstores with escalators. Meaning *multiple* floors. I was in heaven.

There's a large open area on the third floor that the store uses for events. Since Ruby is so popular, there are folding chairs canvassing pretty much every square inch of the space.

"Well, this is an example of what *won't* be happening for my book," Lucy mumbles as we take off our coats.

"Given that Ruby has written like twenty books and you've written one, maybe it's not realistic to make that comparison." I shoot Lucy a knowing look.

"Yeah, yeah. Where's Anne?" Lucy asks, brushing me off. "Wow, they even built up a stage for Ruby. Most authors just sit on a folding chair…"

Lucy's voice trails off as we both spot our boss on the stage. She's waving her hands in a way that only an Italian woman from Brooklyn can, her ringlet curls bouncing with each erratic move of her arms. She's in high heels and a pencil skirt, which both Lucy and I raise our eyebrows at. Because Anne is many things, but coordinated is not one of them. And she should never wear such a constricting skirt with heels.

Anne must have heard Lucy say her name, because she turns towards us. But before the words "Oh my God," can escape Lucy's lips, we watch Anne's knee buckle, and she goes tumbling off the stage.

EIGHT

Oliver

It's the third night in a row that I've let Elle babysit Thor, and I've regretted it pretty much every moment since I agreed to it.

Elle told me she had a work outing tonight, and while I offered to get a dog walker, or leave Thor in my apartment, she insisted that her friend visiting from out of town would want to meet him. I pointed out how *her* leaving him isn't different from *me* leaving him, but I didn't get very far with that argument. Since my schedule is backwards today, I should be home not long after she leaves. Hopefully Thor will be okay for a little while.

So to prove to me that Thor is having a "good time," she sent me a collection of photos she took of him before she left for her event. In every one Thor is wearing a different band t-shirt. The last one was Ed Sheeran. The most recent one is the Jonas Brothers: Thor is sitting on a green chair, perfectly composed, with a pair of huge white sunglasses on his face. He has beaded necklaces around his neck, a bandana tied around one leg, and a cut-up t-shirt that has "Burnin' Up" written on the front in bold red letters.

I'm never letting this woman near my dog again.

I'm pretty much dead on my feet tonight, having worked two twelve hour shifts over the last two days. My smart watch has yelled at me no less than seven times that I've hit my standing goal. The last time I yelled, "No shit, Sherlock!" at it, much to the surprise of all the nurses at the desk I was standing next to.

The same watch also notified me of another missed call from my father. I took the damn thing off after that.

My father has called me three times this week and I've ignored him every time. I've barely spoken to my parents since I moved back, not including the "welcome home" gathering my mother planned at the airport for my arrival. My father wasn't there. Shocking.

I spoke to my mother last week, and she regaled me with all of the stories of Sophia's first two weeks in Italy. It's astounding to me how parents can treat two children so differently. For as long as I can remember, the expectations for me were clear: Go to Stanford, just like my dad. Become a surgeon, just like my dad. Probably marry another doctor, just like my dad. Provide for my family. Live a stable life. All this time, I've never stepped a foot out of line.

Meanwhile, Sophia never had to contend with any expectations. At least, not to my knowledge. She was always bright in school, but there was never any pressure on her to carry on as my dad did. I got a C in Organic Chemistry sophomore year, and I had the fear of God put in me, but Sophia graduated and wanted to "see the world," and my parents didn't bat an eye. I would love for someone to explain these double standards to me, truly.

It's almost nine, and I'm counting down the hours until I can go home and faceplant into my bed. Well, Sophia's too-small-for-my-long-ass-legs bed. Which will be replaced as soon as I have a spare moment to drag myself to the store. I walk past the nurses' station at the entrance to the department and file some manila folders I've been carrying. I eye up an empty chair behind the desk and consider that maybe, just maybe, I'll get to sit in it, but my attention is drawn elsewhere. When the Emergency Department doors open behind me for a brief moment, I overhear a conversation—a *loud* one—going on in the waiting room.

"Please explain to me how this is my fault," I hear a feminine voice say.

"You called my name, I turned, I fell. *Your* fault."

"I didn't *call* your name. I asked Elle, 'Where's Anne?' That's not calling your name."

My head snaps around at the mention of her name.

Instead of plopping in the uncomfortable swivel chair, I take a few steps backwards towards the double swinging doors that mark the entrance to the emergency room. I linger for a moment, trying to catch a glimpse of the waiting room without being too conspicuous. It doesn't take me long to find the source of the squabble. I see Elle's big, curly blonde hair bouncing up and down as she paces past two women sitting in waiting room chairs. One of them is older, with dark hair and glasses that only accentuate the scowl on her face. The other is younger, with longer brown hair, and appears to be trying to comfort the older one.

And then there's Elle.

Holy shit, *Elle*.

She's wearing a dress that hugs every inch of her curvy body—her breasts, her *hips*—and exposes her legs, her muscles working with every step she takes in her boots. She flips her hair, revealing her bare shoulder where her dress cuts out.

I shake my head to divert my thoughts. This is Elle. Nosy, pushy Elle who lives downstairs and is annoying as hell. She just happens to be wearing a flattering dress. That's all.

I walk out into the waiting room and approach them with caution. Elle seems to sense me immediately, because her pacing stops as I approach. When she sees me, what appears to be joy spreads across her face for just a moment before she catches herself.

"Anne, you cannot sue me for workers' comp. That's not how it works. I don't even work for you anymore—" The brunette cuts her sentence short when she sees where Elle's attention has gone, and the expression on her face when she sees me is comical. Her jaw drops and her eyes practically bulge out of her head, like a cartoon.

"Elle—" she starts, clearing her throat.

"Elle," I repeat with a welcome nod to both her and her companions.

"Oliver," she says on an exhale.

"*That's Oliver*?" the brunette says a bit too loudly, considering I'm standing right here.

"Lucy!" Elle whispers harshly. She turns her attention back to me and gives me a half-hearted smile. "Oliver, this is my friend Lucy and my boss, Anne." She gestures to each of the women. Lucy still seems a bit lost in wonder when I shake her hand.

Anne, on the other hand, is laying back in the chair with her hand over her face. "I'd shake your hand, whoever you are, but I'm dying over here, which no one seems to care about—"

"Anne, you're not dying," Elle corrects, crossing her arms.

"I'm in a hospital, *Eloise*, people rarely come here when they are *well*!" Anne replies forcefully.

"Eloise?" I ask Elle with a questioning gaze.

"It's not really my name. Lucy calls me that when she's pissed, and now Anne has picked up on it. Super fun." Elle pinches the bridge of her nose, taking a deep breath. "Anyway, Oliver, maybe you can help us."

"I'm sure he can, given he's a *doctor*," Lucy mumbles, pursing her lips at me. She eyes me up and down like she's evaluating me. She gives a satisfied nod. "A *fine* doctor."

Elle widens her eyes and shakes her head quickly, seemingly trying to regain some control over the situation.

"I'm guessing your event didn't go well then?" I ask, raising my brows.

"Given there was an assassination attempt on my life, I would say no," Anne interjects. Lucy smacks her palm to her forehead, defeated.

"Anne fell off of the stage, *accidentally*. She hit her head and seems to have twisted her ankle," Elle explains. "The cops at the event suggested we bring her in to make sure she doesn't have a concussion."

"Cops?" *What kind of book event has cops?*

"It was a book signing for a pretty famous author. There were a few patrol cars outside for extra security," she explains.

Intriguing. I find myself wanting to know more about this event and her job. We've been texting over the past few days—pretty exclusively about Thor—and I've had to stop myself from trying to move the conversation beyond him. I want to ask her more questions, but I stop myself. Those kinds of intentions always get me into trouble.

I clear my throat and look away. "Do you have any pain in your head, ma'am? Nausea?" I ask Anne. I hear a small giggle come out of Elle when I say the word "ma'am."

"I'm a woman in my fifties, I have head pain and nausea every day," she grumbles, finally making eye contact with me. Elle and Lucy share the same look of disbelief.

"We'll get you triaged and get a head CT to rule out a concussion," I say. "Once you're in the back I can examine your ankle and we'll go from there."

"And how much longer do I have to sit here before that happens?" Anne asks.

"Anne!" Elle scolds. She matches Anne's gaze and narrows her eyes at her.

"I'll have them call you back now," I say, with the reassuring smile I save for the rowdy patients.

"Oh, there were other people here before us—" Elle starts, but Anne pinches her.

"Well, you have an in," I reply with a wink. I can hear Lucy *hmm* in satisfaction as I walk away.

"How do you know that guy again?" Anne whispers as I turn my back.

A beat passes before Elle responds, "We're neighbors."

NINE

Elle

I've been thinking about Oliver Cole wearing scrubs *way* too much.

It's been a few days since Anne's stint in the ER, during which she was diagnosed with a sprained ankle and no concussion. She has to spend two weeks on crutches, which I've heard *relentless* complaints about every day at work since then.

Even though Ruby's signing still ended up being a success regardless of Anne's incident, the part of the evening I found most surprising was my new neighbor. Gone was the impatient jerk I've been dealing with for the past few weeks. In his place was a helpful, and dare I say *charming*, doctor who was downright *neighborly*, even doing me a favor by letting Anne skip the line. Oliver was... *nice*. Pleasant. Cordial. All words I didn't know could apply to him. But beyond that, he was *attractive*. Horribly, massively attractive. The scrubs, the white coat, the charm, the wink. Holy hell, the *wink*.

Lucy will not stop talking about him. Thankfully, when we returned to my apartment we did little else but collapse into bed, but in all of our calls since then, Lucy brings Oliver up any way she can. She's persistent, I'll give her that. Was I this annoying when she met Liam?

It's been over a week since Oliver and I started our new arrangement with Thor. Oliver drops him off before his shifts, which vary from day to night, but I've been able to modify my working-from-home schedule so that I can be home with Thor when Oliver has to leave. And I don't even hear his middle-of-the-night exercising anymore. Two days after the ER incident, Oliver included a present for me in Thor's bag when he dropped him off.

"*What's this?*" I asked when he handed me a white box.

"*It's just something I picked up for you,*" he said awkwardly. He shifted on his feet by my doorway, like he couldn't wait to get out of there. "*Thought it was kind of funny.*"

The box had clear packaging on the top, so I could see what was sitting inside on a bed of white tissue paper. It was the fanciest pair of earplugs I've ever seen in my life.

"*Why—*" I started, looking up at him. We were standing so close together that I could see the moment the corner of his mouth turned up into a small smile.

"*I've been trying not to bother you with my early morning treadmill sessions, but I thought maybe these would help as well.*" He shoved his hands into his pockets and stared up at the ceiling. The tips of his ears were turning red, and it was almost endearing.

I forced a laugh after that, because I just didn't know what to do with the tension of the moment. No guy had ever bought me a gift this nice before. "*Thank you*," I said, a bit breathless.

Oliver smiled wider. I wondered if I'd ever seen him actually smile before. A smirk sure, tons of times, but a genuine, full smile? This was new.

He left quickly after that, and I was stuck standing in my kitchen, trying to decipher the actions of my confusing neighbor. Pretty much every minute since I'd met him had been spent in some kind of bickering match. But now, he'd revealed another side to himself. A softer side that wore scrubs and bought thoughtful presents—a present that I promptly Googled and learned cost sixty dollars.

I don't know how long I stood there, staring at a pair of custom earplugs, but after a while, I unpackaged them and put them on my nightstand, a smile on my face as I did so.

I hate to admit how much seeing Oliver and Thor has been brightening up my days lately. I can tell the good that it's doing for me. For example, if this were a pre-Thor/Oliver morning, I would be staying in bed until at least 8:30, waiting until the last possible second before I would be late for work. I'd probably spend the next hour and a half doom-scrolling through Instagram, admiring the photos of people that I don't even know, wondering when the hell *my* life was going to start.

Instead, a wet nose tries to snuggle its way under my hand.

I roll over to find Thor with his head perfectly positioned on the other pillow, looking up at me. Oliver said not to let him sleep in my bed, because he doesn't let Thor on his own furniture and he doesn't want to confuse him. But I've elected to ignore that.

I consider bringing Thor back upstairs early, just to bother Oliver. It's around seven, which means he's probably just fallen asleep after getting home. I wonder if I have a fog horn around? Maybe I could get one from the store on the corner? I could claim that he wasn't answering his phone...

Thor lets out a sweet little moan, and I decide that I am keeping this dog as long as humanly possible. Maybe I need to be late for work today. For my mental health.

I brush my teeth and throw on a pair of sweatpants and a sweatshirt. It's the end of March now, and the bitter cold is starting to ease, meaning I can get away with a heavy fleece rather than a parka. I put on Thor's leash and take him up to the park. While there are many issues with my apartment, its location is not one of them. I'm only a few blocks from Central Park West, which means I have access to green space to touch some grass whenever I need it. Thor is also thrilled about it, galloping in his too-big paws up the sidewalk, stopping to pee on every patch of mulch that he comes across. I'm probably not supposed to let him do that.

I've just let Thor off the leash at the dog run when my phone buzzes.

Oliver

Got home a little while ago and couldn't sleep. Want me to come grab Thor?

Elle

Us too. We're at the dog park if you want to join us.

Oliver

Be there in a few.

I'm excited for Thor. Maybe Oliver will let him stay at the park later than I'm able to. Part of me wishes I could stay too. I wish I could have Thor for more than just a night. I shake my head at myself as I watch him chase a miniature doodle. *He's not actually your dog, Elle.*

Just as I find a seat on a wooden bench that's not covered in dogs, I see Oliver approaching the gate to the park. I resist the urge to smile at the adorable scene of Thor jumping on his hind legs to get to Oliver as he opens the gate, clawing at the knees of his sweatpants with his tongue lolling out. I've never seen Oliver in sweatpants before. I wonder if they're the same ones he wore to bed. I wonder if he sleeps with no shirt on…

Okay, time to stop the wondering.

He is wearing a zip-up vest over a black hoodless sweatshirt, and a beanie. I mean, maybe he doesn't realize it's a beanie, but it's a beanie. I stifle a laugh as he approaches me, and he furrows his brows.

"What?" he prods.

"Nothing," I say, pressing my lips into a line. He takes a seat surprisingly close to me. "It's just that, you rolled out of bed to come here, and you were like, '*This hat looks good. I'm going to wear this hat.*'" I snort as I finish my sentence.

"It's cold out. Hats are usually warranted in the cold," he says, holding his hands out like he doesn't understand the joke, which makes it even funnier.

"Sure, hats are warranted," I reply with a nod. "But you have to pick the hat that matches your look. That hat reads *skateboarding hipster*. You need more of a black skull cap."

"Yeah well, when I wear a black hat, people tend to think I'm going to rob them," he says, completely serious.

"I see that," I agree. "But that's your look—scaring children, moonlighting as a bank robber. Embrace it."

He grimaces at me. It's like his natural facial expression. I don't think he'll respond well to me calling him Grimace to his face, so I may just troll him with pictures of the McDonald's mascot later.

"And what's your look?" He eyes me. I'm wearing a sweatshirt that says *Read Banned Books*, and leggings from my yoga studio. "Selling people books and reading their horoscopes?"

"Well, you're half right, I suppose."

He opens his mouth to say something, and then closes it again. A moment passes before he tries again. "So the books you work on… They're like the ones with the half-dressed men on the cover?"

I roll my eyes. Over the years, I've gotten over my rage at this response to people learning about my job. People only know what they are exposed to. If you're not part of the romance community, then you don't really see all the amazing parts of it. Sure, half-naked men are amazing, but that's not all romance is. Even though the genre has evolved so much over the last few years, people still like to put unfair labels on it. Romance doesn't get the credit it deserves, and I'm afraid it never will.

I settle for a vague response, because it's too early to get into a heated debate about the intricacies of my job with Oliver. "There's more to it than that."

He raises his eyebrows at my vague answer. "I shouldn't have implied there wasn't," he says, apology in his eyes. He takes a beat before adding, "And that's what you wanted to do? Like those are the books that you wanted to work with?"

"Since I learned that working with books was even a job," I say confidently.

"Why?"

I chuckle at Thor who is mirroring a French Bulldog's playing position. When I turn back to Oliver, a piece of a smile is still on my face. "Why romance?" I clarify. He nods.

"A lot of reasons. Because they're my favorite type of books. Always have been. And because the world could use some more happily ever afters. Or at the very least, people who believe in them."

He studies me for a moment, and I'd love to let the words "*What are you thinking?*" slip out of my mouth. But I hold my tongue. Because I'm not supposed to wonder what he's thinking. I'm not supposed to wonder anything about him, except how best to annoy the crap out of him.

"And that's what you believe in? Happily every afters?" he asks. I almost laugh at the words "happily ever after" coming out of Oliver's mouth. It's an odd thing to hear him say, especially while he is wearing that hat.

I consider if I should be truthful with him. Saying you want an HEA like a Disney princess usually doesn't do anything except scare guys away. As women, we're taught to play it cool in case the guy is afraid of commitment. Then, maybe they will stay with us long enough for us to change their mind. I try my best not to subscribe to this theory. But that still doesn't stop me from pausing when Oliver asks this question. Do I want him to think I'm an all-or-nothing girl?

I mentally scoff at myself. I'm many things, but I'm not a hypocrite—or a coward. I am very much myself, even if myself means being the hype girl and never the main character. I don't lie about who I am or what I want. I think it goes back to those nights looking at the sky with my dog, feeling small and unimportant. It reminds me that our world is too small, too fleeting, to be anything but honest.

"Yes," I say firmly. "That's my business: happily ever after. And I'd love to have one in my own life, too. Someday."

Oliver nods. He doesn't speak for a moment, so I take a chance. "What about you?"

"What about me?" he asks, clapping his hands to get Thor's attention.

"What's your take on happily ever afters?"

Oliver looks away from me, but surprisingly, he doesn't laugh. "I don't think that will be for me. Not anytime soon anyway."

My chest deflates a little. I try to ignore it.

"Why's that?" I ask in my best casual tone.

"I'm not the kind of guy girls like to settle down with," he says, and I scrunch my brows. When he sees the confusion on my face, he adds, "I—uh—I have really bad OCD, and it's pretty much ended all of my relationships." He stretches an arm around his neck, rubbing it with his hand. "I don't know why I'm telling you this."

"Because I asked," I reply plainly. Something twinges in my chest at his confession, at the fact that he felt he could trust me with it. "If those women couldn't appreciate you for who you are, OCD and all, then they probably weren't worth your time anyway," I add, giving him a soft smile.

"That might be the nicest thing you've ever said to me," he says, disbelief on his face.

"Don't get used to it," I reply, giving him a side-eye.

"Plus, I can't imagine being in a relationship right now. Just moving here, my job—" He stops short and drags a hand down his face, an exasperated sigh escaping through his fingers.

"What's wrong with your job?" I ask. "Other than the absurdly long hours, of course."

"It's... complicated, but it just feels like it was forced upon me. Sure, I love medicine, but I don't know if I love practicing it. And I don't have the best relationship with my dad because of it." He pauses, drumming his lips. I can tell he's reluctant to talk about this, but he is anyway, and I appreciate that. It seems hard for him, so I put on my best supportive face.

"Everything in my life is so chaotic right now that I can't think ahead to the next few weeks, let alone consider a long-term relationship." He shakes his head as soon as the words leave his mouth. He's uncomfortable, and definitely looking for a way out of the conversation. He bends down to pet Thor and won't meet my eyes. "Don't you have to leave for work?" he asks, finding a way to change the subject.

I check the time on my phone, and yes, I do. But I feel bad ending this conversation too early. Part of being a hype girl is being a good listener. It's ingrained in me. But I also like to respect people's boundaries, and I don't want to push past Oliver's when we've just had the most civil conversation in recent memory. I hand Oliver the leash and we start the walk back to our building.

I can't help but feel a sort of grief as we walk away from the park, like I lost something while I was there. I know Oliver and I started out at odds, but since I started watching

Thor, we've formed a weird partnership of sorts. Maybe the beginning of a friendship? I thought, maybe *hoped*, that there could something else between us. I don't think I imagined the way we looked at each other some days, but maybe fleeting attraction was all it was. Oliver has made it pretty clear that he doesn't want anything serious. And as Lucy once told me, when a man tells you he doesn't want a relationship, he's rarely lying.

So we continue to be at odds after all.

TEN

Oliver

"Sometimes I can't believe I'm really back in New York," I blurt out as we turn onto Central Park West. It's early in the morning, but cars and yellow cabs are honking obnoxiously and there are sirens in the distance. The sounds of the city don't follow the same timeline as everyone else. Much like medical residents, the city doesn't have a sleep pattern.

"What do you mean 'back'?" Elle asks, trying to fall into step with my long strides.

"I grew up here, but I lived in California for eight years. I went there for college and medical school," I explain, glad the conversation has shifted from what she asked me in the park, and my awkward confession.

"Why did you come back?"

"Residency. You have to go where you get accepted." She nods, considering this. "It's not my favorite place," I add with a shrug.

"New York? It's not your favorite?" She seems a bit stunned by this.

"I don't have anything against the city itself. I just never thought I'd live here again. I don't exactly have many positive memories of this place."

"Would you moving away have anything to do with your relationship with your dad?" she asks, looking up at me.

"It might," I admit, feeling suddenly very uncomfortable with how intimate this morning's conversations have been. Elle reminds me of Henry: intuitive in a way that makes you trust them easily. Thoughtful enough to consider what I'm thinking. She has this demeanor that makes you want to talk to her. And that's saying something coming from me. I don't know why Elle brings this out of me. This morning, she's gotten me to talk more than I have to anyone in months, except maybe Henry or Sophia. And she doesn't even seem like she's trying to be super invasive. It's just how she is.

"So did you really want to be a doctor? Or you just followed that path because you felt like you had no other choice?"

Intuitive, alright.

"My parents are both doctors. My dad is a surgeon. I've always been destined to be the next Dr. Cole. It was understood," I explain, monotonous.

"That didn't answer my question."

"I like some parts of medicine," I say, begrudgingly. "But maybe I wouldn't have chosen this exact path for myself, if I had a choice." I'm surprised that I admitted that out loud, but Elle is removed from that side of my life. I can admit that truth to her without it getting back to my father. I know that's a ridiculous way to think, but it's like my brain is wired to screen every conversation for the possibility of it somehow reaching him.

Elle doesn't have a chance to respond because someone is calling my name from down the block. We come to a stop at the corner of Columbus Avenue and I see Henry jogging across the street towards us. He's wearing shorts, even though it's freezing out, and a hooded sweatshirt with the name of the gym sprawled across the front. His gym is back the other way, so I'm not sure what he's doing heading towards the park this early in the morning.

"Hey man," I say, stuffing my hands in my sweatshirt pockets. "I didn't know you got up this early."

Henry chuckles. "I hate to, but owning a business does that."

"Your business is in the opposite direction, dumbass."

"Yes, but the *coffee* I need to be able to survive at said business is this way," he says, pointing behind me and Elle. "And now that the interrogation is over, maybe you could introduce me to your lovely friend here." He flashes a smile, turning on the charm for Elle. I ignore the weird sensation that sparks in my chest.

"*Friend* is a strong word," Elle replies. "I'm Elle, Oliver's neighbor and sworn enemy." She puts her hand out for Henry to shake, and he holds on to it for a moment too long. Elle gives him a shy smile.

"Oh, so *you're* the neighbor," Henry says giddily, eyeing me.

Elle looks between us warily. "You're spreading your hatred of me to others?"

"Only a little bit." I shrug.

Henry is still holding her hand. When he sees me eyeing it, he lets go. "Well, I have to run. It was nice to meet you, Elle. And if you ever want to get away from this guy, make sure to hit me up." He winks as he pats Elle's shoulder and walks past us. "Later, Ollie."

Ollie? Elle mouths at me, a grin on her lips.

I resist the urge to follow Henry and punch him in the face.

I cross the street, Elle trailing behind. Thor is in a mini-run to keep up with my long legs.

"Well, he was adorable," Elle says once Henry's out of earshot.

"I'm not sure if that's the word I'd use," I grumble. I need to get a hold of myself. Or at the very least, I need to get out of Elle's orbit and give myself a second to think. Elle told me she believes in happily ever after, I pretty much shot her down, and then Henry hits on her. How the fuck did all that happen before breakfast?

I didn't lie to Elle. I didn't say I don't *believe* in happily ever after. I said they don't work out for me. And I certainly can't imagine one for myself anytime in the near future. Which is the truth. Every relationship, or *almost* every relationship, I've been in has ended because I somehow mess it up. A lot of people don't understand that OCD is more than wanting everything to be neat and tidy. It's a compulsion to do certain things and think a certain way. It's thoughts that break into your brain—thoughts that someone without OCD would never have. It's driving through the same intersection every day on your way to work, and picturing being T-boned by a car coming the other way. It's washing your hands quickly and then thinking that if you don't wash them again, for the full twenty seconds this time, you'll get sick. It's having a bad day and imagining harming yourself. Not because you would, but because that's what OCD does. It twists you in ways that you didn't know you could bend.

My OCD makes me rigid. I think in black and white, and I'm logical to a fault. I can't understand why my sister would adopt a dog and then fly halfway across the world. That's not rational. It's why I haven't spoken to her in a few weeks. I avoid things that don't make sense to me.

A relationship that lasts a lifetime makes sense to me. My parents, specifically my father, may be difficult, but a stable marriage is what I've been exposed to my entire life. Commitment doesn't scare me. But I just feel *lost* right now. I'm living in the most stressful city in the world, in a state I swore I would never step foot in again, and my job is quickly destroying me. It's only been a few weeks, and I don't know how I'll keep this up for three more years. Nothing in my life feels stable right now, so I can't imagine trying to maintain a relationship on top of everything else.

Which is why, when I look at Elle—this bubbly, interesting, vibrant person—I can't see a future with her. Because I'll ruin it. I'm not sure how, but I will. I always do.

Plus, I don't even know if I like Elle like *that*. It seems like we've gotten past the nemesis-neighbor stage, and she's so easy to talk to. Of course, I'm grateful for her offering to look after Thor. But just because I shared a bit about myself, that doesn't mean she knows me. That doesn't mean we're going to be actual friends, or anything more, for that matter.

So why does the idea of Henry making a move on her make me feel nauseous?

"Hello, Earth to Oliver?" Elle's amplified voice snaps me out of my trance.

"What? Sorry," I reply, blinking her into focus.

"I said we're home." She points at our building, and I take a moment to look at her. Her hair falls over her shoulders in long waves. It's blonde with a little brown in it, which accentuates the brown in her eyes. Her cheeks and the tip of her nose are a faint shade of pink from the cold, and even though she carries herself as though she's trying to make herself as small as possible, her expression is open and earnest. She has an effortless beauty about her. I'm sure she literally rolled out of bed looking like this.

I look down at the sidewalk for a second, trying to push down the sadness in my chest after appreciating how lovely she is. I wish I found it as easy as Henry does to ask someone on a date, or even just to flirt. It hurts a little that I don't.

When I look up, Elle is eyeing me suspiciously.

"What?" I murmur. I tell Thor to sit because he is pulling to go up the steps into the building.

"I have an idea," Elle says, a grin blossoming across her face.

"Why does that sound terrifying to me?"

"I want to help you fall in love with New York again," she declares, clasping her hands in front of her.

"Huh?"

"This is going to sound weird—"

"That's nothing new," I mutter. Elle narrows her eyes at me.

"My best friend, Lucy, who you met at the hospital—" I nod. "—moved away somewhat recently and I am in *desperate* need of a project."

"A *project*?" I wince at the word.

"Let me show you some good things about New York, *please*." She makes puppy-dog eyes at me, and it's almost impossible to resist.

"It's not like I haven't been here before," I say, gesturing around us.

"Oliver, listen," she says, a firmness in her voice. She hitches her hip and holds her hands out, like she's about to explain something to me in detail. "You said you'd never come back here. But here you are. Maybe you should try to not be miserable the whole time."

"I'm pretty comfortable being miserable, thank you," I jab. Elle rolls her eyes and groans.

"For the love of God," she exclaims dramatically, waving her hands in the air. "You *need* me!"

"I *need* you?"

"This is what I do. I'm a great wing woman. I'll show you great things about the city. New things, things only a true Manhattan local would know. Maybe make you a little *less* miserable about being here."

Her energy is a lot right now.

"Why would I agree to this?" I ask, truly wondering about the answer.

"Because it will be fun!"

I was afraid she was going to say that.

"And why would *you* want to do this?" I don't understand what her friend moving away has to do with any of it.

Elle looks down, crushing a stray leaf with the toe of her shoe. "Because this is what I'm good at. I like to do things for other people." She pauses, darting her eyes up to meet mine before looking away again. She tugs on the sleeve of her sweatshirt. "I told you it would sound weird."

"It does," I say, nodding. "What do you mean it's *what you do*?"

Elle continues to fidget with her shirt and avoid my gaze. "I'm a very good sidekick," she starts. "I take care of people. It's what I've always done."

I tilt my head at her.

"I'm not saying that I want to take care of you, or that you need taking care of—"

The furrow in my brow deepens. She sighs and takes a few steps over to the stoop of our building and sits on the steps, where Thor eagerly tries to jump into her lap. She runs her hand up and down his back and he pants contentedly.

"My parents got divorced when I was six, and my brother has a disability, so I've always been a caretaker. I'm good at it. I help people get what they want. And now that Lucy moved away, my sidekick tendencies haven't been indulged as much."

I'm about to say *"Isn't that a good thing?"* but she takes my momentary silence as an opportunity to continue pleading.

"*Please*, let me be your New York City tour guide. You'd be doing me a favor, really." This is not the same excited voice she had a few minutes ago. It sounds a bit more forced.

I'm surprised by how much I appreciate her telling me something personal about herself. Because regardless of whether I have feelings for her or not, I like getting to know Elle. I *want* to know more about her. Her presence is kind of addictive. Which may or may not make this plan a bad idea.

"That sounds like a lot of you going out of your way. And you're already watching my dog for free..." I look down at Thor, who has moved on to playing with a bug on the ground.

"Then you can do something for me too, if it will make you feel better," she says, her face brightening because she thinks she has me.

"Like what?"

Elle looks around, as if the answer is going to materialize out of the sidewalk. Her gaze pauses down the street for a moment, and I can see her considering something. She opens her mouth to speak, stops herself, and then does it again.

I look back in the direction we came from, and remember Elle calling Henry adorable. I can't believe the next words that come out of my mouth.

"Henry?" I ask, my voice cracking.

"What?" she says, pretending like she wasn't just thinking the same thing.

"I could set you up with Henry, if you want?" I shrug, as if the movement will make this moment hurt a little less. I have no right to be hurt, given that I basically told Elle that I can't be with someone that way, but the sting is still there.

"And what? Tell me what he likes and stuff?" she asks, a hesitant tone in her voice.

"What he *likes*?" I repeat, raising a brow in alarm.

"Food, art, music!" she exclaims, softly punching me. "Get your mind out of the gutter."

It takes a moment for the reality of this situation to sink in. A moment ago, the thought of Elle calling Henry adorable was enough to make me nauseous, and now I'm, what... her dating coach? What kind of rom-com alternate dimension is this?

Everything in my brain wants me to say, *no! Say no! We can't go out with her, but that doesn't mean Henry should!*

"That's kind of weird, don't you think?" I say, contorting my face to match the uncertainty in my chest. I suggested telling Henry he could ask her out. This is taking it to another level.

Elle doesn't answer right away, and I can see her swallow, as if pushing down something she wishes she could say. "Why would it be weird? You're like *almost* my friend now. Or at the very least, my not-completely loathsome neighbor. You can help me win him over, can't you?"

Can't I?

There's no reason that I shouldn't be able to do that. That's what she's saying. She's giving me the chance to say *no, actually, I can't do that. Because I think you're funny and cute and* I *want to ask you out.* But I can't. God, throw some self-sabotage into this alternate universe, why don't you?

"Sure, I can do that," I say, clenching my jaw. I feel something twist in my gut when the words leave my mouth.

Elle nods, and I swear I see the same bob in her throat. She holds out her hand. "Friends?"

I try not to focus too much on how her soft hand feels in mine, or the warmth in my chest at her touch.

"Friends."

ELEVEN

Elle

A lot happened Wednesday morning with Oliver at the park, and I'm not quite sure what to make of it all.

Oliver and I have somehow fallen into an unlikely friendship. A few weeks ago, I was berating him at his door and now I'm almost... disappointed our relationship won't turn into anything more. I'm not exactly sure how we got here, but here we are, and it's all a bit confusing.

When I asked Oliver if it would be weird for him to set me up with Henry, I wanted him to say *yes, it would.* And for a moment, I thought he was going to. I don't think I've hallucinated all the times he's checked me out, or leaned in a little closer than necessary when I'm talking. I think about the way he was nice to Anne at the hospital, or the overpriced earbuds he bought me... Did I really imagine all of that? I know he said he wasn't in the right place for a relationship, but he must *really* not be interested in me if he would rather set me up with his friend than ask me out himself. Right?

My heart hurts a little at that thought. It wasn't a formal rejection, but it feels a bit like one. I can handle a lot of things, but no one wants to feel unwanted.

So naturally, I'm going to push that feeling down somewhere deep in my brain and focus on the task at hand. Oliver needs to love New York again. And I am here for it. Hype Girl Elle is back and she is ready to New York the *shit* out of this guy.

I'm practically giddy as I wait for Oliver and Thor on the steps of our building. It's late afternoon, since he needed some time to sleep after his shift. He picked Thor up at about eight this morning, and he looked gray. Like the color of his face was *gray*. I don't know a lot about the medical field, but I'm pretty sure your job is not supposed to literally suck the life out of you.

When he finally emerges from the building, Thor immediately finds me on the steps and licks my face, his tail wagging so hard that his butt wiggles. He has grown a bit since I first met him, and he's finally starting to fit his paws, but I don't think he'll get much bigger. I gather him up in my arms and hold him like a koala. Oliver shakes his head, but I can see him hiding a small smile. He looks much better after a few hours of sleep. Color has returned to his cheeks, even though there are still shadows under his eyes. His hair is damp from a shower, and I try to ignore the fresh scent of some kind of woodland shampoo that emanates off of his body. *He's not interested in you, snap out of it.*

It's the end of March, so there's still a chill in the air, but the humidity is already starting to creep in. The threat of rain is always looming, and I hope we won't get caught in a downpour, but my weather app says it won't rain until tonight.

"So, where are we headed first?" Oliver asks, yawning into his hand.

"The Highline. I figure you haven't been there since it was only finished a few years ago."

"Yeah, I've heard of it," he replies unenthusiastically. He rubs his hand up and down his face as if it will magically wake him up.

"Coffee first?" I ask, giving him a knowing look.

"Definitely." He stifles another yawn.

We walk to the end of our street, in the direction of the Natural History Museum. I'm not sure Oliver even knows where he is going. He just seems to be following me in a sleepy haze. Thor trots alongside us, happily sniffing each square of the pavement in a strategic order. I lead us to a small coffee shop on the edge of the park. It's one of my favorites because it's not a big chain. There are glass windows along one side and a double door leading into the small space. There are a few plush benches and some high-top tables scattered throughout the café, but most of the space is taken up by the line throughout the store.

Oliver hands me his credit card when I order the coffees, and I take it. The interaction is so natural, it's like we've done it a thousand times. We grab our coffees and go to exit the store, but there's a rush of customers getting in line and trying to leave at the same time. I find myself awkwardly pressed between Oliver's chest and the frame of the door, my face inches from his chin. I make the mistake of looking up, and I see that his eyes are piercingly clear for the first time today. And they're staring back down at me.

The interaction lasts less than a few seconds, but for those few moments, every inch of me is pressed up to every part of him, and it feels like everyone around us is moving in slow motion. We're frozen in the middle of this doorway, the people around us a blur of color, the two of us posed among them.

When the doorway finally clears, Oliver and I are funneled out with the crowd, awkwardly stumbling onto the sidewalk. The street is quiet because it's Saturday in our mostly residential neighborhood, so the hustle and bustle of the workweek is replaced by the muted hum of a few cars passing by along Central Park West.

I mentally shake off the—*whatever* just happened between Oliver and me and start walking. I head towards the subway station, thinking Oliver will follow me.

"So we can take the A or the C—" I say, turning around to find Oliver still standing in front of the coffee shop. Thor is pattering his feet impatiently to catch up to me. "What's wrong?"

"I—I don't take the subway," he says in a low voice. He shuffles uncomfortably from one foot to the other.

I guess he expects that to surprise me, but it doesn't. I could understand how being in an underground tunnel on a rickety tube of metal would be unsettling for him.

"It's just, I don't like not having an *in case of emergency* plan. I lose my shit in the tunnels to get on this island," he adds. His shoulders creep up to his ears as he says this, like the thought of it alone is making him cringe.

"Okay, no subway then," I say quickly. "Well, that definitely eliminates my plan to ride up and down the escalators in Penn Station." Oliver's eyes go wide and I giggle. "Kidding!"

"Not funny." Oliver narrows his eyes at me in mock-annoyance, but then relaxes.

"So how do you get around?" I ask, genuinely curious.

"I walk mostly. If it's anywhere too far, I take a cab."

I consider that for a moment. "So, we can Citi Bike it," I finally reply.

"You ride those death traps?" he asks, in such shock that his voice actually breaks. I start walking in the direction of the nearest collection of bikes, because by the time we decide on transportation, we could be halfway there.

"You're not the only one who doesn't love the subway," I say with a shrug. His pace matches mine in a few quick strides.

"Do you think that's a good idea? I mean... if you got hit by a car you would—"

"I feel a double standard coming," I mutter, giving him a sideways glance.

"It's not because you're a woman, it's just because you're small! If you crashed, you'd go flying!" He's actually getting himself worked up about this. Is... is he concerned about my safety? Seriously? That's what's happening here?

I lead us to a bike docking station and get set up. I swing my backpack around to my front and pull out a travel pack of disinfecting wipes and hand one to Oliver, who is standing awkwardly next to a bike. He looks at the wipe suspiciously, and then catches my gaze and gives me a look I can't quite identify. Maybe he's surprised that he's not the only one who thinks about germs? Or by the fact that I knew he would need one without him saying it? He watches me wipe down the handlebars on one of the bikes and blinks a few times before speaking.

"I'm a big girl. I can handle a bicycle. I'm a very experienced rider." I shoot him a wink as I throw my leg over the bike, putting one foot on the pedal and leaving one on the ground until Oliver makes his mind up.

"I would be happy to pay for an Uber."

"Come on, live a little." I'm worried about pushing him too far out of his comfort zone, but I can tell in this instance, he needs a little shove. I decide not to give him a choice and begin to pedal, giving him a chance to catch up by waiting at the next intersection.

"I'd like to state for the record that this is a bad idea," he says, riding up beside me. I cackle when I see Thor strapped into a basket on the front of the bike. His tongue is hanging out the side of his mouth and he looks like he couldn't be happier.

Oliver on the other hand…

The only way to accurately describe how Oliver looks on a bright blue bicycle is like a clown on a tricycle. His knees look like they might knock into his chest every time he pedals, and his brows are so furrowed I'm surprised he can see from underneath them. I have to stop looking at him after a while, because laughing distracts me from paying attention to the road.

There's not much traffic until we get more into Midtown, at which point Oliver shouts, "We should be wearing helmets! This is a bad example for the children!" He yells so loudly you would think we were in a convertible sports car with a revving engine and blaring wind, rather than a relatively calm city street.

While I do agree with him that helmets should be more common practice, I take the opportunity to jab, "Duly noted, *Grandpa*!"

When we park our bikes on 34th Street, about a block from the Highline, I feel like I could go home happy for the day.

"I'd say mission accomplished already, right?" I joke, as I watch Oliver awkwardly get off the bike. His foot lands in one of the many puddles against the curb and he curses. I try not to laugh. When he gets up on the sidewalk, he puts his hands to his knees and lets his head hang. I put a hand on his back, my stomach clenching a bit when I feel the grooves of his spine. I pat him gently. "You made it, buddy."

"That was way too stressful," he says on an exasperated breath. I shake my head and start walking. I've found that if I keep moving, Oliver catches up eventually. I think he intended for this day to go differently, but clearly he hasn't seen the full-force of the hype girl that is Elle Thompson.

When Oliver finally recovers from his ordeal, I lead us towards the steps that go up to the park. I'm trying to remove the smile that is plastered onto my face from watching Oliver ride a Citi Bike down 10th Avenue, but failing miserably. I start talking instead.

"So this used to be an elevated subway line. It was built in the 1930s and was used up until the 80s. It was supposed to be demolished because people thought it was an eyesore. It was overgrown after not being used for years, and that's what inspired them to make it a public park."

"Do you just walk around with this knowledge in your head?" Oliver asks as we reach the top of the stairs and emerge onto the platform.

"Yeah, me and *Google*," I deadpan.

I've been here too many times to count. It's one of my favorite places in the city. I much preferred it a few years ago, before the final stages were finished and it was less popular. But still, it feels like a hidden oasis perched above the craziness of downtown. I love the history of it too. As we walk, the old rail tracks follow alongside us, now covered with short grasses and small plants. The old lining the pathway to the new.

Thor zigzags in front of us, sniffing every inch of the platform that he can get his nose on. I watch him for a few moments, before returning my gaze to Oliver, who is looking over the edge of the platform, and up at the buildings that tower above us.

"This is pretty cool," he murmurs. I nod and stifle my "*I told you so*," until later.

"It would be different if we came in a month or so, everything would be in bloom," I say, gesturing to the bare trees.

"I still think it's pretty beautiful. It's like we're in a different universe, even though we're only a few stories up." I look down and smile at how similar his thoughts are to mine. "What is that?" he asks, pointing to the large structure to the left of us.

"It's called The Vessel," I say, stopping to lean against the railing. "This is Hudson Yards. It used to be a rail yard that was empty for as long as I can remember. They built all these new apartment buildings and shops here over the last few years."

"And what's the point of it?" Oliver asks, skepticism on his face.

"You climb up it and get good views of the city," I say with a shrug. We keep walking as the path narrows between several blocks of buildings.

"It feels like the world was just built around this," Oliver comments, gazing up at the buildings that feel so close to us we could touch them.

"Yeah, I think it's cool that they've repurposed it instead of demolishing it. It's a nice place for tranquility in the midst of all the chaos that comes with living here." I close my eyes for a moment and let the wind brush past my face. When I open my eyes, Oliver is watching me. I offer him a small smile and keep walking.

We walk in silence for a while, until the pathway opens up again to reveal some modern art structures and a pavilion with benches.

"This would be a great place to go for a run," Oliver says, gesturing to the pathway ahead of us.

I scoff. "Well, you have fun with that."

"You're trying to sell me on this place, but you wouldn't come for a run with me here?" he asks, as if that is even in the realm of possibility.

"I wasn't kidding when I said I only run when someone is chasing me. Have you seen these boobs?" I gesture to my chest. "What do you think happens to these when I run?"

Oliver coughs awkwardly. "I... um..."

"And don't get any ideas. It's not *Baywatch*, buddy. It's like running with two ten-pound sandbags on your chest that are *not* well secured. I've gotten hit in the face with these things during a cardio session." Oliver's eyes widen as I talk, my voice getting louder as I rant. "You know mountain climbers? That shit could knock me out!"

I nod to prove my point, a serious look on my face. Oliver presses his lips into a line. He's trying not to laugh, but he can't help it, and a bark escapes from his lips, his eyes squinting from his smile. I playfully hit his side. "It's true!"

"I'm sure it is," he says, wiping a tear from under his eye. "You paint quite a picture."

I push him again and he stumbles to the side, still laughing.

"Just for that you're buying me lunch," I say pointedly. "And I'm getting a lobster roll."

TWELVE

Oliver

"Sophia, I'd really love to know what it's like to live in your brain," I say, rolling my eyes at my sister, thankful that she can't see me through the phone.

"Oliver—"

"Sophia—"

"Don't use that tone with me," she chides. I can hear clinking dishes and mumbles of conversations in the background behind her. I picture my sister sitting in a piazza in Tuscany, wearing one of those obnoxiously big hats and oversized sunglasses, her whole outfit screaming "*I'm an American!*"

It's the first time I've actually spoken to my sister since she left, other than text messages here and there. Sophia and I have always had a weird relationship: we're six years apart, so we weren't exactly close growing up. By the time she was in middle school, I was at college. And the truth is, I only see her as much as I see my parents, at holidays and a handful of times in between. But it wasn't easy growing up with a father like Andrew Cole, so my sister and I do have some kind of trauma bond that makes us close, even if we don't talk to each other every day.

"I can use whatever tone I want, Soph," I snap back at her. "You left me with a dog I never asked for."

"Oh shut up, Oliver! It's a dog! Who doesn't want a dog?"

"A guy who doesn't like surprises!" I exclaim, my patience with my flighty sister wearing thin.

"He was at a high-kill shelter, Oliver. What was I supposed to do? Let him be *killed*?"

Ugh, the good old guilt trip. Sophia is getting almost as good at it as my mother.

"Did it even occur to you to ask me why I'm in Italy?" she adds, a hint of anger in her voice. I'm confused by the change of subject.

"Mom said you're taking a course or something," I say, rubbing my temples. I'm dropping Thor off at Elle's after I get back from the gym, so I'm collecting Thor's toys and putting them in the big bag that Elle and I pass back and forth during our co-parenting pick-ups and drop-offs.

"I'm enrolled in the most *selective* and *prestigious* fashion program in the world, Oliver. Twenty people get in every year. Out of the *whole world*. Mom didn't tell you that?"

Aw, shit. Maybe she *is* better at guilt than Mom is these days.

"She said a fashion program. She left out *prestigious* and *selective*."

"Of course she did, because if you're not going to Stanford Medical School in this family, you don't matter." I can hear the hurt behind her words.

I stop what I'm doing and sit on the couch. Thor patters his feet, getting impatient with me. He knows I have a bone in the bag and he wants it. He sits down in front of me, his awkward hind legs sticking out from each side of him as he plops his butt down. When I look in his eyes, I'm reminded of my little sister, who has eyes that can look just as pathetic when she wants them to.

"Look, Soph, I'm sorry, okay? I've—" I start, but I'm not sure where my sentence is going. I am sorry. I guess I'm usually stuck on how my parents are hounding me and think that they leave Sophia alone. But maybe being the kid without expectations comes with its own set of problems?

Sophia scoffs on the other end of the phone. "You're apologizing, but you don't even know what for."

"Soph, you're giving me some serious guilt right now, can you lay off a bit?"

"I'll lay off when you get your head out of your ass, Ollie. You're not the only one with problems."

"Soph, come on—" I start, but she hangs up before I can finish.

She's right, I don't know what I'm apologizing for. I don't know what Sophia wants from me. I don't know what everyone wants from me. I just want to scream, "*I'm doing my best! This is me trying!*" at all of them.

I run my hands through my hair, trying to ease the tension out of my head. And then a cold, wet nose presses against my arm and I smile. This dog…

"What is this?" Henry asks. I've just sent him a text message even though we're right next to each other.

"It's Elle's number," I say through gritted teeth.

Henry looks at me funny. I'm lying on a towel on the cushioned floor of his gym, waiting for him to close up for the night. I would never actually lay on this floor without something under me. Plus, there is so much sweat pooling off of me that I could probably make a sweat angel with my arms and legs. But I can't try because Thor is laying on the mat next to me. His back is up against my side, and he's out cold. I spent a good half hour at the punching bag, getting out my frustration from speaking to my sister. My conversation with her just cemented why Elle is better off with Henry. Clearly, I did something to upset Sophia, and I don't even know what it was. Wherever I go, relationships crumble.

"I'm confused," Henry finally says.

"I figure you're used to that feeling by now," I snap back, unable to laugh at my own joke.

"I thought you two—"

"We're not," I answer too quickly, my tone harsher than I mean it. "We're actually kind of... *friends* now. It's weird, but she asked me to tell you she's interested, so do with that what you will." I wave my hand at him flippantly.

"She's *interested*?" He purses his lips to the side, like he is unsure what that wording should mean to him. I know I signed up for this self-torment, but I think I underestimated how much it would suck to see someone else, let alone my best friend, go out with Elle. Especially since, the more I think about it, they have a lot in common and want the same things. While Elle and I... don't.

"Well, she thinks you're cute," I reply, closing my eyes, willing this conversation to end. I try to keep my face stoic, so he can't see how much encouraging him to do this is hurting me.

"Ugh, *cute*, really? She used the word *cute*?"

"Well, the exact word she used was adorable."

"Fuck off, you're messing with me." He kicks my leg and makes Thor jump.

"Not a word of a lie, I swear!" I say, kicking him back, and I can't stop myself grinning at his annoyance. Busting Henry's balls is one way to help me forget the cloud of sadness that is hanging over this situation. "It's not my fault you have a short man complex."

"I'm 5'10", I am *not* short," he says, talking more to himself than to me.

"Whatever you have to tell yourself, bud," I say, putting my arms behind my head.

"And you're sure you're okay with this?" he asks, trying to match my gaze.

"Yes, so please stop asking," I reply, my patience wearing thin. "Now text her so you can finish cleaning this place and we can get some food. I'm starving."

THIRTEEN

Elle

Everything about Henry Sanchez screams *happily ever after*.

He's charming. He's funny. He understood the yellow picture frame that I have around the peephole in my apartment. He's very handsome—the perfect combination of high school football captain and dark romance love interest. His hair is short and neat, and thankfully, he doesn't use product. Guys who put gel in their hair instantly give me the *ick*.

He's smart. He went to *Stanford*. He runs his own business, which he wants to franchise. He is close with his family and has one older sister. She has two kids who he loves immensely. They live in Connecticut, but he sees them as often as he can.

He shows me pictures of himself holding freaking *babies* with a huge grin on his face. That is how perfect he is.

I'm determined to make this date amazing. I want so badly to forget about the nagging thought I have in my head, the one about a certain doctor who wears beanies and buys the most adorable toys for his dog. Because that thought isn't going to get me anywhere. I have a great guy sitting in front of me, and I refuse to focus on anything but him.

"It's funny. When we met the other day, I thought I'd seen you before." He twists his face, like he is trying to remember where he knows me from. "Around my gym, maybe?"

"Where is your gym? I ask, playing with the bucatini on my plate.

"75th and Amsterdam."

"I teach at the yoga studio there. I didn't realize that was your gym. What a small world!" I say, maybe too enthusiastically. I add another item to the list of things we have in common. All this time, Henry worked at the gym beneath where I teach. As someone who fully believes in fate, and the universe giving you things when you need them, I take this as a sign.

"How did you get into yoga?" He crosses his arms—his extremely *large* arms—on the table and leans forward, his full attention on me.

"I started in college and never stopped. It's... I don't know. Kind of a happy place for me," I say, blushing. "That sounds stupid."

"No, it doesn't," he says, shaking his head. "The gym is my happy place too. It's a safe space, where I feel the most comfortable. That's what you feel when you do yoga, right?"

I nod, letting a small smile spread across my face. "Yeah, exactly."

From our conversation so far, I've noticed that Henry is very thoughtful. He asks questions because he genuinely wants to hear the answer, not just because he thinks he has to. He considers what I say and builds on it. Talking with him is like getting a hug from a big, warm teddy bear.

"Let me guess, you didn't have a space that was just yours growing up? Maybe an annoying older sister that wouldn't let you near any of her stuff? Because I definitely have one of those." He chuckles.

"I have a little brother. But in a way you're right, I didn't really have my own space in our house. My parents divorced when I was young, and Nick and I stayed with my mom in our tiny three-bedroom."

"Are you close with your brother?" Henry asks, genuine interest in his eyes.

I nod, a smile spreading across my face. "He's my favorite person in the world. He has Down's syndrome, so he needed a little extra care growing up. I guess that's why I didn't have a place that was just for me. I think people assume that I must resent him for it, but I could never."

Henry's gaze flicks down to my mouth and I can feel the heat of a blush creeping into my cheeks again. When he looks back up, I hold eye contact for moment and put on my best flirting face, then look back down at my plate. I relish in the feeling of him watching my every move. There's not exactly fireworks going off in my body, but I feel *wanted*, and that's a start.

Even though Henry is amazing, in the amount of time I've been sitting in this restaurant, I've decided that I hate dating. Specifically, I hate first dates. I hate feeling like I'm on a job interview while also trying to discern whether someone is attractive. It's weird, and frankly a little messed up, the way we have to sit here and pretend that we're both not thinking about whether we want to have sex with the other. We're making small talk about families and jobs and hobbies, and using that to decipher whether the other person might suck in bed. The whole process is awkward and I really want no part of it anymore. Why can't I skip this step and just find the love of my life? Forget the whole courting process and be in a settled relationship? But also find them without leaving my couch? That would be the dream.

We opt to walk back to the apartment, stopping for gelato on the way. Henry gets pistachio and I get chocolate and strawberry. I laugh as he tells a story about a client who visited the gym last week and got stuck under the bench press.

"I'm sorry for laughing! I'm sure it wasn't funny in the moment," I say, putting another spoonful of gelato into my mouth. Henry's gaze lingers on my movements, but he recovers quickly.

"No, it was pretty funny in the moment. There was no weight on the bar. The poor guy was just trying the gym for the first time. I felt so bad, but I couldn't help laughing either."

"*No*! You laughed at him?" I cover my mouth.

"I couldn't help it!" Henry admits with a smile. "I don't think I'll see him at my gym again."

"You better hope he doesn't have a vengeful side and do a whole one-star review rampage on Yelp."

"Oh shit, I didn't even think of that." Henry rubs his temples. "That's what I'll be doing when I get home then."

We slow to a stop outside of my apartment building, and I notice that Oliver's window is illuminated. I'm surprised he's up this late on his night off, but more likely, he and Thor just have fallen asleep watching TV and he didn't turn the light off. When I turn back to Henry, I can tell that he saw what I was looking at. I smile and act like it's nothing, because it *is* nothing.

"I had a great time," I say, and I genuinely mean it, but an awkwardness has fallen between us.

"Me too," he replies, putting his hands in the pockets of his coat. "Can I call you again?" My heart melts a little. He is literally a textbook dreamy romance hero. Lucy would be screaming at me right now if she saw this interaction.

I think back to the beginning of the night, when Henry put his hand on the small of my back and ushered me into the restaurant. If there was a jolt of excitement, I can't recall it. I don't remember if I got butterflies in my stomach when he smiled at me as we ordered our meals. But I'm excited to see Henry again because he is full of possibilities, not necessarily because of how I felt on *this* one date. There will be a spark next time, I'm sure.

"Yeah, I'd like that," I say with a flirty smile.

Henry leans forward and places a quick kiss on my cheek, saying he'll see me soon. I wait for the imprint of his lips to leave a searing sensation on my skin. It doesn't happen.

I look up at the building before climbing the stairs. The apartment above mine is now dark.

FOURTEEN

Oliver

"We'll have two orders of the pork fried dumplings, a shrimp ball, *har gow*, and *siu mai*," Elle says, pointing to the variety of woven baskets on the cart next to us.

"Wait, I think there's one thing you didn't order," I say sarcastically.

"This is just round one," she replies, a dead-serious look on her face.

It's Saturday afternoon, and Elle has invited me to a traditional dim sum brunch in Chinatown. She let me pay for an Uber this time, because it's the weekend and the roads are clearer, so it didn't take next to forever to get downtown. On the way here, I Googled the place we were going and found out there was one right by our apartment.

"*That's not the same. This is the original in Chinatown. It's more authentic,*" she'd said, rolling her eyes like this was something obvious I should have known.

"*They have the same stuff on their menu,*" I'd deadpanned.

"Shut up, Oliver, and prepare to watch me eat my weight in dumplings."

And that, she wasn't kidding about.

We're sitting outside because she insisted that we bring Thor, even though I hate eating on a New York City street. I should only be eating outside if I'm looking at a beautiful view. Not smelling the subway fumes.

I'm pretty sure Elle has already eaten about twelve dumplings, and the cart has only passed by us once. Frankly, I'm impressed. She loves the fried pork ones, which I do too. But I only take two and leave the rest for her. I reach for the plate of *har gow* and put two on my plate.

"So, how was your date?" I ask, feeling like a glutton for punishment. I think back to Thursday night, when I saw Elle walk up to the building stoop with Henry. I remember the way my stomach dropped when he kissed her. I can only hope that Elle doesn't bring up the fact that I was on the treadmill for an hour that night, unable to sleep with that image in my head.

"It was good," she replies, not making eye contact with me. "He's really sweet."

A beat passes between us. "*But?*" I prod, gesturing with my silverware.

"No *but*," she says with a shrug. She's lying. She looked down and back up again quickly. She always does that when she lies. I know this after asking if she gave Thor peanut butter with his dinner most nights. She has no poker face.

"Do you think you'll go out with him again?"

"I think so," she says, popping another dumpling into her mouth. "Any advice?"

I think for a moment. "I don't know, Henry's pretty chill. He loves his family and his business. Big into Formula 1. Giants fan—"

"Please stop listing sports things, that's not helpful," she interrupts.

I think for a second, getting lost in her doe eyes, before I settle on, "He'll like you for who you are." There's a moment between us, when I give Elle a shy smile, and something feels unsaid. But I can't find the words.

"You might be the worst dating guru ever," she says plainly, shaking her head.

"I'm okay with that. That's not really something a guy wants to be called."

"What about Hitch? I'm sure he would like to be called that," she rebuts, raising a brow.

"Oh please, don't get me started," I scoff. "That was the most unrealistic plot of a movie ever. What New Yorker goes on a jet ski in the Hudson? We all know what is in that water!" I reply, getting a bit animated. Elle smiles knowingly. "What?"

"You called yourself a New Yorker," she says cockily. Her grin spreads wider.

I visibly roll my eyes at her, and return to my plate. I swat away a fly that won't leave our table alone. *This* is why I don't eat outside.

"Q-tip," Elle says, mimicking the dance move that Kevin James does in the movie.

"*Throw it away!*" We say in tandem. We both cackle so loudly, we gain the attention of our neighbors, and the unhappy waitress pushing the dumpling cart. Elle's face goes red as she puts her fist in front of her mouth, trying to suppress her laughter. I continue laughing so much that Thor even jumps up to see what the commotion is about. I swat the fly away from him.

"Fucking bugs," I mumble.

"You're afraid of bugs?" Elle asks, curious about my frustration.

"I'm not *afraid*," I say, narrowing my eyes. "I just don't like them."

"No one likes bugs. Except the people who work in the bug section of the zoo, I suppose," she says, pursing her lips. I give her a dubious look. "But you're giving off a horse being afraid of a mouse vibes."

I grimace. I cringe and bring my shoulders up to my ears as another fly buzzes by me. Or maybe it's the same one, and it has a serious vendetta. "I'll rephrase, I fucking *hate* bugs."

Elle grins. And my frown deepens. I know that face.

"You're a very strange person," I say to her, as she fills a bowl with bug-shaped candy.

"I don't find that to be an insult," she replies, taking one of the gummy worms and pretending to slither it around my counter.

"It wasn't meant as an insult. It was a factual statement. But whatever you have to tell yourself."

A month ago, I would have never expected to spend an afternoon eating dim sum with Elle Thompson, the nosiest and pushiest neighbor I've ever had. I would have also never predicted that on the same day I'd be sitting in my apartment with the same pushy neighbor, now betting me to eat a bowl of candy.

"*Not just candy*," she'd said as she emerged from the convenience store that she made Thor and me wait outside of. "*Bug candy*."

"*So your torment of me has reached new heights then?*" I said, as she showed me the bag of cockroaches, spiders, worms, and who knows what else.

"*Precisely*," she said with a wink. And like a fool, I followed her back to our building and let her into my apartment.

"Explain to me why I should do this again," I mutter, plopping down on one of my bar stools after putting Thor's dinner bowl down.

"Because, *Oliver*—" I try not to focus on the skip in my chest when she says my name. "I have a bet for you. I bet that you cannot eat a bowl of insects. Creepy, crawly, *crunchy* insects," she says, pressing her palms into the counter and bouncing on the balls of her feet, her expression one of pure joy.

"*Crunchy*?"

"Yeah, the cockroaches have lifelike exoskeletons made out of processed sugar of some sort."

"And if I don't?"

"Then you have to attend a yoga class at my studio." She raises her brows as if to say, "*What do you think?*" as the smile on her face turns into a devilish smirk. I break off our staring match to look down at the bowl of bugs in front of me. Part of me is intrigued to see Elle teach a yoga class in a pair of those leggings. But the other part of me knows I have absolutely zero flexibility. And I'm sure Elle knows that too, just by looking at me. She probably realizes what a fool I would look like in front of a room full of yoga people. *Yogi people*?

"Yoga?" I repeat, like the answer is somehow going to change.

"Yoga," she says confidently, raising her brows. "Have you done it before?"

"I've seen it. It's just like stretching."

Elle lets out an audible, "*Ugh*," before leaning forward against the counter. "Please try the cockroach. *Please*," she says through gritted teeth. Her voice is stern, like it's taking everything in her not to smack me.

"Again, I have to ask: *why* would I do this?"

"Because it would be good for your anxiety."

I scrunch my face at her. *Where did she come up with that?*

"I don't have anxiety. I have OCD. It's different," I say plainly.

I can't believe I just said that out loud to her. I never talk so openly about my OCD, not even with my family. I mean, everyone knows about it, but it's kind of just swept under the rug, ignored.

Elle looks at me from beneath her brows, her eyes calling me out on my bullshit.

"Why do you think I have anxiety?" I say, and she rolls her eyes, taking a deep breath. *Those fucking eyes.*

"Fine, let's say you *don't* have anxiety," she says, trying to placate me. "Maybe I just want to torture you in public. Plus, it's another New York City experience. It's only a beginner class. Will you do it?" I don't miss the fact that she didn't answer my question.

"Do you know that you don't have to spend every minute of every day trying to think of ways to help people?" I mirror her previous knowing look.

"What does that mean?" she replies, scrunching her face in surprise. She looks offended.

"It means that you're always thinking of your next project, of what someone else needs. You don't have to do that." I say, flicking a gummy bug at her. I think she's surprised that I remember her speech about supporting people, the one she gave me when she suggested being my New York tour guide.

Elle doesn't say anything right away. I get the sense that people don't tell her like it is very often. I want to say something like, *"It's annoying to have someone point out your bullshit, isn't it?"* but I don't.

"I know I don't *have* to—"

"Do you?"

"Stop trying to change the subject. Eat the bugs!" she whines, pushing the bowl towards me. I groan internally at her insistence on talking about anything besides herself. She thinks she's sly when she puts the focus on everyone else. But I'm starting to see through her.

"And what if I do eat the bugs?" I shiver at the thought. "What do I get?"

"I don't know..." she muses. "You can come up with another form of public humiliation for me."

I contemplate this for a moment. I'm not really sure how that is a "win" for me, but if I've learned anything in the past few weeks, it's that resisting Elle's schemes never works for long.

"I should mention that the main thing I don't like about bugs is the buzzing, so this game doesn't even really—"

"Yeah, uh huh, that's great. Start with the cockroach," she prompts. I pick up the gummy worm instead, side-eyeing her, and throw it in my mouth.

I should have swallowed it whole.

My stomach convulses as the candy crunches against my teeth, the texture so much worse than I imagined it would be. *Oh my* God. *Do not let me throw up in front of this woman.*

I quickly swallow the worm and try to un-contort my face, to pretend like that wasn't actually physically painful for me. When I make eye contact with Elle again, she raises her brows at me, a hint of a smile on her lips. She pushes the cockroach shaped candy at me. As soon as my front teeth crunch down on the exterior shell, I spit it right back out.

"Fuck it! Fuck it!" I shout, grabbing a napkin. Thor jumps as I propel myself from my chair.

Elle laughs hysterically, hunching over on the counter to steady herself, her face flushing red. Thor jumps up on her, just as amused by her laughter as I am, because it is the most infectious sound I've ever heard. Once I've gotten the disgusting candy out of my mouth, I realize that I'm smiling, just from looking at her.

Elle's laugh is the best sound I've heard in a long time.

Now *that* is a dangerous thought.

FIFTEEN

Elle

"This game is totally rigged!" Henry shouts, throwing his hands up.

The white glow from the air hockey table illuminates his body and shows the defined muscles beneath his white t-shirt. It's a really good look for him.

"Why do I get the feeling you were the kid that went way too hard in gym class?" I reply, retrieving the pucks from the middle of the table.

"I am neither going to confirm or deny if that's true," he says, leaning over the table. "Best out of three?"

"Let's put some money on it, so I can get something out of this except just kicking your butt," I joke. "Ten bucks if I win the next game."

"It's probably not the most gentlemanly thing to agree to taking money from a lady on a date, but my competitive nature is outweighing my manners right now." His smile sparkles as he pulls out his wallet and places a ten-dollar bill on the table. "Winner gets to keep that."

"Bring it on, Sanchez," I say, slapping my own ten-dollar bill on the table and hitting the puck off to the side.

When Henry suggested we go to the arcade tonight, I was pretty surprised. I've never been on a "game" date before, and it made me excited to see if this night would show me that Henry is different from other guys.

And it's true. Henry *is* different. He makes me laugh. He's playful. Our conversations flow naturally. I smile a lot when I am with him. Overall, he seems perfect on paper. Perfect for *me*. He checks all of the boxes on my imaginary checklist. But the whole time I am with him, I am making a mental pro/con list, and I hate myself for it. Henry deserves better than someone who is making a subconscious comparison in her head. Which is why when he walks me home that night, I give him a quick kiss on the cheek, and tell him I'll text him tomorrow.

Because as much as I *want* to fall for him, I'm afraid my feet have already reached the ground somewhere else.

As much as I try to throw myself into being interested in Henry, I find myself more enthusiastic about planning my next New York City adventure with Oliver. My Oliver Cole Elle-ter-vention is in full effect.

The other day, when Oliver told me he didn't like bugs, my instinct was to scoff at him. But I didn't. Because I could see that his concern was genuine. I thought back to Oliver's apartment and how immaculate it was. Coupled with the fact that he can't wind himself down without hitting the treadmill at 6 a.m., and the brief conversation we had about his family, I'm starting to think that what I assumed was stress from a high-pressure job is actually a lot more complicated.

As big and intimidating as he is, Oliver doesn't give off a *macho man* attitude. He's kind, funny, and sweet. The custom pair of earplugs on my nightstand and his spoiled dog are proof of that. He has quirks, but who doesn't?

I know anxiety takes a lot of forms, and is different for everyone. I wish I could come out and ask Oliver what his triggers are, but I don't want to push too hard. I want him to trust me enough to show me that side of him. Now that we're friends (which the me from a few weeks ago would never believe), I want to understand what goes on in his head. And I'm not sure if he's ready to share that with me yet. Which is why I think yoga will be perfect for him.

We've been to the Highline, Hudson Yards, Chelsea Market, pretty much any non-touristy New York places I could think of over the last few weeks. But I think tonight's expedition is going to be my favorite.

"Hey, before I forget—" Oliver says as we walk towards the West Side Highway. "Can you watch Thor next Sunday when I go to my parents' house?"

"Only if you say please," I tease.

"*Yeah right*, like you would actually say no to spending the day with my dog." He matches my expression and for a moment, we're locked in a *who knows who better* stare off. Oliver wins when I look down at Thor. He's got me there. When my gaze meets his again, he chuckles. "Yeah, that's what I thought."

"Why don't you take him with you?"

"It will be quicker if I take the train to Long Island rather than renting a car and driving out there. And I can't take him on the train," he explains.

"Then sure, I can watch him." I lean down to scratch between Thor's ears. "What's the occasion?"

"My mom's birthday," Oliver replies on an exhale. "Can't get out of it." I'm about to ask why he would want to, but he changes the subject. "So, where are we going?"

Thor and I met him at the hospital at the end of his shift. He was pissed about it, having just worked fourteen hours, but I refused to listen to his complaints. He can be out one more hour before crashing into bed for the night, and it might actually help him sleep. It's the first day shift he's had in a while, and the change in time frame is wearing on him. I can see it on his face.

He's still in his scrubs, which honestly, I'm not mad about. It's a good look. He told me these are clean ones he put on in the locker room, not ones he wore around patients. I didn't ask, but he told me all the same. He's very conscious of germs like that.

"Pier 97. It's going to be beautiful tonight, and I think you'll love it."

"And why did it have to be tonight? Why couldn't it be a day when, I don't know, I didn't just keep people alive for seventeen million hours?"

"Because, you *whiner*, seeing a New York City sunset is a rite of passage. And tonight's is supposed to be *epic*." I resist the urge to put my arm through Oliver's so we can walk down the street in tandem. Friends don't do that. Friends just walk next to each other. "It can feel a bit dark around the city sometimes," I continue. "And it's good to remember that there's a beautiful world out there, one that doesn't smell like garbage."

"And the sunset helps us do that, how?"

"By reminding us that we're small in the grand scheme of things, even though this island feels like a world within itself," I say, looking up at the sky.

"Very profound, Miss. Yogi Master," Oliver says, nudging me with his elbow.

"That's not yoga. Just my obsession with looking up. Stars, sunsets, they're my thing." I shrug.

"How come?" he asks, following my gaze up to the sky.

I let out a calming breath before responding. "I love when I look up at the sky and I'm reminded that we're on a planet with ten billion people, in a universe that is bigger than we can even imagine. I like the perspective."

I get a bit of a pep in my step as I talk. Oliver grabs my shoulders and pulls me closer to him so I don't collide with another person while I'm preaching about my sky theories, but even after they've passed he doesn't let go instantly. It's another movement that feels so natural. I try to remain as casual as possible when he finally releases me, and fall back into a natural walk, as if that didn't just happen.

"Plus, I've always loved astrology," I add, trying to hide the hitch in my voice from the unexpected contact. "If we ever leave the city, I can show you how I go full nerd on my Sky View app."

"Do I want to know what that is?"

"It's an app that lets you hold your phone up to the sky and see all the constellations!" I whine. I can't believe he's never heard of it. "And when the planets are visible, it is so cool!"

"Wow," Oliver says, feigning sarcasm. He pauses for a moment, before adding, "How come you're so interested in that kind of stuff?"

"How come you're so interested in the gym?" I challenge, mimicking his question. I can't tell if he's being sincere or making fun of me.

"I was trying to give you a compliment, *Eloise*," he says, barely able to say Lucy's nickname for me without cracking a smile.

"It didn't sound like one."

"Well, it's not every day that you meet someone who can name the constellations and talk about the effect the lunar phases have on the tides."

"Still waiting for the compliment," I murmur, gently knocking into him.

"It's impressive, that's all. You and your yoga and the deep-seeded musings on the universe. You're kind of brilliant," he says with a shrug. We make eye contact for a second, but he quickly looks away.

I'm not sure what to make of that comment. "Thank you, I guess."

We walk in companionable silence for a while before I speak again. "And because of my brother, I think." Oliver scrunches his brows. "To answer your question about why I'm interested in it. I mean, I always liked it on my own, but I loved teaching Nicky about the stars and the moon. It made him so happy." I don't realize I'm smiling until I see a soft smile on Oliver's face as well.

I lead us to the pier, which is a long building that stretches out into the Hudson. There are some public spaces, playgrounds, a few sports courts, and grassy areas for people to lounge on. Oliver and I stop for ice cream at one of the markets, and take it out to the end of the pier with us. I get a bit of déjà vu. I was eating ice cream with another guy recently, and it felt very different.

Part of me really wants to understand why Oliver *only* wants to be my friend. I don't want to sound conceited, but I *do* think he is attracted to me. The way he looks at me sometimes, I can see there is something more behind his eyes. I think about our moment in the coffee shop doorway, how being close to him made me... *breathless.* I can't be making that up, can I?

But if he *is* attracted to me, *why* would he want me to go out with his best friend? Why would he tell me that Henry is the best guy he knows? Honestly, it's all a bit confusing, and I'm not sure how to handle it. It's one of those times when having my own hype girl would be helpful. My heart aches when I think of Lucy. I miss my friend.

As the sun starts to slide behind the Jersey City skyline, I tell Oliver to look behind us, at the glow that illuminates 57th Street. I watch Oliver as he takes in the orange and yellow haze along the street. His eyes widen ever so slightly, and a contented look comes across his face. I feel a big smile squeeze my cheeks. I am so happy that he appreciates this. This isn't a big New York City landmark or tourist trap. It's just a small thing that makes me smile most days, and I can see it has the same effect on him. I can only hope it's changing his mind about New York, even just a little bit.

"That is a pretty good sunset," he says. He looks down at me, his smile growing, and I don't look away. I feel a warmth in my chest, a burning that moves my body closer to his, just by an inch. When I notice myself gravitating towards him, I pull back and clear my throat.

"I wish it was Manhattanhenge. That would have made this way more dramatic," I say, leaning over the rail to watch the river play with the shoreline.

"What's that?" he asks, either ignoring or oblivious to the moment we just shared.

"It's when the sunset lines up with all of the east-west streets of Manhattan. Like Stonehenge—"

"Shut up," he interrupts. "That can't be a thing!"

"It is! It happens three weeks before and after the summer solstice. If my New York City tour was a few weeks later, this could have been even more awesome."

"There's no way they could have planned that," he replies, still skeptical.

"They didn't, you goose. It's just one of life's coincidences." Oliver looks at me for a moment, and I get lost in his eyes. They're the kind of dark brown that feels like melted chocolate—a pool of it that I could drown in.

I walk over to a nearby bench, coaxing Thor to sit with me. He can't manage the jump with his short legs, so I pick him up and hold him in my lap.

"He's not a baby, you know," Oliver scolds, sitting beside us.

"Do we know him, Thor? I don't think we do," I say in my baby voice, smushing Thor's face between my hands. Oliver shakes his head at us. He yawns and leans forward, placing his head in his hands.

"These hours are killing you, huh?" I ask. Oliver nods, interlacing his fingers behind his neck. "I'm not sure how you're doing this when it's not something you're truly passionate about. I can't imagine losing sleep over a job unless it was a lifelong dream come true or something," I say, ignoring my instinct to reach out and rub his back. "Actually, no, not even that could sway me from a full night's sleep."

Oliver turns his head towards me, still holding it with both his hands. A shy smile appears on his face. "You're weird," he mumbles.

"Duly noted."

He sits back and puts his arms along the back of the bench, and his hand just barely grazes my shoulder. "It is a lifelong dream. It's just my father's, not mine," he says, his voice gravelly. "I thought he was going to disown me when I didn't match for a surgery residency." I tilt my head at him, unsure of what that means. He clarifies, "After med school, you have to match with a hospital to do your residency."

"Like on a dating app?"

He lets out a short laugh. "Kind of. Well, I didn't match with anyone. I'm not the most personable guy—"

"*Nooooo*!" I say sarcastically. Thor licks my face, surprised by my deep voice. Oliver scowls at me. "Sorry, so how did you get here?"

"Good old Andrew Cole and his connections," he says, flipping his hands up. "Straight-up nepotism."

"You don't sound happy about that."

"No, it's not a great feeling when you're doing a job you don't feel like you deserve to be doing," he says, drumming his lips. "I like to earn things. I've had to earn my father's approval all my life."

"So all these extra hours…?" I ask, trying to read between the lines.

"Well, those are just part of being a resident," he rebuts. "But yes, I want to prove to myself that I deserve to be here."

"Because your mind is constantly telling you that you're not?"

He looks at me in a way that tells me no one has ever said that to him before. "Exactly." He pauses for a moment. "Sometimes my brain gets in a cycle of negativity that I can't get out of."

"I get that," I say with a nod. "It makes sense that since you've been under so much pressure to be perfect or to excel your entire life, your mind is kind of stuck in that mode."

No wonder this guy is anxious. I feel for the child version of Oliver who had this intense pressure from such a young age. I'm so glad I made him eat bugs and come to yoga. It's good for him. Check one for *Project Oliver*.

Oliver doesn't say anything for a moment, and it takes me a minute to notice that he's twirling the ends of my hair between his fingers. My hair is so long I couldn't feel it, and I don't think he even knows he's doing it, because when I look at his hand, he seems surprised and drops it like he's been burned.

"Were you under pressure too, growing up? Is that why you got into yoga and stuff?" he asks hurriedly.

It seems like an odd question for him to ask, but apart from clearly trying to cover up his embarrassment, I think he's trying to match my own questions. It feels even more weird that I answer him naturally, without overthinking what I should say.

"Not pressure exactly," I say, fidgeting with the bottom of my shirt. "Just a lot of responsibility. A lot of sweeping my own problems under the rug. I don't know if that's why I like yoga. Maybe." I force a smile.

I feel a sense of contentment when I realize that Oliver asked me that question because he knows little things about me—about my brother and my passion for yoga. He put the two together and found things inside of me that I didn't know were connected. It's weird, having someone... *understand* me. I don't think I've ever felt that before.

Usually, when I find myself in a predicament, my head is saying one thing and my heart is saying another. But in this instance, they're both in agreement. My mind and body are equally confused with what to do with Oliver Cole.

SIXTEEN

Oliver

I think I may have underestimated the level to which Elle wants to torture me.

That's what I'm ruminating on when I enter the yoga studio at 8 p.m. on Thursday. Since our dumpling brunch, Elle has been texting me gifs of men in tights doing yoga on the daily. There was also one of a big, purple, Muppet-looking thing doing yoga. That one was particularly disturbing.

Thor and I take the stairs next to Henry's door up to a humble-looking studio. There's only one room, which means the number of people who will witness this should be minimal. One point Oliver. I walk up to a cranky-looking woman at the front desk who raises her brows as soon as she sees me. She whips her red ponytail in my direction and suppresses a smile.

"You must be Oliver," she says, trying to keep her voice neutral.

"Oh, great," I mutter. She's got other people in on it. I'm so screwed.

"You can set up wherever. Class starts in a few." She pauses for a moment and looks down at Thor before adding, "She usually ties the dog's leash to a chair by the side."

"Thanks," I mutter. I don't like the way she said *"the dog,"* but I don't say anything. Elle brings him here all the time. Why is this lady so cranky about it?

I walk into the studio, which has a wall lined with mirrors. All the other yoga people have their mats lengthwise, facing the mirror. I take the mat at the end of the back row, placing my water bottle off to the corner. I discreetly take my sweatshirt off, but I still feel the side-eyes of everyone in the room. How did I get myself into this?

There is one mat set up horizontally in front of the mirror. It must belong to Elle. As soon as I think of her, she appears from a door on the adjacent wall. She is wearing skin-tight blue leggings and a black muscle tee that she has tied in a knot behind her back. The shirt says *"Nama-stay-in-bed"* in large script letters. Before I can appreciate her long hair, she flips her head over and throws it up in a bun. She turns to look at herself in the mirror, tucking a few strands behind her ears. As she reaches for a headset on the floor, she sees me in the reflection. An evil smile spreads across her face.

This is going to be painful.

She scampers over to Thor to give him a quick kiss on the head, then turns around to stick her tongue out at me before returning to her place at the front of the room. I flip her off in return.

"Welcome, friends," Elle says, her voice amplified. I see her cringe when she says "friends."

"Okay, so this is a beginner yoga flow we're doing today." Elle speaks with a confidence that I don't usually hear from her. I find myself feeling... proud of her? Happy for her?

Elle keeps to herself a lot. Not that I know everything about her, but from what I do know, she's home and at work. Occasionally she mentions her friend Lucy or her brother, but not a whole lot else. It's refreshing to see her in a space where she is in control, where she can shine.

"For those of you who are new, my name is Elle. I am by no means a master yogi—" *Yogis! That's what the yoga people are called!* "—but I like to flow my own way and I hope you have some fun today." She smiles and instructs everyone to take a seat on the mat.

I fold my legs under me and sit in the middle of the mat. I don't think I've sat like this since fifth grade. Mainly because my legs are so long that I look like a contorted pretzel when I try to cross them. When I sit down, the mat curls up under me, so I shift to fix it, lining it back up with the line of one of the planks on the wood floor.

"Let's take a moment to settle and arrive on the mat," Elle says, folding her hands over her chest. The rest of the class mimics her movements. I just can't get on board with the group "*ohmmm*" mentality, so I watch silently from my corner.

"Let's take stock of our expectations for this practice. I want you to release any ideas or preconceived notions of what this is supposed to look like." Her voice is monotone, gentle and calm, and I get the feeling she's talking to me specifically. "Let's just move our bodies and be open to failure. But let's also have some fun. Some of us are beginners. Some of us are just taking time for ourselves today. I think this is going to be an awesome class." She opens her eyes and shoots me a wink. "Take a deep breath in, and as you exhale, flutter your eyes open and let's get this thing rolling."

She prompts everyone to come to all fours. I move at a beat behind the rest, watching to make sure I'm doing everything right. We do things that are called "cat cows," which I don't fully understand. How is sticking your head and butt up in the air similar to a cow?

We go into a downward-facing dog, which surprisingly doesn't suck because it stretches out my hamstrings and my calves. I awkwardly turn my head to see what everyone else looks like in this position, to make sure I'm not the only *schmo* with my butt up in the air.

"Take a few moments to pedal out here," Elle says, and I watch as she moves her heels up and down off the mat. That must be pedaling. "Feel where you are in your body. If anything I cue is not working for you, please feel free to modify and do what is best for you in your body."

She takes a breath and I can hear her shallow exhale through the microphone. "Now find stillness in your downward dog, and stay with me because I like to do some funky sun salutations. Because, well, it's my class and I can do whatever I want," she says with an airy laugh. A quiet ripple of laughter moves through the room.

Elle guides us through a series of movements. They get repetitive after a while, but five minutes later, sweat is starting to bead on my skin. Is this hot yoga? Is that why I'm sweating? I didn't realize I could sweat from stretching.

We're back in downward dog again, which seems to be our home base. Apparently these sun salutations are just a warm up? I hope there's less down-dogging in the rest of this, because my shoulders are tired already.

I take a break from the next down dog and stretch out my wrists. Elle continues, "Let's flow. Inhale, lift your right leg up and back."

I watch as she kicks her leg to the ceiling behind her. I can see every muscle in her leg working, and she points her foot gracefully as she bends her knee towards her face and comes down into a lunge.

"Crescent lunge," she pronounces, lifting her arms over her head. She looks like a statue. A beaming, bubbly, blonde statue that could care less how she looks in front of all these people. She is flowing to her own rhythm. Even the music she is playing is... *sexy*. I expected there to be chanting or soothing white noise in the background. But these sound like songs I would hear on a Spotify playlist. They pair perfectly with the intensity of Elle's movements.

This whole scene could be such a turn on. But Elle is my friend. Who is currently dating my other friend. No turning on allowed here.

In my daze, I don't notice that Elle is staring at me. Her hands are still raised and she flicks her wrist as if to say, "What are you doing?" I'm the only one in the room that is still sitting on his heels, so I stumble to mirror Elle's position. I make a face at her, and I hear a hint of a chuckle in her microphone.

When Elle says "warrior two," which for some reason makes me think of ancient Chinese warriors with samurai swords, she actually looks like a goddamn warrior. Her arms are taught when she stretches them out, her bum is flexed and her legs look so strong beneath her. I try to shake the image of those thighs clenching around my waist from my head, but I lose my balance admiring her. I try to be as subtle as possible as I find my footing again.

"If you feel yourself falling, come back to your breath. Find that *ujjayi* breath, focus on one thing, find your *drishti*." She looks at me directly when she says that word. "One thing that's constant, not moving. Focus on it and don't let go."

When she finally blinks, she loses her balance and teeters to the side. She laughs immediately. "And know that if you fall, that's your muscles learning. Just get back into it."

The crowd laughs with her, a few of them losing their balance as well. I think my expectations of this class were very misguided. I expected… more of a facade, I guess? Serious chanting and vogueing and shit. But Elle is so *real*. She is authentic to who she is, and she's just trying to enjoy the movements. The people in the room gravitate towards that energy. They love her.

"Drag your right hip back and straighten your right leg, triangle pose," Elle instructs. I watch her lean forward with both of her legs straight, her body so stealthy and lean, she looks like she's moving through water.

"Touch down to your shin, the floor, or a block on the inside of your foot." She holds her position for a moment and then stands up and starts wandering around the room, critiquing the poses of the other people.

I study the women around me, who are literally scoffing under their breath at my attempts to mirror their positions. I try to match my legs to the legs of the woman next to me, but when I spread my legs that wide, the mat shifts. I step off of it to line it back up with the wood plank on the floor.

I spread my legs again, but closer together this time, and keep them straight as I try to touch the ground near my front foot. I notice that the woman in front of me has a foam block under her hand. I grab one that is lying next to my mat and stack it as high as it goes to alleviate the stretch in my legs. Elle's voice gets closer, but I know if I move my head to find her, I'll lose my balance, so I let out my best inconspicuous exhale and try not to move.

"Your left shoulder should be in line with your left hip," she says softly. *God Almighty, this is like a game of Twister.*

"Lift your left hand up and twist slightly." Her voice sounds closer now. I see two bare feet out of my peripheral vision, and I resist the urge to stand upright.

Elle comes in front of me, and reaches a hand out towards my body.

Okay? she mouths. I nod.

And then, Elle is touching me.

Her touch is like a feather, gently grazing my arm. Her hand is warm, but it feels electric against my skin. She takes hold of my wrist and guides my left hand into the air. Her hand traces a line down my arm and she gently cups my hip, guiding it towards her. Her touch is so light, goosebumps rise on my skin.

"Imagine yourself as one long line, from the crown of your head to your hip," she instructs to the group. I feel Elle move towards my head, and I wonder if she realizes what this is doing to me.

"Let this feel good," she says, trailing her finger down my neck to my shoulder.

I turn my head slightly so I can see her. Surprisingly, she's not smiling at my torture. Her face is focused, her lips barely parted, and she meets my gaze with such intensity that I feel like I could melt down onto this floor from the weight of it.

I let out a stifled groan when she places a hand on my lower back. She jumps at the sound and immediately pulls her hand away, and I see heat flush to her face. She doesn't make eye contact with me as she struts back to the front of the room. My gaze follows her backside, and my pretzel/Twister shape crumbles to the floor, earning me gasps from around the room. And one very loud laugh.

Elle repeats her flow again and again, moving quicker each time. I give up trying to keep up with her, and start skipping whole moves so I can look like I'm on the same step as the rest of the class. I slip and slide across my mat, and my neighbor glares at me as I rearrange it for the twentieth time.

As the class winds down, Elle brings everyone back to a downward-facing dog and instructs them to "ripple like a wave" into a plank. At this point, I'm so frustrated, I'd like to tell her where she can take her rippled wave and *shove it*.

I move myself into a plank position and am brought face to face with the edge of the mat. The left corner is closer to me than the right again, making it misaligned with the line of the hardwood floor.

This. Fucking. Mat.

I'm really trying to stay focused. Elle is saying more words, something about folding your legs under you and finding a seat, but my gaze is glued to the mat.

A few moments pass and I feel a hand on my arm. My instinct makes me grab it, and warm, soft flesh meets my grasp. I open my eyes to see Elle's big brown ones staring at me, but my mind is racing so furiously that at that moment,

I can't understand the words coming out of her mouth. She is still wearing her headset, still teaching, which means everyone's eyes are probably on me. But I can't move. I can't fast forward this slow-motion freeze frame in which our eyes are locked and her hands are on mine.

She lowers me to the floor and I sit back on my butt. A quick look in my periphery tells me that in fact, no one is looking at me but her. Everyone else is sitting on the floor, their eyes closed.

I reach out with my other hand to straighten the mat to line up with the floor again, but Elle stops me. Her hand reaches for my outstretched arm first, and then she gently cups her palm around my chin, guiding me to look at her.

"Left hand heart, right hand belly," I hear Elle's voice murmur through my foggy trance. Once my eyes are locked on hers again, she takes each of my hands in one of hers.

And I let her.

I'm too far gone into my spiral to be embarrassed about what is happening. I'm too far gone to think about the way she'll mercilessly roast me for losing it in her yoga class. She'll probably make me buy her a donut or eat another bowl of bugs after this, just to prove that she was right, that yoga was fucking hard.

She presses her palm to the backside of my hand, entwining our fingers, and presses our joint hands against my chest. "Inhale," she commands, but the tone of her voice is comforting, like it could envelop me in a hug.

I look into her eyes again, and she inhales with exaggeration. That's when I realize I'm still holding my breath.

And the mat is still crooked.

She must notice my gaze briefly dart to the corner, because she presses firmly on the hand on my chest.

"Exhale all the air out." I listen, feeling the tension slowly release from my muscles. "Again. Take a long, smooth breath inwards." She exaggerates her breath again, squeezing the fingers on the hand against my chest.

I find myself closing my eyes as I sharply inhale.

"Picture the air filling your lungs, your belly."

Usually, I would be laughing right now. How am I supposed to picture breath? It's invisible. But then I feel Elle tug on my shirt, trying to instruct me to move my shoulders. "Feel the inhale, feel the air fill your body."

I lift my shoulders, tensing my grip on my chest as my mind snaps back to the mat, and Elle tightens her grasp on me as well.

"There is nothing but this moment. Right here. You and your breath. Exhale all the air out." Elle makes a loud, long exhale, and I sense the faint smell of mint on her breath. That's how close we are. "Fall into rhythm with your own breath. Find that *ujjayi* breath. Make it intentional."

I know what she's trying to do. The fight or flight part of me is telling me to resist it. Resist the hold she's trying to have on me. Resist the path she's taking my mind down. *Resist.*

She squeezes my hand, and I feel centered. *Calm.*

She's grounding me.

And it's fucking working.

"Focus the mind, find comfort in your body. You are safe in your own space. Your home." She pauses. I resist the urge to look at her and let myself be transfixed by the sound of her voice instead. "As you inhale, say silently to yourself,

I am calm in this moment." She pauses again, letting her hands move in rhythm with my breath. "As you exhale, *I can find peace in this moment.*"

I feel the pressure of her hand lighten on my chest as she says, "Bring your hands to prayer and bow your head." I don't listen to her. I gently open my eyes and observe her. A bead of sweat falls from behind her ear, but she doesn't move to catch it. I steady my hand to stop myself from reaching for it. She is sitting so close to me that our heads would touch if I bowed mine like hers. She touches her forehead to her hands and says, "Be grateful for showing up today. Gently flutter your eyes open, and sense the world around you again."

She opens her eyes, directly into mine, and smiles.

SEVENTEEN

Elle

"Show me a picture of him!" Lucy squeals on the other end of my phone.

"You're ridiculous," I mutter, rolling my eyes at her.

"Well, you won't tell me his last name, so I can't stalk him myself," she complains. I text her the link to Henry's Instagram for the gym just to stop her complaining.

"There, are you happy now?"

"Holy crap," she says, putting the phone so close to her face I can only see her nose. I put my head in my hand, waiting for her investigation to conclude.

Lucy just happened to call me as I was getting ready for my date with Henry, and if I didn't answer the phone, she would have called in a SWAT team. So I was caught. I got a fifteen-minute lecture for going on dates that she A) didn't know about and B) wasn't able to track my location for. I told her Oliver knew where I was. Which led to a ten-minute rant about how she's been replaced. I didn't counter with the fact that she's the one who moved away, because then I really would have been late.

When Lucy is finally done stalking Henry's Instagram, and I'm finished with my makeup, both of our attentions turn back to the screen. I'm sitting at my bar top and she is laying on her couch. I can just barely make out the tip of Blue's nose on her chest. If I wasn't already dressed, I'm sure Thor and I would be in a similar position on the couch. Oliver is working until midnight tonight, so I told him I'd text him if I got home later than that, so he could come in and get Thor. Thor is getting better at being alone, but not for twelve hours at a time.

"I have to admit, I'm conflicted," Lucy finally says.

"About?"

"I think Oliver is cuter. I mean Henry clearly has the bigger muscles, but I worry he is overcompensating for something. Oliver though, there's no way that it's not *huge*—"

"Okay, stop!" I interrupt too loudly. "Lucy, it's not a competition. I'm going out with *Henry*. Oliver is not... We're not..."

There's an awkward moment of silence between us.

"Are there ends to those sentences?" she asks plainly.

"Ugh, I can't have this conversation right now," I moan, looking at the clock. I'm meeting Henry in a few minutes.

"What conversation?" Lucy sits up abruptly, and Blue whines in annoyance. "What is there to talk about? Did something happen with you and Oliver?"

"Okay, *calm*, please," I beg, putting my hand out to the phone. "Nothing *happened*, it's just... I don't know. We've had *moments*."

"*Moments*?" Lucy echoes. "Well, I *must* alert the church elders." She laughs at her own joke.

"I'm going to hang up on you."

"Did you use protection?" she adds, cracking herself up even more. When I give her a death glare, she tries to stifle her giggles. "I'm sorry, I'm sorry! But come on, Elle. Be honest. Are you just wasting your time with Henry?"

"I definitely can't have *that* conversation right now. He'll be here any minute!"

"Do you feel attracted to him, yes or no?" Lucy asks.

"Attraction isn't everything—"

"It's a *big* thing."

"He's really sweet—"

"Candy is sweet."

"You're not helping!" I whine. I shake my head, trying to somehow escape the awkwardness of this conversation. After a deep breath I say, "It doesn't matter, Luce. Oliver doesn't want me. He—"

"I don't want to hear what *he* wants. I care about *you*." Her voice is stern, all sarcasm gone. She's gesturing with her hands as she speaks. "Yes, Henry is gorgeous in a *short king* kind of way. But there is never, *ever* any reason to settle if there's no fireworks. Don't settle for less than what you deserve."

I feel a pressure in my chest as she says those words, and I think my eyes might start welling up. I refuse to cry. I *just* got my eyeliner right.

"I'm just tired of being alone," I finally whisper. I gulp down the knot in my throat after the words leave my lips. *I'm tired of being there for everyone else and no one showing up for me.*

"Oh, Elle—" A knock at the door interrupts whatever she was about to say. Thor erupts into a barking tantrum.

"I've got to go, Luce. Henry is here. I'll call you tomorrow," I say.

"I love you babe," Lucy yells at the phone, as if to stop me from hanging up.

"Love you too," I reply, and end the call.

I don't let myself think about what she just said. Henry is nice and he does not deserve to be left standing at my door. I stand at the entrance to my apartment and put one hand on my heart and one on my belly, and breathe in deep. I exhale as I open the door.

"Favorite food?"

"Chinese, definitely," I answer easily.

"Dessert?"

"Chocolate chip cookies."

"Beach or mountains?" Henry asks, taking another bite of his chicken.

Oh for the love of God, I feel like I'm on a dating game show.

Lucy has ruined this date for me. She's put thoughts in my head about doing what is right for me and not settling and I can't shake them.

"Beach," I say. "Unless it's going to the mountains to visit my friend Lucy," I add, regretting that I now have to go into the whole Lucy and her mountain man story.

I feel bad calling Henry "settling," but this feels like work. I'm putting on my "Third Date Elle" face, laughing at all the right moments, being dainty about my napkin on my lap, and even letting Henry touch my hand from across the table. With another glass of wine, I would probably go home with him. But with Lucy's voice echoing in my head, not even an extremely attractive buff guy can do anything for my libido.

Henry is great. He is. He's just not—

I don't want to finish that thought. But I can't help the slew of images that flood my brain of my time with Oliver. Most days he sees me without makeup, unlike the full cat-eye look I put on for tonight. Sometimes I'm not even wearing a bra. I never feel like I'm pretending with him. I'm just me. I feel like I know more about him than I could glean on a thousand dates with Henry, and I didn't get that information from endless trivia questions. I can't blame Henry. He is doing what people do on a date. He's trying to get to know me. I just don't have the energy for it.

But I'm nothing if not a people pleaser, so I schmooze my way through dinner, all the while trying to find something that I really like about Henry. In fairness, there's a lot to like. Family oriented. Cute. Funny. Doesn't judge when I order an appetizer and an entrée for myself, and neither of them are salads. And yet, my mind keeps drifting to a guy who clearly stated that he wants different things than me.

Henry walks me back to my apartment again, and I spend the whole time thinking about how I just want to put my pajamas on and cuddle with Thor. Then I feel terrible for that thought. Henry shouldn't settle for me either. He walks me to my door and there's an awkward moment of expectation between us. When neither of us says, we both laugh nervously.

"Listen, I—"

"I had a—"

We smile sheepishly at each other for a moment. This is ridiculous. This man is great. Perfect, even. If there was a list for a man I should be inviting up to my apartment, he would check all the boxes. Why can't I just be attracted to him?

I start to speak, catch myself, and then take a step towards Henry. "Can I just—" I put my arms around his neck tentatively. My fingers find the hair that trails down his neck and run my fingers through it. How long has it been since I've been pressed up against a man? And this is a nice man! I want to *will* myself to feel something…

"I just want to try something here, if that's okay," I say, running a thumb along his jaw. Henry nods. I bring my lips to his and kiss him firmly. He's surprised at first, but quickly tightens his arms around me and splays his hands over my back. His lips are soft, and the kiss is tender and gentle. Our lips move together like they're supposed to but…

I pull away, leaving Henry and his puckered lips frozen in time. I purse my own and furrow my brows, a bit frustrated. Henry awkwardly opens his eyes and says, "Well? Good experiment or…"

My arms are still around him, his hands low on my waist. It was a nice kiss. I mean, the best one I've had in a few years, but I don't feel anything.

"Let me try again," I say, really trying to push myself into the kiss. I slide my tongue between his lips, which should instantly get some reaction between my legs, and yet, there's no fireworks.

Damn, I hate it when Lucy is right.

I pull back, settling down from my tippy toes and laying my hands on Henry's chest. "What do you think?" I ask him.

He tilts his head. "I mean, very enjoyable. You'll hear no complaints from me," he says with an airy laugh.

"But did you feel any—?"

"Spark?"

"Yeah," I say with a sigh.

"I really want to say yes," he says, a defeated expression crossing his face.

"Ugh, me too!" I say exasperated. I step away from him, one hand still on his shoulder.

I look down at the ground. Letting someone down is so *not* something I do. I try to make things work until the very end. Heck, the last guy I dated I kept around until I literally forgot about two dates in a row. What was his name again? John? Lucy would know.

I sway nervously. "I really like you, Henry. I'm not trying to sound cliché when I say you are such a great guy."

"But..." he starts. "Things just aren't clicking."

A wave of relief comes over me, and my body unclenches. "You feel it too?" I say, a sigh in my voice. He nods shyly.

"Ugh, I am so sorry," I say, exasperated. "Like, you don't even know how sorry—" And for some reason, I reach out and hug him. I don't know why, but it happens so fast, both Henry and I don't know what to do about it. We stand there awkwardly for a second, his arms barely around my back and mine laying limply on his shoulders. Our faces are so close, I can feel the heat radiating off of him.

"Hey, Elle, you have nothing to apologize about," he says, resting one hand lightly on my hip. "You go out with people and sometimes it doesn't work out. I still think you're a great person. Not to sound cliché." A small smile turns up the corner of his lips.

Good God in Heaven, why can't it be him? Why am I so broken that I can't accept this nice man in front of me for what he is? Why do I have to want more? Am I asking for too much?

Never settle for anything less than fireworks.

"I think you're great, too," I say, a pathetic look on my face, cringing at the fact that I'm repeating myself. I start to say "I'm sorry" again, but the look on Henry's face stops me. "Oliver is going to be so disappointed in his first attempt at matchmaking," I add instead.

Henry cackles. "Yeah, I wouldn't be so sure about that." I give him a questioning look. "Never mind. Hey, I'll see you around, yeah?"

"Yeah," I reply. Henry backs up, holding on to one of my hands until the last moment, before letting it drop. As I watch him walk down the street, I should feel some disappointment, like I'm letting a good thing go. Instead, I feel relief. I was putting on a show for Henry, and trying to please Oliver by keeping up my end of the deal. But this is what is right for me.

And doing something that is right for me feels like its own form of fireworks.

EIGHTEEN

Oliver

When Sunday arrives, I spend way too much time explaining to Thor that I'll be back in a couple of hours and telling him to be a good boy. I talk as I put his leash on, which he has become quite fond of chewing. I'm sure Elle doesn't reprimand him when he does it. I shake my head at the goofball, who has his butt in the air while he bites the leash into submission. I genuinely don't think he cares about me leaving him.

I do think he's definitely done growing. His legs are still stout, but his body is longer, and I can see the muscles of his shoulders becoming more defined. I take a photo and send it to Sophia as a form of peace offering.

When I drop Thor off at Elle's door, she's still in her pajamas. I usually see Elle in her work attire or loungewear, so "sleepy Elle" is a bit of a shock to me, reminding me of the night we first met. What's more of a shock is that she's wearing shorts that can barely be seen under her oversized t-shirt. A t-shirt that is once again extremely threadbare and white, which leaves little to the imagination. Today's shirt reads: *I like my books like I like my tacos, just a little bit SPICY.*

Her hair is up in a sloppy bun, which might be my second favorite way to see it, aside from it laying long across her shoulders. She looks adorable when it bobs on top of her head as she talks.

I'm dying to ask her about her date with Henry last night, but I have no right to ask that. Although, I am the one who set them up. But maybe it would still come off as creepy? I decide to let myself stew in agony for a little longer, because it seems like the right thing to do.

Oh fuck it, I'll text Henry when I get on the train.

Elle brightens when she sees Thor, and gets down to his level to greet him. "Finally! I have you all to myself for a whole day! What do you want to do today, bud?" she says in an animated voice. She scoops up Thor's belly and awkward legs and sways him in her arms. "Pack a bag and head to Canada? He would never catch us."

"I have connections. I would catch you," I say, folding my arms.

"I'm sure. You have a real mafia look about you," she agrees.

"A mafia look?"

"Have you looked in a mirror? You look like the young, hotter guy they should have cast as Michael Corleone instead of Al Pacino."

"And that means I know the mafia?"

"Definitely," she nods, bouncing Thor like he's a baby.

"Have you eaten breakfast yet? You're being weird."

"No comment," she mumbles, visibly annoyed that I can make such a deduction about her.

"Alright, *God-willing,* I'll be back by five, maybe six o'clock. Lay off the treats and don't let him bite his leash so much," I say, a little too commanding. I place a hand on Thor's head and scratch behind his ears.

"Remember the whole *free* dog-sitting thing? This is a no-rules zone. Take your treat-limiting talk somewhere else, pal," she says, taking a step back and closing the door on me.

A second later she opens it again, a remorseful look on her face. "I'm sorry, say a proper goodbye. I was just trying to be dramatic."

"How unlike you," I say, giving Thor a pat on the head. As I get closer to Elle, I'm hit with a wave of vanilla and citrus. I have to swallow hard before leaning back. Our eyes lock, but the moment ends quickly when Elle takes a more pronounced step back, adjusts Thor to one hip, reaches her hand out slowly, and whips the door closed. I try to muffle my laughter.

As I stand facing the closed white door, I imagine what it would be like to forgo the trip home, stay here with Elle and watch Netflix all day. Maybe take a walk to the park. Get some take-out. Friends can do that, can't they?

But instead, I get on the Long Island Railroad—my own personal monorail to hell.

Oliver
How did it go with Elle?

Casual message. Hard to read anything into it. Just a friend checking in with a friend.

Henry
Didn't work out. She's super cool tho.

I jerk forward in my seat, the few passengers around me giving me a sideways glance.

Didn't work out? What does that mean? She thought it didn't work out? Or him?

I can't ask any of that. I'm not *that* needy. I'm just overthinking this whole thing. I'm being obsessive. I have to get Elle and her yoga class and her cute pajamas out of my head. I have to break the cycle of thinking. Because *this* is the very reason why I'm not the guy for her.

And what better way to get my mind off of it than to spend the day crammed into a small house with my extended family?

It's my mother's birthday, so everyone and their second cousin are coming. Literally. My grandparents and two aunts live within a two-block radius of my parents. We have a little monopoly on the zip code, especially given that my two *other* aunts live next door to my parents. It's a lot.

And I feel like every time I go away and come back to my family home, they get louder.

Like, *much* louder.

Come to think of it, maybe this is why I'm so sensitive to the volume of music playing in my headphones or the volume of the TV. I've been audio-traumatized by my overly loud family. I can't be the only one. I should form a support group for this to go with the one for residents.

When I arrive, I take a deep breath and embrace my fate. Two minutes later, I wish I had brought face wash, because I have layers of grandma and auntie lipstick smothered on my cheeks.

"You look tired, Ollie," my mother says, forgoing any niceties and wrapping her arms around my midsection.

She's the smallest of our family, with coarse black hair that has strands of gray strewn throughout. It's a wonder that Sophia and I got my dad's height.

Once I greet everyone and slyly wipe my hands down my face, I take a spot on the most uncomfortable leather couch in the world, next to my dad. He's already parked himself in the corner recliner and has the TV remote in hand. He must be on call today because he has a Diet Coke beside him rather than a beer. I dread the following conversation before it's even begun.

"Dr. Cole," he says. He holds a hand out to me.

"Dr. Cole," I repeat, indulging him. He looks thinner than the last time I saw him, not that I can recall when that was. Christmas maybe? His face is more drawn, and there's more gray than black in his hair. His hair is gelled back and his thick glasses are high on his nose. He's wearing a collared golf shirt and dockers, eerily similar to my own attire.

Is this my future? This—sitting on a recliner waiting to be paged for an emergency? Tired from hours of working, only to be called to work some more? And for what, a good salary? What about everything else?

What about *life*?

"Have you had lunch with Steve yet?" my father asks, his eyes never leaving the TV.

Who the fuck is Steve?

"No, not yet," I reply, not bothering to even try and figure out who that is. I'm sure it's one of the hospital administrators that my father brown-nosed to get me into this position. Of course, I have no proof of that, just a lifetime's worth of experience with this man.

"You have to make connections, Oliver," he scolds, gesturing with the remote in his hand. "These first two years are crucial. If you don't make a mark now, you won't even be considered for Chief Resident when the time comes."

Thank God, I think to myself. That sounds more like a prison sentence than an opportunity. But I can't say that out loud, of course.

"I mean, it's bad enough you're in *medicine*," he practically spits the last word, like it is poison in his mouth. "But I suppose it's good you're in a hospital at all."

Am I even part of this conversation?

Part of me admires my father for being so passionate about what he does. Maybe that's the reason I butt heads with Sophia too, because she is so sure of what she wants in her life. Me? I was always good at science. Medical school, residency, that was always the plan for me. There was no Plan B. And I'm not sure that I've ever had the same passion for it that Dad does, or that Sophia has for fashion. Do I really want to tie myself to a career that I don't love? That I dread going to every day?

As I listen to my father drone on about his connections at Mount Sinai, my thoughts drift to Elle, because I can't get Henry's text out of my head. Part of me is surprised by how easy and effortless the time I spend with Elle has been lately. Since the pier, I've only seen her for a few minutes a day, at Thor pick up and drop off, but those are the times of my day that I look forward to the most. One time there was a giddy smile on her face, and it turned out she met someone on the street with a baby corgi. That was my favorite day in the past week. I literally want to track down the corgi owner and pay them to walk past our building at the same time every day.

Most days, I'd rather be home with Elle or out on one of her New York City excursions than at work. All days, actually.

When my colleagues at the hospital talk, they're eager to get called in to assist in surgery or consult in the ER. I dread it. Part of me envies Elle for her predictable work schedule. What would my life be like if I only had to work five days a week, nine-to-five?

Structured, stable, predictable. Literally the things my brain craves.

Most aspiring medical students would give anything for what I have right now. I feel like an ass for even suggesting that I take it for granted. I worked hard to get here. But it still feels unearned. And that is a feeling I'm worried I'll never be able to shake.

"Oliver, are you even listening to me?" I blink a few times to bring my father into focus. I look him up and down again, the furrow in my brows growing as I evaluate him. Before I open my mouth to speak, not even knowing what to say, his phone rings. The Caller ID for the hospital lights up the screen.

Is this really where I want to be in thirty years?

If not, what the hell am I doing right now?

I forgot how overstimulating my family can be after having been away for so long. I don't know what to make of the day I just had, but as I open the door to my apartment, I know one thing: I need to sit down.

I stumble into the living room, cursing this stressful day. As if seeing my family wasn't stressful enough, being trapped on the train always gets to me. Driving there would have been so much more difficult, but at least I wouldn't have had to go under the East River in a metal tube. The tunnels don't make sense to me. How do they build them? How are they not the eighth wonder of the world?

To make matters worse, it started torrentially raining on my walk home from the train station, so my socks are soaked in my shoes.

After my father left for the hospital, my cousins proceeded to scream—what I call "screaming" is their normal speaking volume—at each other for the entire dinner. Between the heat blasting at 78 degrees and the overworked oven, it was sweltering in there. I could barely eat anything. I was too busy discreetly wiping my head with my napkin and trying to zone out from my cousins' banter. What must it be like to look forward to spending time with your family?

I sit down on the bed of the treadmill, my knees almost reaching my shoulders. I don't know why this is the spot I chose, but it'll have to do for right now. I wish I could get up and wash my face, but I can't seem to find the wire in my brain that connects to my legs and tells them to move. I haven't had a panic attack in so long, I almost forgot what it felt like. But I could never *really* forget this.

I rub my hands up and down on my cheeks until the stubble turns my hands red. I try to inhale deeply, and my exhale comes out shakily. *This is panic*, I tell myself. *In a minute I'll get up and take a shower, and I'll feel better.* These and other mantras are the strategies therapists have given me over the years, and in theory, they're a good idea. But in the moment, when your body feels like the slightest touch could make you explode, they really do jack shit.

My legs still won't move.

I try to remember more of the exercises the therapist I went to a few years ago taught me, but I'm coming up blank. Again, the strategies are great when you hear them, but when panic wants to take you over, then that's exactly what it does. Panic has the power to freeze every muscle in your body, every neuron in your brain. It's the invisible enemy that no one talks about, but whose power is all-consuming.

Inhale, I hear Elle's voice say. My memory takes me back to the yoga class, when her hand was on my chest, her fingers laced with mine.

"I'm sorry I ran out of treats, but we're going to find some, I promise," a muffled voice says in the distance. My mind doesn't fully register it, because I can still hear Elle's voice commanding me. *Exhale all the air out.*

"Oliver?" Her voice sounds closer now, not as muffled as it did in the memory. My eyes flutter open and I see Thor bounding towards me, licking my face as soon as he reaches me. He shakes in front of me, flicking me with water. They must have been outside too. I hear Elle's footsteps close behind him. "Oliver? Are you okay? Are you hurt?" I try to meet her gaze, but my vision is blurry, and she won't come into focus. I can feel her hands on my arms, like coal branding my skin.

"I'm having a… panic attack," I mumble, my voice shaking.

"Okay, okay," Elle's voice sounds rushed, the complete opposite of the voice in my memory. "Just breathe," I hear her say as she moves away from me. I can feel the imprint that her hands left behind.

She returns seconds later and takes my hands. I close my eyes again, breathing deeply. "Hold this," she says, placing something cold in my hand. The sensation shocks me, and my eyes fly open.

"Wh—Why?" I stutter. She closes my hands around an ice cube and lifts them to my heart.

"I actually have no idea, but apparently it's supposed to help," she says.

"Well it's just fucking cold, so I don't know what it's doing for me."

"You're not shaking anymore, so that's progress."

I lean my head against my knees, trying to slow my breathing. Elle is running her fingers through my hair, her nails gently massaging my scalp. Her other hand is holding my shoulder and it is so steadying, so *sure*, that I feel like if she lets go, I'll fall over.

"Tell me something you feel," she commands.

"The cold ice cube you just gave me, dummy," I reply.

She flicks my shoulder. "Something else."

"Your hands. They're warm."

"Now tell me something you hear," she says, putting her hand back on my shoulder. She kneads circles into my muscle and my breath hitches.

"Thor licking himself," I mutter. Elle snorts and I can't help but smile. "I know this trick," I add, calling her out.

"Yeah, well, it's working, isn't it?" she says, her fingers finding the side of my face. I let my head lean to the side and inhale sharply when she cups my cheek in her palm. My eyes open and I'm greeted with her brilliant brown ones, so close to me our foreheads could touch. She's kneeling down on the floor in front of me, holding me. Her hair is wet, her cheeks flushed. She gently takes the hand away that was stroking my hair. "Tell me something you see," she whispers, her gaze flicking back and forth between my eyes and my mouth.

"The gold outline around the brown in your eyes," I whisper shakily, the lids of my eyes drooping as our eyes meet. Elle's hand lands on my forearm, and I'm transfixed by the way she grips it. I can't stop looking at her. Every stitch of panic is gone from my body, but I'm still frozen.

I lean my head close to hers and drop my gaze to her mouth, and once I see her take a small breath between her small pink lips, the energy shifts between us. Our eyes don't move for a while, but it's Elle who finally breaks our gaze.

She looks down for a moment, and then jumps backwards as Thor barks loudly behind us.

Elle tumbles backwards from her kneeling position, and Thor abandons his post at the window, where I'm sure a pigeon was threatening our safety and demanding to be barked at. Thor clearly thinks Elle is playing with him by the way he gallops over to her and puts his front two paws on her chest. She giggles as Thor licks her face and starts digging in her hair. When she sits up, I see that her face is red from laughing, and I let out a nervous laugh, shaking my head at the situation. This day has really gone off the rails.

Elle pulls Thor onto her lap and flips her hair behind her, threading her fingers through the wild curls that Thor just knotted. I hold my hand out to Thor and he sniffs the ice cube suspiciously, before grabbing it and carrying it over to his favorite spot on the corner of the area rug. He tosses it in the air a few times, jumping into playing position each time it lands on the floor. Elle and I watch him, laughing hysterically when he dives into the carpet and ends up with his legs in the air. Eventually he settles down and starts chomping on the ice cube. That's when Elle turns her attention back to me.

"You know I gave you that key for emergencies," I say, eyeing her.

"We've been at the park all day and then it started pouring so we ran back. I knew I was out of treats this morning, but it totally slipped my mind to stop at the store."

I raise a brow at her.

"That qualifies as an emergency in my book," she admits, raising her hands at me. I roll my eyes at her seriousness. She studies me for a moment. "So what brought this on?" she asks, gesturing to me and folding her legs underneath her. She holds onto her ankles and sits up straight, like she is doing a yoga pose.

I should feel embarrassed about what just happened. I should apologize for Elle finding me like this, although she did come into my apartment unannounced, using the key I gave her for *emergencies*. I should try to recover this situation somehow, but I don't really know what I can do. She just witnessed me at my absolute worst, for the *second* time. That's more than any person I've ever dated has seen me break down. And Elle isn't running for the hills.

Of course she isn't, *banana head*, you're not dating.

I rub my hand on my forehead, trying to get my story straight in my head.

"Family dinner, always a triggering time," I say. As if there aren't enough reasons that I feel like my life is in a spiral, seeing my parents and being reminded of the toxic relationship with my father just adds another layer to the dysfunction. I come with too much baggage. Elle *should* run for the hills.

"I get that," she says, nodding. "Want to talk about it?"

"Never. I guess that's half of my problem," I reply, hanging my head. Elle purses her lips at me, but I know she won't push me. I wrap my hand around my neck, wondering what must be going on in Elle's mind. She really got a handful when she decided to camp outside my door that night. "Where did the ice cube thing come from?"

She doesn't answer right away, turning her attention to Thor for a moment before speaking. "I don't know. In my research for yoga or my brother or something," she says with a shrug.

"Your brother?"

"I told you he has a disability," she says, and I nod. "He has Down's syndrome. Sometimes he'll get upset and hard to console, so I've picked up some tricks along the way."

A beat passes between us, and I think we're both not sure what to say next. I hate how much focus is on me, so I ask about Elle's brother. I think it's one of her favorite topics to talk about.

"Do you miss him?" I ask.

Elle smiles to herself, still looking down at Thor. "Of course. But he likes to FaceTime me. The other day, he called to tell me he got a promotion at the grocery store where he works. He was so excited about getting to stock the shelves instead of just bagging." She looks up at me, and I can see the cheerfulness in her eyes as she talks about him. "And then last night, there was a category about vegetables on *Jeopardy!* and he got all the questions right. He had to call me about that too," she adds with a chuckle.

Elle so rarely talks about herself. Usually on our expeditions she'll ask me about work and my family. She doesn't offer up too much information about herself, so when I get it, I feel like I have to soak up every morsel and hide it somewhere safe, so I won't forget it.

I lean my arms on my knees and don't shy away from admiring her. She takes a few moments to play with Thor, poking his nose and tickling him, prompting him to roll in his back. When she finally looks back at me, I can see a blush in her cheeks, and I wonder if she is thinking about the moment we just shared.

She reaches her hand out to me and squeezes my forearm, her hands a little less scorching than before. She gives me a half-smile. "All of us have a little crazy, Oliver. I guess we just have to embrace it."

She watches me for a moment, and I manage to give her a sheepish smile. I don't want her to let go of my arm, but her phone buzzes. Her face is confused when she sees the contact on the screen. "Why is the landlord texting me?" she mumbles quietly, more to herself than to me.

"Everything okay?" I ask.

"Yeah, he just wants to check something in my apartment. I'll be right back." She presses a quick kiss on Thor's head and is out the door in a flash.

I finally stand from the treadmill and get a towel to dry Thor, but only a few minutes pass before I hear a sound that sends ice through my bones.

Elle screaming.

NINETEEN

Elle

"Oh my God!" I yell, rushing into the apartment. "There's water everywhere!"

I stand in the middle of my studio in horror. At least three inches of water lines the entire floor of the space. I feel my heart sink to my gut when I see the murky brown water touching the bottom of my bedspread, and gasp when I realize the water has reached the cushion on my favorite green chair.

"I'll get the Shop Vac, grab anything you want to save," Mikey, the landlord, says behind me. I don't wait for confirmation on that plan before I race into the room, my socks and shoes already saturated inside my breathable sneakers. I squish with every step. The water is up to my ankles.

"*Elle*?" I hear a frantic voice behind me. I turn and find Oliver in my doorway, a towel in his hand. "Are you okay?" He's breathless and panicked.

"No, I'm not okay! Look at my apartment!" I shriek.

Oliver throws his arm on the doorframe and plops his head against it, like he's exhausted. "Elle, I thought you were being *murdered* down here," he says, and I can practically see the adrenaline leaving his body in waves as he leans against the wall.

"And what were you going to do? Strangle my murderer with a towel?" I say, gesturing to his hand.

"I wouldn't need the towel," he says matter-of-factly. The deep tenor and seriousness of his voice travels right through me.

I shake my head and go back to my task, lifting everything I can on to a higher surface. My rug is destroyed, my comforter and bed skirt are as well, but luckily the clothes in my closet are at least a foot off the ground. As I gather my books off of the shelves by my TV, Oliver finally enters the room, surveying the damage.

"Has this happened before?" he asks, inspecting the window where it meets the ceiling.

"Yeah, that's why I was *super* prepared for it and didn't leave anything on the floor!" I snap, harsher than I mean.

"Sorry, what can I do?" he asks, stumbling through the water. He doesn't seem concerned at all that he's up to his shins in muck, something that would usually throw him into a tailspin. He's too focused on getting to me, helping me, that his germaphobia took the back burner for a second. At least, I hope so. I hope he's not internally panicking just for my benefit.

"Save my green chair," I whimper. "I love that chair." Oliver gives it the once over. It's pretty low to the ground—it stands on wood pedestal feet with fabric lining the bottom. Oliver lifts it up and places it on the kitchen counter, upside down.

Oliver, Mikey, and I don't spend long in the apartment. There isn't much we can do. Mikey clears out the water and temporarily fixes the leak, but he said he'll need a few days to fully clean out the damage. I was able to save most of my books, including my yoga sutras and my collection of books I've edited, but my television equipment is questionable. As is my DIY wooden nightstand and any toiletries and paper products I was storing on the floor in the closet.

Oliver saved my green chair. The bottom was just barely touched by the water, and he assures me I'll be able to find someone in the city to restore the wooden legs.

By the time most of the water has been excavated, it's almost 9 p.m., and I'm exhausted. All I want to do is cry, but I refuse to do that in front of Oliver, who's hovering outside the door to my very soggy apartment.

"Why don't you grab some stuff and meet me upstairs?" Oliver finally says, the towel he originally came down here with slung over his shoulder. I lean against the wall and stare at him in confusion.

"For what?"

"So you can stay at my place tonight," he says, like that is not a totally absurd suggestion.

"Don't joke with me right now," I say, defeated.

"It's not a joke. You can't sleep in here. You know the amount of mold that is currently growing on your baseboards? Not to mention the—other *grossness* that is here already," he says, cringing. I'm honestly not sure if he's telling me I can't sleep here because of my safety or because it simply grosses him out too much. The germs finally caught up to him now that the water is gone and he can see all the dirt lining my floors.

I look around my apartment. There is a layer of black muck on every inch of the floor. Even though Mikey got the water out, the remnants of the city sidewalk are strewn everywhere. Leaves, cigarette butts, and just *gunk*. Black gunk. On *my floors*.

"Hey, it's okay," Oliver says, placing a reassuring hand on my shoulder. I'm not actively crying, but I must look like I'm on the verge of tears. I slump against the wall even more. "This will get cleaned up and everything will be fine, right Mikey?" he calls out into the hallway, where Mikey is still fiddling with his tools.

"Give me a few days to answer that," Mikey says back.

"A few *days*?" I snap, my mouth agape.

"I have to check the appliances, check for mold, make sure the floors will survive—"

"Stop, I can't hear anymore," I say, holding my hand up. I let my head fall into my hands and fold over against the wall. I feel Oliver wrap his arms around me and pull me into his chest. I'm so caught off guard, I let him do it. And then I melt into him.

We're both still in our wet clothes from our respective outings in the rain. Our skin is sticky, but Oliver smells like oregano and minty cologne and *him*. I let him hold me, because it's been so long since anyone has, and I don't care how much I enjoy it. I don't remember the reasons why I shouldn't be getting so close to him, and I just let myself *be*.

"It's just some walls and floors," he says, rubbing his hands on my back. "Those things can be fixed."

"But they're *mine*," I say, pulling away from him to look at the destruction again. "Mine," I whisper. Oliver nods.

I only take a few minutes to gather some clothes for work, my toiletries, and my electronics. Oliver says I should come back for some more clothes tomorrow, so they don't get musty. I ignore him, pretending like I'm not going to stay at his place for more than one night. Because this is *not* happening.

"I'm sleeping on the couch. I don't want to hear anything else out of your mouth about it," I say sternly when I wobble into his apartment with my bags. I look like a college student on move-in day. I only have one small overnight suitcase, so I stuffed everything else into my reusable grocery bags. I throw them all on the couch and see Oliver open his mouth to speak.

"No! I don't want to hear a peep!" I say, pointing at him. His eyes widen and he raises his hands, like he's really not sure what he's done wrong. But I'm not in the mood to explain.

"Okay, I'm going to take a shower then," he says, backing away from me slowly. He pulls his shirt off as he walks towards the bathroom and I'm sure my mouth drops. I can only see the back of him, but *Good Lord*, it's a nice back. His shoulders are defined by taut muscles, two of which line his spine and travel downwards. I have to shake myself to stop staring, and I'm grateful that Oliver didn't catch me openly ogling him. I plop down on the couch and Thor hops up beside me, putting his two front paws on my lap, so half of his body is curled on top of me. I don't see how that's comfortable, but I let him do it. He must be able to tell I need comforting right now. I pull out my phone and text Lucy.

Elle

BURT

BURT!!

BURT!!!!

Lucy

Are you okay? This is Lucy. An almost asleep Lucy, I might add

Lucy

Since when do you know someone named Burt? Like and Ernie?

Lucy

OH! Our code word for danger!

Elle

I'm disappointed in how long it took you to get there

Lucy

My apologies to Joey and Chandler

Lucy

Wait… what kind of danger?

Lucy

Have you been kidnapped?? BLINK TWICE IF YOU NEED HELP!

Elle

We're texting, how would I blink??

Lucy

That sounds like a kidnapper talking. Quick, tell me something only Elle would know

Elle
Your code word for danger is Burt

Lucy
Damn, you're a smart kidnapper

Elle
LUCY! We do not have time for this! I am in a crisis
My apartment flooded…

Lucy
Oh no! Hold on, I'll call you

Elle
No I can't talk
I'm in Oliver's apartment

Lucy
YAAAASSS

Elle
THIS IS NOT A TIME FOR CELEBRATION!
I cannot sleep in the same room as this man.
HE IS NOT WEARING A SHIRT

Lucy
Take a picture please

Elle
I cannot be here, but he insisted
There is ONLY ONE BED

Elle
My life is in shambles

Lucy
This stuff doesn't happen in real life

Elle
Says the girl living a small-town romance!

Lucy
But what are the chances your apartment floods and you just HAPPEN to have a beautiful man upstairs who offers you his couch?

Elle
I'M AWARE OF THE ODDS LUCILLE!

Lucy
Calm down. Nothing bad is going to happen. You're going to sleep on his couch, hear him snore, get up, and go to work in the morning. It's not like you have feelings for him, so it's just physical attraction. He's a nice-looking man in close proximity. You can handle that. Right?

Lucy
Right?

I plop the phone on my lap and turn to Thor. He's laying upside down, with his head in my lap. He looks up at me, an ear flopping to one side, and I chuckle softly, rubbing his belly.

I look over to the bathroom door and watch the steam sneak out from under it. My brain wanders, picturing what's on the other side of that door, wrapped in all that steam. I shake my head vigorously.

Elle

Right.

Oliver exits the bathroom and thank *God* he is not wearing a towel, because I might have just cackled at the irony of that. He's wearing a white t-shirt with a faded Led Zeppelin graphic and basketball shorts.

I take a shower after him and it is sensory overload. As soon as I walk into the steamy bathroom, the scent of him surrounds me. His shampoo bottle reads "fresh scent," but it smells like cinnamon and minty aftershave, undeniably *him*. As I stand in the shower, I can just imagine him standing in the same spot, water running down his body, soap lathering in *all* the places.

It's possibly the fastest shower in the history of the world.

When I exit the bathroom in my oversized pajamas, I see that Oliver has made the couch up into a bed. Two pillows are stacked on one end, and a sheet has been tucked over the cushions. A Stanford blanket is folded in the middle.

"You didn't have to do this," I say softly. Oliver shrugs. He is laying on the bed scrolling through his phone, one hand bent behind his head as a pillow. When I move the blanket to lay down and get settled with Thor, I see a glass of water on the side table next to the couch.

"Is there anything else you need?" Oliver asks, putting his phone down.

"I'm good, thank you," I say, pulling Thor to my chest and petting his head. I'm glad the back of the couch hides my face from Oliver, because I can't seem to stop smiling. Oliver Cole made a bed for me. He got me water. He's *taking care of me*.

"Hey," Oliver says, making me turn around. He's leaning forward on the bed, resting on his forearms. I've been around Oliver for a while now, but something feels different. *Something* has changed. I'm suddenly taken aback by how beautiful he is. His hair is wet and a few long strands rest on his forehead. A faint stubble shadows his face, and his Adam's apple bobs with each breath he takes. He looks like the Mediterranean version of Chris Hemsworth, and I almost let out an obnoxious laugh at the idea that I'm about to sleep on his couch.

"Hmm?" I ask, trying to reign my thoughts in.

"Will you tell me what happened with Henry?" he asks, and I'm so caught off guard that my stomach drops a bit, like I've been caught doing something wrong. I had almost forgotten about Henry. "He said things didn't work out."

I'm not really sure what to say. My conversation with Lucy from the other night is screaming at the forefront of my mind. But what is the point? It doesn't matter if I feel... *whatever* for him. Oliver doesn't want what I want, right?

"There's not really much to say," I finally admit. "He's great. Literally everything I want on paper, but—"

"But?" Oliver prods.

"Something didn't feel right, I guess," I say, barely above a whisper. Oliver inhales sharply. He nods, swallowing audibly. There's more words hanging in the air between us, but they float away as Oliver adjusts himself in the bed and lays his head down.

"Goodnight, Elle. Get some sleep."

I sigh, resting my head on the pillow, knowing it won't be that easy to fall asleep now. "Goodnight, Oliver."

As it turns out, living with Oliver doesn't change a whole lot about our established dynamics. When I wake up in the morning, he's still sleeping, so I sneak into the bathroom and get dressed quickly, opting to grab breakfast on my way to work. I can't help but take in the sight of him as I tiptoe past him. He is asleep on his stomach, an arm thrown across a pillow and his face mashed into another. Thor migrated to his bed during the night, and is curled in a ball next to Oliver. I smile, thinking of when Oliver insisted Thor wasn't allowed to sleep in the bed.

Oliver's hair looks long, strewn across his face and hiding his eyes. I'm transfixed by the outline of his shoulder blades and the defined muscles that sculpt his neck. I imagine running my fingers along them, feeling the soft, sensitive skin of his back. The very idea makes me shiver, and I scurry away.

Monday and Tuesday pass quickly, since I only see Oliver for the brief period between when I come home from work and he leaves for his night shifts. I also schedule myself for yoga classes those nights, to keep our time together in the apartment to a minimum.

When Thursday rolls around and Mikey tells me that it's going to be at least a week to fix the window and patch some floors in my apartment, I know I have to do something.

I can't afford to live in a hotel for a week. I'm going to have to go home and commute for the time being. In the meantime, I've decided I have to do something to thank Oliver for letting me sleep on his couch. I've just returned to my desk after our weekly editorial meeting when I take out my phone to text him.

Elle

I'm cooking tonight. Don't make plans.

Oliver

You could simply say Oliver, would you like to have dinner with me tonight?

Elle

That's what I said.

Oliver

No, you told me not to make plans. Telling not asking.

Elle

I'm offering to make you dinner because you've been letting me sleep on your couch for three days!!

Oliver

It's not what you said, it's how you said it.

Elle

Did you just quote Friends at me?

Oliver

Do you think you're the only one who watches that show?

I don't notice I'm grinning until my cheeks start to hurt. I quickly put my phone down and cover my mouth with the back of my hand, trying to focus on my computer. But I just look past the document on the screen, seeing my reflection. It's not lost on me that my mood has been uncharacteristically upbeat over the last few days, and I wish I could say it wasn't because of Oliver.

I feel less stress since breaking things off with Henry, as terrible as that sounds. It's just that I felt like I had to try too hard with him. And I am so jaded from imagining my life as it could be—a life like Lucy's, with a partner that I feel comfortable with, that understands me, that wants me to be happy—only to have my hopes crushed every time. It just seems so impossible to me. But now that Oliver is in my life, I feel the possibilities running across my brain again. I look forward to the brief few minutes a day I get to see him. It's the thing that's keeping me going right now

However much I like spending time with Oliver, though, hope turns back to disappointment when I remind myself that he is not my partner. He's my friend. Just my friend.

TWENTY

Oliver

Elle lets herself into the apartment, two bags of groceries hanging from her arms, along with the three other canvas bags she carries to work with her every day. When I first saw her carrying them, I couldn't imagine what she lugged back and forth in those things. It's not like she packs her lunch. I snuck a peek last night when my insomnia was in full force, since I can't exactly run on the treadmill when Elle is asleep on the couch. And the answer is books.

The girl carries books around Manhattan for no apparent reason.

No wonder she is freakishly strong.

"Hey," I say, rising from the couch as she closes the door behind her. She is in casual work mode today, no chic dress with black tights—I'm a big fan of the tights. She's wearing a high-neck, white sweater with khakis. It's the end of April, I'd be sweating in that outfit if I was her. She has a shy smile on her face when she walks in the door, so I ask, "What are you so happy about? Did you see the baby corgi again?"

"Ugh, I wish," she says, dropping the bags on the counter.

"I could have gone shopping," I offer, leaning against the bar top.

"Well that would defeat the purpose of my cooking dinner, now wouldn't it?" she says, emptying a pack of chicken thighs on to the counter.

"And why are you suddenly feeling so domestic?"

"I told you, as a thank you for letting me stay here." She takes a cutting board out of one of my cabinets and starts dicing the chicken. She moves with such ease, it's like she's always lived here.

"It's really not a big deal—"

"Baked chicken and mac and cheese," she says, interrupting me. She turns the oven on and jumps when the gas turns on. "It's my brother's favorite."

I smile. I love when she talks about her brother. Her face lights up in a way that I don't see any other time, except maybe when she talks about Lucy.

We're quiet for a few minutes as she moves around the kitchen, cooking the chicken and chopping some vegetables. As I watch her, curiosity sneaks in my brain. "Can I ask you something?" She hums and nods. "You said you needed a project when we started our New York deal."

"Yeah," she replies.

"*Why*? And don't say because Lucy moved out."

Elle shrugs. "It's what I do. I help people. Make them feel better. I'm a really good hype girl." When I don't say anything, Elle continues. "It's just the way I am. I told you my parents got divorced and my brother needed some extra attention, so I picked up the pieces. As I got older, I guess it became a habit, taking care of people." She smiles as she adds a bag of shredded cheese to a pot.

"When is the next time you're going to see your brother?" I ask.

"Well, that's what I want to talk to you about. Next weekend, Lucy is coming for our final dress fittings. And then she'll be back the following week for her book launch party."

"Uh huh," I mumble, setting two dishes out for us on the counter. I keep an eye on Thor, who is inhaling his food like he'll never get another morsel again.

When I turn to face Elle, she's dropping a box of pasta into the boiling water. She seems hesitant to speak again, avoiding my gaze and stirring the pasta more than she has to.

"Mikey said it's going to be at least another week until my apartment is livable," she finally says. "So I'm going to have to stay at my mom's and commute next week. If you don't mind me staying tonight, then I'll take the train tomorrow after work."

I look at her for a moment, trying to figure out the logistics of what she just said. She's... going to commute from her mom's in Jersey? She'd rather do that than stay here with me? I think back over the past few days, wondering if I've been a terribly annoying roommate. I don't think I snore that loud, and I know for a fact I am not a messy person...

"Oliver," Elle says, snapping me out of my thoughts. I meet her gaze, my face still contorted in confusion. "I'm really grateful for you letting me stay here, but I can't impose—"

"You're not imposing. I *asked* you to stay here," I say, a sharp edge to my voice. I don't know why I'm getting so...

territorial about her staying here. It's just the thought of not seeing her for a whole week. Should it bother me this much, just the idea of that? Especially when she clearly doesn't think the same way, so much so that she's planning a way to avoid this situation?

"Plus, who would watch Thor next week while I'm at work?" I continue, ignoring the fact that Thor would probably be fine on his own at this point. If I have to leave him and Elle isn't around, he's usually okay. I find him upside down in his anti-anxiety bed when I get home.

"Ugh, I didn't think about that," Elle says, brushing some stray strands of hair off of her forehead. She thinks for a moment before speaking again. "But it's a little weird, me sleeping on your couch for so long, don't you think?" she says, shrugging her shoulders up to her ears as she leans her back against the counter.

"Why would it be weird?" I ask, my brain racing for a way to change the direction of this conversation.

"Well, it's not like we're dating—"

"If we were dating, you certainly wouldn't be sleeping on the couch," I say impulsively. I can't say I haven't imagined the picture of Elle in my bed, her soft skin wrapped in my sheets. I gauge her reaction, expecting her to snap back with some witty remark, but instead her eyes just widen at me, and her cheeks flush pink.

"Are you... *blushing*?"

She turns around immediately, shutting the stove off. "No! No, I just—"

"Was imagining being in my bed," I say, a newfound confidence in my voice.

A minute ago, I thought Elle was trying to avoid me, but now, after seeing her reaction to that idea, I can't help but wonder if she's pictured the same thing I have. If she's been thinking about the day she found me panicking and we almost kissed, or at least I thought we were going to.

I take a step towards her, boxing her between me and the counter. When she turns around to get an oven mitt, she comes face-to-face with my chest, and a delicious gasp escapes her lips. I clench my fists beside me to prevent myself from reaching out for her.

"What are you—?"

"I want you to stay here, Elle, and I think you do too," I say in a low voice.

Her eyes slowly make their way up my body until she meets mine. "Why would I want that?" she whispers. I inhale as she speaks, and I'm met with the scent of her shampoo—fruity smelling, mixed with vanilla.

My stomach tightens with anxiety at the thought of what to say next. I have no right to want Elle. I threw her at Henry because I thought he was better for her. But she said it herself the other night. She didn't feel right with him. And things have felt different since then. It can't just be on my end.

"Why did you end things with Henry?" I finally say, my gut saying *fuck it* to my brain for the first time in years.

I think Elle might actually burst from the color that rushes to her face. She literally cannot hide a single thing behind her expressions. Her mind is right there on her face, a book for anyone to read.

"I—I told you, we just didn't work out," she stammers. She looks around me for a way to escape the situation, pressing her hands against the counter, dropping them, and repeating the motion. She won't meet my eyes again.

"Elle—" I say, reaching out and tracing a line down her arm. I see goosebumps rise along her skin. "Look at me."

She nods her head so she's looking even more at the floor. "I—I… We can't…"

Her reluctance feels like a punch to the stomach. What was I thinking? *I'm* the reason we can't do this. *I'm* the reason I pushed her away all those months ago. *I'm* the guy who told her he doesn't want a relationship. The guy who is so unsure of his career, his family, himself… And here I am acting on impulses, being completely selfish.

I take a step back, a chill falling between us. "You're right, I'm sorry. I don't know what came over me," I say, my words stumbling over one another.

"Oliver, nothing has changed for me. I still want—"

"I know," I say, nodding, but not meeting her eyes. "I lost myself for a moment I guess." I swallow hard and finally look at her. She looks small against the countertop, and I want nothing more than to take her in my arms. I've hurt her, which is the last thing I ever wanted to do. "You're my friend. I don't want to lose that."

She nods. "I agree."

"But I still think you should stay here. It's just another week. Thor would miss you too much." At the mention of his name, Thor trots into the kitchen and plops into a sit, waiting to see if he'll get anything. Elle laughs when he tilts his head at her expectantly.

"I would miss him too," she says. When I look back up at her, she's smiling.

TWENTY-ONE

Elle

"So, you've officially gone from *enemies-to-lovers* to *only one bed*? What's next?"

I can hear the disbelief in Lucy's voice. She pokes her head out of the dressing room and wags her eyebrows at me. "And I thought a small-town trope was pushing it for me," she adds, conducting this conversation with a casual tone, as if we're not standing in the middle of a dress store with customers and employees all around us.

"Lucy, can we maybe discuss this later?" I ask in a rushed whisper. In a moment, she will emerge all pinned up and white and I'll stand here and "ooh" and "ahh" and then we'll get lunch. Hopefully. There definitely should be food involved in this deal.

Lucy's head pops out from behind the curtain again. Her long brown locks are tied up in a tight bun on top of her head, stray hairs falling on her cheeks. I can see the outline of the dress around her neck, but am quickly redirected to her face as she scowls at me.

"No, we cannot discuss this later. You can't honestly expect me to believe that you don't have feelings for this man. And him for you."

"Trust me, if I can believe it, you can too," I mutter, crossing my legs in an attempt to make the velvet pedestal I'm sitting on more comfortable. Lucy is not one for big and flashy, so she chose to buy her dress from a mom-and-pop shop on the Upper East Side. I honestly don't know how she found it, but it's adorable. It's two floors of racks on racks of dresses, piled on top of each other so tightly that I could get lost in between them, and no one would find me for weeks. May is almost upon us, as the warm weather suggests, and it is *stuffy* in here. As in, hair-sticking-to-the back-of-my-neck stuffy. I've already tried on my dress and gotten the all clear, so I shoved myself back into my jeans to sit here and wait for Lucy. I wonder if I can DoorDash some Mister Softie up here.

"Do I sense some bitterness in your tone?" Lucy's voice sings from behind the curtain.

"I don't know if I'd call it bitter. It's just—I don't know. I thought maybe things had changed for him."

"In regards to?" she calls from behind the curtain.

"The possibility of a relationship, I guess," I reply with a huff.

"And you definitely don't see a friends-with-benefits thing happening?" Lucy asks, again too loudly for our current setting.

I shake my head, even though she can't see. "No. That's just not what I want. I feel like with Oliver—" My voice trails off. "It would have to be all or nothing." My mind wanders, imagining the possibility. What would *all* look like with Oliver? I think about the small things he's been doing for me since my apartment flooded, and even before then. Pulling me out of harm's way when we're walking down the street, opening doors for me, folding the blanket on the couch, rushing downstairs after hearing me scream... If he let himself, Oliver would probably be a romance-book-level boyfriend. Sure, he can be stubborn at times, if our first meetings were any indication, but he's protective, and smart, and loving. Or he could be.

"Some might say you're never happy."

"Ugh, I hate that about myself right now," I groan, rubbing my temples. I hate how whiney I am. I can't expect Oliver to read my mind. I'm more rational than that.

But romance books aren't. And romance books are my daily life. I believe that every story needs an HEA, otherwise it's not worth my time. But what if, with Oliver, getting to know him, *exploring*, actually *is* worth my time? I haven't had a partner in so long, I forget what it feels like. What if Oliver could be that someone for me, even if it's not forever? I feel such a strong connection to him, and given what almost happened in the kitchen last week, he must be attracted to me. All this time, I thought he was pushing me towards Henry because he wasn't interested, but now I know there's something between us. That night in his apartment proves it. I just don't know if either of us will ever compromise on what we want.

I hear Lucy scoff. "You've seen him almost every day for the past three months. You've been sleeping on his couch for two weeks." When I don't respond, she continues, "I remember having a discussion a lot like this last year, and our roles were reversed."

"My situation is very different," I say, remembering how I encouraged Lucy to be honest about her feelings for Liam. "And I want things that you didn't."

I want a connection. I want epic love that consumes me. I want a person, an everything, a universe.

And a part of me wants it to be with Oliver.

I just don't know whether he can give it to me.

"There's one thing that's the same." I can practically hear Lucy waving her hands around as she speaks. "You need to decide what you want. You need to stop believing that happy endings or romance are never going to happen for you. You need to get yourself out of a book and into real life."

I rest my head on the heels of my palms. "I don't remember my speech being so harsh."

"Love is harsh sometimes, babe," Lucy's voice says, closer this time.

"I'm not in love—" I look up, stopping mid-sentence as Lucy emerges from the fitting room, seamstress in tow, beaming. Long strands of hair that didn't make it into the bun cascade down her neck, falling on a high white neckline made of intricate lace. The rest of her bodice is solid, fitted to her curves, and falling away from her into a short train, lined with lace. She looks beautiful.

"Wow," I whisper, standing to meet her. "This dress is so... *you*." And it is—simple, elegant, and stunning. Lucy looks up at me and smiles. Other women might cry right now, but we giggle softly at each other, relishing the ridiculousness of this moment. All the nights we spent on our couch, talking about becoming hermits in a tiny house and owning seven dogs, or becoming rich on a Shark Tank idea and buying a mansion on the beach. Never did we think they would lead to this. The moment when one of us gets our happily ever after.

70 percent happy, 30 percent jealous, I swear.

"Where do you want this, Elle?" Liam asks, holding my green armchair like it's a paperweight. Mikey finally let me back in the apartment today, and I conveniently have two non-volunteer movers to help me get the place in order. Liam and Lucy are staying at a hotel for their one-night visit. I'm sure Lucy would like to stay longer, but she said she's not sure which Liam is more anxious about—leaving his restaurant to his sous chef or his dog with his friend Brett. And they'll be back next week for her book launch party, so Liam had to choose his time away from the restaurant carefully.

"Um, Liam," I say, my tone obvious. My eyes point to the *one and only* spot in front of the TV. "There's kind of only one place it can go."

"Just trying to help, *geez*," Liam mumbles, placing the chair in front of the TV.

"Are you planning on feeding us dinner for all this unpaid labor?" Lucy calls from the bathroom, where she is sweeping the tile floor. The bathroom made out the best in the Great Flood of Apartment 1A. The wood floors, which probably haven't been replaced since the Gilded Age, were not so lucky. Mikey had to patch a few spots by the far wall, and sand them to match the rest. It's a bit mismatched, but I'm not mad about it. It gives the place character.

"You literally carried one box," I deadpan, eyeing Lucy from my spot atop my bed. I'm hanging up the photos that I had to take down so Mikey could spackle and paint around the window—the window that is literally the size of a shoebox—that caused all this chaos.

"It was a heavy box," Lucy groans as she stows the Swiffer against the wall and plops onto my bed. "I got the one with all the yoga books in it. The ancient knowledge and wisdom really weighed it down."

I chuckle. "What do you want to eat?"

"Let's go to that bar down the street. I saw something about a cheeseburger on their sign," Liam says, fussing around in the kitchen.

"Liam, I haven't lived here for two weeks, bud. There's no food in there," I call, smacking the final picture on the wall and sitting down next to Lucy.

"Guy can't even get a Cheerio around here," Liam mutters. "Yeah, I'm going to need sustenance, like, *soon*."

"Okay, let's go before Liam turns into Marsha Brady from that Snickers commercial," Lucy says, throwing her phone on the bed and heading for my closet.

"What are you doing?" I ask, watching her rummage through my clothes.

"I just looked up the place. It says Saturdays are DJ nights. You can't go looking like that." She raises her brows at me, and I look down at my outfit. I'm wearing yoga pants, with a baggy t-shirt that says: *Sorry I'm late, I saw a dog.*

"What are you talking about? These are my *nice* yoga pants," I say matter-of-factly. Lucy rolls her eyes and throws a sequined shirt at me.

"I'm not wearing this, it scratches my arms," I say, throwing it back at her.

"Then why do you own it?"

"Because it was sparkly and I was having an off day."

Having Lucy here makes me happy. Aside from the tall blonde man standing in the kitchen—the same one who waits for traffic lights to be red before crossing the street, and therefore could not look more out of place in Manhattan—it feels like old times. Exchanging banter with Lucy, the comfort and familiarity of her presence brings a warmness into my chest. I miss her.

In the corner, a box of books falls off of the hall tree by the door.

"Lucy, that was literally the one place I told you not to put anything. The wall shakes when the neighbor slams their door." I make my way over to the pile of books on the floor and start scooping them into my arms.

"I may or may not have been listening when you said that," Lucy admits, a guilty look on her face. I fall to my knees to pick up the rest of the books. "Need help?" Lucy asks from the other side of the apartment.

"No, I got it—" My voice trails off as I pick up a journal I recognize from years ago. It was the one I used when I was studying the yoga sutras. I bullet-journaled my way through it. It's a small red journal, one I'm sure I picked up as an impulse buy at a Barnes and Noble register. The edges have faded with time, and the exterior of the pages have a yellow tint. I can't remember the last time I found this. It must have been stuck at the back of my bookcase and was thrown in a box when I was saving my books from the water.

I turn the book over in my hands, feeling the soft faux leather crease in my fingers. When I flip it over, I find an explosion of color on the pages. Both pages are filled with a blend of colors—yellow, red, purple, and orange, vibrant streaks stretching towards the edge of the pages, centered around meticulously outlined words in the middle of the space.

"You are the sky. Everything else—it's just the weather."
— Pema Chödrön

The hair on my arms raises and goosebumps spread across my skin. I get the exact same sensation every time I read that quote or hear it in a meditation. I haven't thought about those words in a while. I try to pinpoint the moment when I created this entry—it must have been a few months after I moved to the city. I had my first internship at a small press. I missed home and I believed every intrusive thought that burrowed into my head—that I was a bad daughter and a selfish sister for moving away. I remember the guilt, the pressure to be present for my mom and Nick, to do everything I could to make their lives easier. I was cracking under it. I thought I was ridiculous for thinking I could live on my own and I blamed myself for every bad day Nick had and the toll it took on my mother.

It's just the weather.

I close my eyes and picture an open sky, blue and cloudless, and try to remember what I felt the first time I read that quote. Understood. Heard. Comforted.

How different the weather in my life is now, compared to back then. I was so young, so optimistic. I still feel the same pressure I did when I first saw these words years ago. I'm still unsure of the future. I'm still alone. I'm older, but I'm still waiting for things to get better.

My thoughts drift to Oliver, and the way I feel... *lighter* when I'm with him. My world is a little less lonely with him in it. He thinks of things before I ask for them, or even know I need them myself. I've never met someone who can read me like that, which is why I want him in my life, in whatever form he is willing to give me. I don't know what our future together looks like, or if there even is a "together" for us, but all I can say is that Oliver makes me feel good. And it's been a long time since I've been able to say that.

"You okay, Elle?" Lucy says as she takes a few steps towards me.

I turn around and snap the journal closed, taking a deep breath. "Yep. Let's go."

TWENTY-TWO

Oliver

"So do we need to talk about it?" Henry asks as he spots me on the bench press.

"What?" I grunt.

"You know what," he says in an obvious tone. That's the thing about Henry. He's so sure of himself. He sees the world around him for what it is, and he is so damn perceptive it's annoying sometimes.

"For once, could you not be so mature and communicative?" I say, placing the bar on the rungs and sitting up. I wipe the sweat off of my forehead and hang my head, waiting for the lecture I know is coming.

"What I don't understand is why you set her up with *me* when *you* clearly like her," he says, coming around the cage and leaning against it. He crosses his arms in front of him and glares at me.

"I never said—"

"You didn't have to say it, asshole," he snaps back. The few patrons that are still moseying around the gym give us an awkward glance. I glare at him. "Sorry, but you are being a dick. You like this girl. She's awesome and is clearly into you. Why is this such a Greek tragedy? Just do something about it."

"A Greek tragedy?" I ask, tilting my head.

"Yeah, that didn't make sense. But you get what I mean. What is all the *melodrama* about?"

"Melodrama? Have you been watching the Hallmark channel or something?"

"I *may* have gotten sucked into a cheesy, romantic movie when I was at my sister's house last weekend, but that is beside the point. What is your problem?"

"She wants things that I can't give her," I admit, rubbing my temples.

"I swear that was a line in the movie," Henry says. I scowl at him. "That's ridiculous. What can't you give her?"

"She's *literally* a romance editor, she believes in happily ever afters and—"

"And you're the most relationship-centered guy I've ever met. I'm sure if I told all the girls who come into the gym that my friend is a single doctor who works out, there would be a stampede."

"Well, thank you for the boost to my ego, but I can't get myself into that again."

"Into what?"

"A relationship," I say, standing up. I'm so embarrassed by this conversation that my voice has turned into a whisper. "I'm too fucked up. Yeah, girls might like me to start with, but once they get to know me and the crazy shows, I fuck it up. They run. I don't want to do that anymore." I let out a loud breath, avoiding my own gaze in the mirror. "And it's not just that. I'm not a doctor yet. And I don't know if I ever will be." I haven't admitted that out loud to anyone, and I can't believe it just slipped out.

"What do you mean?"

I lean against the wall, pulling my shirt around my waist. Thor picks his head up from his spot behind the front desk when he sees me move.

"I mean I'm miserable. Internal medicine was never my first choice. Neither was the ER." I slide down the wall until I'm sitting on the floor, and Thor bounds over to sit next to me. I scratch behind his ears when he plops down. "And I didn't even earn the spot I have. Nothing about it feels right."

"And what does that have to do with Elle?"

"She wants a future with someone. How can I give that to her when I don't know what mine will look like? I'm thinking about quitting a residency that thousands of medical students would kill for and completely upending my career." I wave my hands too enthusiastically on the last part, so I let them drop to my sides and I rest my head on the wall behind me. Thor twists his head to look up at me, confused about why I stopped petting him.

Henry blows out a breath, considering everything I just said. "That's a fuck ton of pressure you're putting on yourself man. You're thirty. Contrary to popular belief, you don't have to have everything about your life figured out." I squint an eye open at him. "And if I know Elle like I think I do, she would want you to do something that makes you happy. If it takes you some time to figure that out, I think she'd be pretty supportive of that."

"*That* sounds like too much pressure, right there," I say, pointing at him.

"So you're going to be alone all your life?" he says, looking at me like I'm an idiot. Which, honestly, I can't blame him for. "How does that make sense, Oliver?"

"If I admit that it doesn't, then can we please stop having this conversation?"

"*No!* I have a whole speech prepared from the movie." He clears his throat. "You see, Oliver, when life gives you opportunities—"

"Oh, would you shut up?" I stand up and wrap an arm around Henry's neck, grunting as I pretend to strangle him. He chuckles and ducks out of my grasp, cracking up at his own joke as he walks towards the back of the gym. I shake my head.

He makes it all sound so simple. I wish it was.

"DJ Night? Seriously?" I ask Henry as I follow him into a restaurant at the end of my block.

"Yeah, we can ignore that. It's a nice bar with good food, and I'm starving," he says with a grunt. We've just closed his gym for the night, and after a few miles on the treadmill, I'm pretty hungry as well, so I'm in no position to argue. Thankfully I was able to shower in his locker room while he closed up, otherwise it would not be acceptable for me to be out in public. We dropped Thor at my apartment quickly and set him up with his dinner and a chewing bone, and headed back out before Henry crashed through the wall like the Kool-Aid man looking for something to eat.

We take a seat at the bar and order some beers and appetizers. I check the camera on my phone and see Thor chomping away at the bone I left him with. I'll only be gone an hour or so, so hopefully he won't tear up the carpet before I get back. My thoughts drift to Elle. I know she had a dress fitting or something with Lucy today. Just as I get my phone out to message her and see how it went, I stop myself. My conversation with Henry has given me a knot in my gut that I can't shake.

Henry shoves me when I yawn. "Twelve-hour shifts are not for the weak, huh?"

"Yup," I grumble.

"Is there anything about it that you like?" he asks, and I wish he hadn't. My stomach drops at the thought of having to answer that question. Because the answer, truthfully, is no. I'm not dreading every second of it, but I'm dreading the thought of having to go through *years* of this. It's only been two months and I already feel like I've lost my sense of self. I don't care enough about my work. But maybe that's the way everyone feels, and I just have to get over it?

I don't say any of that to Henry though.

"Is that—"

I stop hearing the words coming out of his mouth when I turn around to follow his gaze. Everything becomes slow motion when Elle walks through the door, followed by her friend Lucy and a man. Her hair is curled into voluptuous waves, bouncing as she moves. She flips her hair over her shoulder as she takes off her coat, placing it on the rack by the door. She's dressed in black jeans that look like they are *painted* onto her legs and a literal triangular piece of fabric for a shirt. It's red and sparkly, and is only held on to her by a thin strap around her neck and one around her back.

I've never seen Elle like this. My body—and my mind for that matter—doesn't know what to do with it.

Inhale. Exhale.

Very important to keep breathing.

Get yourself together, Oliver.

Suddenly, I realize that Henry is no longer sitting next to me. I whip my head right and left before I see him heading over to Elle and waving like a dork.

"Elle! So good to see you!" I overhear.

He's a *dead man.*

When I slide off of the barstool, Elle is giving Henry a hug. I have to stifle a gasp when we make eye contact. She looks *stunning*.

When they approach me, I realize I haven't actually moved an inch. Henry comes beside the bar and steps on my foot, trying to shake me from my trance.

"Ol, look who's here!" he says, slapping me on the back. His voice is annoyingly patronizing. I throw an arm around him and give him an equally harsh slap on his shoulder, pushing him forward with the force of it.

"I have eyes, asshole," I mutter under my breath.

Elle and Lucy lean against the bar and a tall blonde man stands behind them. "Oliver, you remember Lucy. And this is her fiancé, Liam," Elle says, nodding to the man behind her. He lifts his hand in a small wave.

"Nice to meet you," I say in a monotone voice. Henry steps on my foot again. "What are you guys doing here?"

"Well, we understand this is the type of establishment that serves food and drinks, is that correct?" Lucy says sarcastically.

"Right, of course," I murmur. Elle gives me a weird look.

"Should we sit at the bar instead, Elle?" Lucy asks. Just as she does, a couple slides into the seats beside Henry and me.

"Well, I guess we'll be over there then," Elle says awkwardly, and the group heads off towards a free table on the other side of the bar.

When she's out of eyesight, I lean against the bar and drop my head, trying to regain my composure. I hate being caught off guard. I'm already on edge because I've never been to this restaurant, so I didn't know what to expect when I walked in. I like to know what I'm walking into, from the menu to the layout of the place. Henry knows this, but two guys should be able to walk into a bar and get a bite to eat without one of them freaking out.

And then there's Elle. The one thing in my life that has caught me so off guard that I'm still trying to recover, months later. Add to that the fact that she looks *amazing* tonight. I might actually lose my shit if she gets up to dance in that outfit.

So of course, that's exactly what happens.

About a half hour later, a familiar song comes on that gets Elle and Lucy excited. The pair skip to the dance floor, and it's not long before I'm the schmuck sitting at a bar, watching the most beautiful woman I've ever seen shake her body in a way that should be illegal, too scared to do anything about it.

She looks ridiculous. Not in the usual sense of the word, but in the sense that there is no way she can be the same person that I found sleeping on the floor outside of my apartment three months ago. Every set of eyes in the place has been on her since she walked in, including mine.

Her blonde waves bounce beautifully off her shoulders any time she moves. She keeps doing this thing where she runs two fingers down her part and fluffs the back of her hair—and it is literally driving me wild.

Her shirt—if it can even be called that— lays longer on her front than her back. Every time she sways her hips, I can see the gentle curve of her lower back, and I don't know what to do with myself.

"You alright, Ol?" Henry asks, nudging me with his elbow. I shake my head and down the rest of my beer. I need to get a handle on myself. "You need to go for it, man. This is painful to watch. She's a great kisser, if that sways your decision at all."

I turn my head so fast I get dizzy. "*Excuse me?*" Henry just chuckles.

"You're proving my point for me, man. I can't wait until you're back in your right mind so I can give you so much shit about this."

Liam doesn't let his woman go solo for very long. A few minutes after Lucy and Elle move on to the dance floor, he follows, putting his arms around Lucy and taking her attention away from Elle. Elle doesn't seem to mind though because she quickly finds someone else to dance with.

I squeeze the edge of the bar so hard my hand starts to ache.

Elle's hips move left to right with the beat of the song. The guy she dances next to, a real greaseball, puts one hand on her hip and takes a sip from his drink with the other. Elle lifts up her arms and runs her hands through her hair. The guy's fingers trail up her back as he presses his front against her.

I push my chair away from the bar so violently I nearly knock it over.

"Oh, here we *go!*" Henry says like he's announcing a boxing match.

I promise, I really don't know how I got to the middle of the dance floor. The moment is a complete blackout. All I know is one moment I had a death grip on the bar and the next, my hands are wrapped around Elle's waist, pulling her away from the stranger. The other guy curses at me and I square off with him, not really sure what my next move is. My brain has completely lost its ability to reason. I stand a foot taller than him, and he quickly realizes he wouldn't have a chance.

Suddenly, I feel a warm hand grasp my forearm. I let myself be turned around because I know it's her. She pulls me flush to her and wraps her hands around my neck.

"No," she murmurs, pressing our foreheads together. The concern in her eyes brings rationality back into my head.

Elle runs her fingers down my arms and settles them on the loops of my jeans. I feel her breath hitch as she presses herself flush against me. I have no idea what she is doing, but the smell of her berry shampoo and the feeling of her chest pressed against mine leaves me with no reason to tell her to stop. I think she's trying to center me, to calm me down, but she's really doing the opposite.

She applies pressure to each side of my hips, willing them to move. I gently place my hands on her back, and the burning feeling of her skin against mine feels like a brand. I move with her, swaying our hips left and right, riding the beat.

A wicked smile spreads across Elle's bright red lips and I realize the trap I've let myself fall into. She's trying to tease me. She turns around and presses every inch of her back against my front, and I'm sure she can feel the bulge growing in my pants.

"You're killing me," I murmur against her ear. I've lost control. Every pent-up emotion—confusion, disdain, annoyance, desire—I've had for Elle since the moment I met her feels like it's building up inside me, and I have no way of stopping it. My grip on her hips gets tighter as I guide them to the beat of the music. She presses a little harder against me and I think my world might just explode.

I grab Elle's hand and she lets me lead her to the back of the room. I slam open the back door of the restaurant and pull us into the alley. I turn around quicker than she expected and press her against the brick wall that lines the back of the restaurant. There's no one around us and we're at least twenty feet from the street. We're alone.

Elle gasps when I cage her in with my arms, and I can barely contain myself when she flips her hair out of her face.

"What are you doing?" I growl, pressing my forehead against hers. I let my lips graze her cheek and her neck, her sharp inhale making my arms flex around her body.

"I was dancing," she says, breathless.

"You were doing a lot more than that."

Elle doesn't answer. She looks me hard in the eye and a conversation passes between us, one powered by months of yearning, and I pull her closer to me.

Then her gaze flutters to my lips.

She crushes her mouth against mine, her lips hot as they open against my mouth. She gasps again when I groan into her mouth, pressing every inch of my body that I can against her. I move my arms to her backside, lifting her up so her legs are around my waist. She breaks us apart for a brief moment to whisper against my lips.

"Take me home."

TWENTY-THREE

Elle

A lot happens in a short amount of time. And most of it is a blur.

Somewhere in between Oliver hurrying me back into the restaurant and then pulling me out the front door, I tell Lucy that I'm going home and I'll text her in the morning. I distinctly remember the look Liam gave her after I left. I'm pretty sure he slid some money across the table to her.

I'm in a daze on the walk back to Oliver's apartment. It's not until we stumble through the door, say hello to Thor, and make our way to his bed that the moment feels real.

Like *really* real.

Like *Elle Thompson, what did you get yourself into* real.

After Oliver assures Thor that he'll take him out in a bit, we find ourselves standing on opposite sides of his dark room, staring at each other like one of us will disappear if we look away.

"Are you sure—"

"Yes," I reply before he even finishes the question. It's not lost on me that this is the most impulsive thing I've ever done. But I don't want to deal with that fact right now. I want to do something impulsive and emotional and not care about the consequences.

I want *Oliver*.

I walk backwards until the back of my legs find the bed, and Oliver's gaze follows my every movement. He takes small steps towards me and towers over me. I look up at him, taking a moment to scan every inch of his face, like I could keep a photo of it in my mind forever.

I reach behind my neck and untie the delicate string that is holding my shirt on my body. I let it drop to the floor next to me. Oliver's eyes go dark as he inhales sharply.

"My imagination did not do you justice," he growls, trailing a gentle finger across my collarbone.

"And how much have you imagined me, exactly?" I tease. A gentle moan escapes my lips when his hand cups my breast, his thumb sliding over my hardened nipple.

"I probably shouldn't answer that," he murmurs, as his hands continue to search and tease me.

Oliver takes my head in both of his hands, his fingers snaking through my hair, and presses his lips against mine, increasing his firmness with each passing second. He traces my mouth with his tongue and bites my bottom lip. He moves his lips to my neck, his teeth grazing my earlobe.

"Every day, since the first time I found you sleeping outside my door. That's how much," he whispers, the feel of his breath against my sensitive skin making my stomach tighten.

I sneak my hands under his shirt, sliding them up his chest, and tracing the lines of his stomach. I gasp a little too loudly when he pulls the shirt over his head, and I would feel embarrassed if this was anyone else. But I can tell Oliver is just as desperate for this as I am. I run my hands up his chest and back down along his abs.

"I've waited so long to do this," I say, my voice cracking. I kiss over his heart and run my lips down to his ribs, my fingers gripping the muscles of his stomach, desperate to get my hands on every inch of him.

Oliver threads his arms around me, picking me up and laying me down on the bed. He crawls over me, bracing himself on his forearms above me. I reach down for the buckle on his jeans, but in an instant he is gone, standing beside the bed. He takes my foot in his hand, placing a gentle kiss to my ankle before he pulls at the hem of my jeans. A grunt escapes him when he realizes what a task that is.

"I knew these things were painted on," he groans.

I giggle, any lingering nerves fading away with the sight of a smile on Oliver's face.

He eventually pulls the jeans off, and my underwear after them, leaving me exposed in front of him. He doesn't return to the bed right away, taking a moment to look at me. He unbuckles his pants with one hand and when they drop to the floor, I swallow hard, my hips swaying with anticipation.

Woah.

"You know you just said that out loud, right?" he chuckles. I put my hands in front of my face, hiding from him, small giggles escaping me. Oliver leans over me and takes one of my hands, kisses my palm, and guides me to his shaft.

"This is what you do to me," he says, his body twitching as I tighten my grip on him. I run my hand up and down his length and lick my lips. I bring my mouth close to the head, and I just barely have my lips on it when he wraps his arms around me and moves me up towards the top of the bed.

"If you do that, we won't be here for long. And I want to take my time," he says, kissing the area below my belly button. A small whine escapes me as he kisses my hip bones, up my stomach and between my breasts, his hands exploring every inch of my body. I arch into him when he takes my breast into his mouth, feeling his bare chest against mine, and wanting us to be closer. He swirls his tongue around my nipple and I moan. When I grab him and pull him to my mouth, I can feel the smile on his lips.

He circles his fingers around my nipple and I moan into his mouth, my hips rising, searching for him. His hands grip my shoulders as if I'm grounding him in this moment. I run my fingers through his hair and throw my arms around him, pressing every bit of skin I can against him, but it still doesn't feel like enough.

It feels like we stay that way for hours—kissing, biting, teasing. Oliver takes his time on each part of me—my neck, my breasts, my lips, and around again. All the while his hands roam across my body, his rough palms squeezing my softest parts, his fingers entwining with mine over my head. It's months of anticipation, of waiting, of wondering, all coming together. It's everything we've been afraid to say—every touch a secret we've been too nervous to share, every kiss a feeling we couldn't place. But now that we're here, everything is understood.

Finally, Oliver's hand slides down my side and over my hips, his movements full of purpose this time. I widen my legs for him and he curses when he feels the wetness between my thighs. Without missing a beat, he kisses me hard, his tongue licking the inside of my mouth while he presses a finger inside of me. I grip his shoulders, feeling a high that I have never experienced. I've been touched before, but it's never felt like this. His thumb finds my clit, and he starts with slow circles, testing my reaction. He takes his fingers out of me and massages my clit with two fingers, increasing in pace. I can feel the heat building in my face and pressure between my legs. I know Oliver is waiting for something, but it doesn't come, and a brief moment of worry passes through my mind, afraid that I've disappointed him. I feel the same pressure I remember from other times men have used their hands on me. The pressure to perform.

"Don't disappear on me," Oliver says in a low voice. I open my eyes when I feel him brushing strands of hair out of my face. "Stay here."

He gently traces his fingers around my opening, his eyes never straying from mine. I take a deep breath and tell myself to relax, try to forget about what I'm supposed to look like or sound like in this moment, and just be. It's a lot harder than it sounds.

"Keep your eyes on me," Oliver commands when they start to flutter closed. "Tell me what feels good." He gently pushes a finger into me, curling it inside me.

"Well, that doesn't suck," I say, breathy.

Oliver chuckles. He removes his hand and puts his thumb in his mouth, before putting his hand back, pushing two fingers inside me and rubbing my clit again. As he moves his hand, I feel a warmness in my belly, the instinct to move with him. He puts his arm down on my hips, keeping me in place.

"That—" I say, my voice shaking. "That feels good."

Oliver keeps his movements steady, watching my reaction. My urge to put on a show comes naturally, and I can't shake the feeling like he somehow knows it. He would call me out on it. I relax against the bed and his hand slows.

I take a deep breath and sit up, pushing myself back towards the headboard. I open my legs as I rest my head against his pillows, his scent enveloping me.

Without either of us saying a word, Oliver reaches into his nightstand and slides a condom on. He kneels on the bed above me, a few stray hairs falling in front of his face. I reach up and push them back with my fingers, and Oliver hums as he presses his cheek into my palm. He hovers for a moment just above me, his arms on either side of my head, our breaths ragged. His eyes never moving from mine, he reaches a hand down and guides himself into me.

There's pressure, and then a sense of completeness. I gasp as I feel him fill me completely, in a way that I didn't know was possible. I squeeze his shoulders and he catches my open mouth in a kiss. I press my forehead against his while we both catch our breaths, and then he starts to move.

It seems like everything before this moment was a fog. Like what have we been doing since we met, if not this? Being connected to Oliver in every way possible feels *right*, and I want to be as close to him as possible, in every way I physically can.

His hands play with my breasts as he moves his hips, and he leans forward so that more of him rubs against my clit. The moan that I let out at that sensation is nothing short of animalistic, but never has anything felt as good, as incredible, as this. He takes my leg in one hand and bends it towards me, opening me further, his thrusts becoming deeper and more delicious.

I feel a tingle in my toes as he moves faster, a clenching feeling spreading through my belly. Oliver crushes his mouth against mine, tangles his hands in my hair, and my senses are in overdrive.

Feeling Oliver inside me makes me tighten more, as if doing so could make us any closer. I grab Oliver's ass with one hand and scratch down his back with the other. Oliver curses. A lot.

"*Fuck*, Elle," he groans, his head next to mine. He bites my neck right beneath my ear and I grip his shoulder harder, in disbelief that this kind of pleasure exists, and rage that I've never felt it before. I'm torn between craving the release and never wanting this to end.

"The times I've pictured this moment," he whispers in my ear. He licks the spot where he just bit. "Never thought it would be like *this*."

That makes two of us.

"Oh my God!" I gasp, gripping the muscles of Oliver's shoulders like they're the only thing tying me to life. Oliver buries his face in my neck, and I open my mouth in a soundless cry, completely lost to the pleasure in the center of my body. My legs squeeze around his hips and my nails dig into his skin, his neck, his hair. I feel his warmth fill me, and the sensation pushes me over the edge. Every part of my body tenses, and for a moment I can't breathe. I barely hear the words of encouragement he whispers in my ear, my senses reduced down to a single point. He kisses me hard, then tenderly, until there's nothing left of me but a quivering mess beneath him.

I feel an emptiness when he slides out of me. He disappears for a moment, but I'm so blissed out I barely notice. When he returns, he wraps his arms around me and pulls us together, my bare chest against his, our legs tangled beneath the sheets. I don't know how long he kisses me for, but I know I want it to be forever.

When he finally lays back, I rest my cheek on his chest, and we breathe together, and it feels like the air is a little bit easier to take in than before.

TWENTY-FOUR

Oliver

There's something surreal about waking up next to someone that you never want to leave.

In recent years, I've been so intent on not getting attached, for fear of someone getting to know the *real* me and wanting out. I've rarely entertained the possibility that I could ever be with someone long-term.

But as I stand here, the smallest ripples of sunlight peeking through the plain curtains of the apartment windows, making lines on Elle's pale face, I realize something.

I don't want to be apart from Elle Thompson.

And that is equal parts exhilarating and terrifying.

I reach my hand out and gently smooth her hair away from her face. I don't want to wake her up, but leaving a note doesn't feel right after last night. And I want to see her eyes before I leave for work.

I manage to extract myself from the twisted sheets without waking her. Once I'm dressed, I kneel next to the bed and gently rest my arms on the mattress next to her.

Her lips are pursed, like they're begging to be kissed. But I've never kissed a sleeping Elle before, and I'm not sure if it would end with me being punched in the face. Knowing her, that is a very plausible outcome.

I caress her bare shoulder blades and see goosebumps start to spread across her skin. I lean forward and place a kiss on her shoulder, eliciting a quiet moan from her. Her eyes scrunch, but don't open.

"Do that again," she whispers in a hoarse voice. The corner of my mouth lifts up. I kiss her in the same place, letting my lips linger there for a moment longer. And then I blow a small puff of air on the spot.

A longer moan this time.

She rolls over, the sheet dropping below her breasts, and I'm struck again by how gorgeous she is. She smiles lazily before squinting her eyes open. When she sees me in my scrubs, she pouts.

"You're dressed," she mumbles.

"I am," I say with a nod. I crawl my hands towards her and trace one finger over her breasts. "But you, beautiful, are not. And that is *fucking* killing me right now."

Her pout lifts slightly. "Then join me," she replies, and I nearly give in.

"I would love to, but duty calls," I respond as I stand up, adjusting my pants in the process. I have to cover a day shift, today of all days, even though I'd like nothing more than to get right back into bed.

"You don't even like your job, just quit and stay here. I could plan a much more fun day for us than saving lives," she says, wrapping the sheet around her and sitting up.

"I don't doubt that for a second, sweetheart." I say, the pet name rolling easily off my tongue.

Elle runs her fingers through her knotted hair and turns to face me. I lean down and kiss her plump lips, still swollen from all the times we woke up during the night and found ourselves kissing again. She puts a hand around my neck and tries to pull me towards her but I resist. I let my tongue touch hers for just a second, give her one last peck, and pull away.

I look at the clock on my nightstand. "I have to go," I say, leaning over the bed to kiss her on the forehead.

"Ugh, you can't do that," she groans.

"Why?"

"Because a forehead kiss is one of the most *endearing* ways a love interest shows affection. And we don't know what we are yet." She looks up at me from underneath her full lashes. Something feels uneasy in my chest when she says that, but I try to ignore it. We clearly can't have the "what was last night" talk right now, and she respects that.

"Right, uh—" I stutter. Then, awkwardly, I put my fist out. "See you later, bro."

Elle tilts her head at my fist and scrunches her face. "Better. I guess," she says, giving me a fist bump. "Later bro."

I turn to leave and Thor jumps up on the bed to join Elle. She plops back on the pillows and allows Thor to cuddle up beside her, both of them knowing full well he is not supposed to be on the furniture. I shake my head fondly. Leaving that sight to work for twelve hours. I should get a fucking medal for that.

***

"Dr. Cole, can you consult on a broken arm in Room Three please?" the nurse at the station asks me without looking up from her clipboard. I rub my eyes from exhaustion and immediately regret it. Germs. I cringe and promptly take some hand sanitizer from the nurses' desk.

"Sure," I say with a yawn, looking at the clock. One hour left on my shift. *One hour left until I can see Elle again.* "Has it been splinted?"

"It has, but they need sutures as well. Some glass is stuck in the wound on the same hand. Car accident. Ortho was consulted but Dr. *Penistown* didn't have time to evacuate the contents and suture it before a trauma came in," she explains. She finally looks up from her chart, realizing what she just said.

I'm taken aback and widen my eyes at her. She does the same. "I'm *so* sorry," she stutters. All of the color drains from her face and I'm worried she might pass out from the shock of what she just did. "I meant Dr. *Penniston*. Dr. *Penniston* wasn't able to—"

"I like *Penistown* better, frankly," I say with a chuckle. The nurse's shoulders relax and relief floods her expression. She's an older woman, with black hair braided into cornrows that lead to her ponytail. I don't remember her name, but she's always been stoic with me. Until now, that is. I grin at her.

"I'm so sorry," she repeats as she shakes her head. "It's a name one of the other nurses came up with as a joke and I wish I never heard it." She places her palm over her forehead.

"I don't, just made my day. *Penistown* is a turd," I whisper to her, taking the chart from her hands and winking as I walk towards the exam room.

Penistown. I can't wait to tell Elle about this.

I can't wait to tell Elle about this.

Shit. I shouldn't think like that.

I brush it off as I pull back the curtain on Exam Room Three, and I'm surprised when I see a young boy sitting on the bed. He has dark hair and eyes, which are swollen from crying. His mother is sitting next to him on an uncomfortable looking plastic chair and is absorbed in something in her phone. I should have read the chart before I came in, but for some reason, I wasn't expecting a pediatric patient.

"Hey there," I say, jolting the mother to attention. The boy looks up at me with a miserable expression on his face. A quick look at the first page of his chart tells me he is five. He is wearing a blue Spiderman shirt that is spotted with blood on the sleeve and Spiderman shoes that look too small for his feet. He's sitting at a ninety-degree angle because his arm is placed on a tray table beside the bed. There is a soft cast on the underside of his wrist and the wound on the top of his forearm is covered with gauze. He looks terribly uncomfortable, and also like he could fall asleep at any moment. I wonder how long he has been sitting in this position, unable to move his arm. It's probably numb at this point.

I tilt my head at him and something comes over me. I've never been a *kids* guy, but in this moment, I find myself wanting to make *this* kid a little less miserable.

And for some reason, making shit up is the only way I can think to do it.

I sneak another quick look at the chart before speaking. "I'm sorry, but are you Riley? The hero who saved the neighborhood?"

"Huh?" he says in a weak voice.

I look at the chart again. "Riley Chen, the kid who used his *spidey* senses to stop a bank robbery and save the neighborhood. I heard all about you. You're a superhero!" My feigned voice is pathetic, but I try not to let my internal cringing show on my face. I'm doing my best.

The kid's shoulders straighten as he tilts his head. His interest piques at the mention of "*spidey* senses."

"That's how you hurt your arm, right?" I raise my brows at him, trying to get him to play along with my game. I pull a wheeling stool up to his bed and sit on it. I give him a reassuring smile and his lips lift a little.

"Yeah, I was, um, battling the Green Goblin," he says, a hint of excitement in his eyes.

"Wow, you are so brave. The Green Goblin scares me so much! I always have nightmares about him." That isn't entirely made up. The Green Goblin from the live-action *Spiderman* movies actually scared the crap out of me when I was a kid.

"I used my webs to trap him!" Riley squeals back.

"Nice work, man! Tell me all about it while I wrap up this arm." I slide closer to the table where his arm is laying and I see his little fingers are so swollen they are touching each other. "Make sure you look at Mom the whole time though. She wants to hear the story too." I smile at the mom, and she gives me a knowing smile back.

"Eyes on Mom, okay kiddo? I'm just going to check out these web shooters on your arm, but keep telling me, what did you do to the Goblin?" I squeeze a small amount of skin to distract him from the pinch of the needle that I use to inject lidocaine near his wound.

The kid regales us with a made-up story of how he defeated the Green Goblin, and by the time he is done, I have his arm stitched and wrapped. Not only was it a good stitching job, but I was also proud of myself for being able to make this kid's day after it started out with an accident that landed him in the ER. When I walk out of his room, I have a grin on my face until I have that unnerving thought again.

I can't wait to tell Elle.

That thought makes something squeeze in my chest, an all-too familiar feeling of dread. A flood of thoughts fill my brain: images of my night with Elle, her smile this morning, her comment about "what we are." The scene of her consoling me on the treadmill pushes in, followed by a made-up image of her being hurt, or in danger. I shake my head and try to push those thoughts away, and replace them with reality. Elle is fine. She's home with Thor. She was in my bed this morning. And I loved it.

I pinch the bridge of my nose as I make my way to the on-call room. I need a second to myself. I can feel panic rising in my chest, and I need to get a handle on it. I can't fall apart, not here. There's a flare of anger in me—I was literally fine a minute ago, helping a nice kid and feeling proud of myself, and now… now my mind is trying to sabotage me. As per freaking usual.

I close the door behind me and lock it. The stress of this shift is evident in my shoulders, and I turn my head to crack my neck, trying to release the tension from my muscles. The on-call room consists of a twin bed and a desk, much like there would be in a prison cell. The walls are white cinderblock and the chair is a rickety swivel chair that could collapse at any moment. I sit in the desk chair and hang my head between my legs, trying to steady my breaths.

The intrusive thoughts about Elle fade, replaced with questioning ones about my job, my future, and what the hell I'm doing with my life… and now they've circled back around to how, or *if*, Elle is going to fit into that. God, my mind is such a fun place.

My thoughts drift back to all of my conversations with Elle and Henry about my job. And then to what I said to Henry last night. I could never really quit residency, could I? I am anything but spontaneous. My life has been planned since my first science class. How could I throw all that away now? That moment with the kid was good, right? Maybe I could find more moments like that?

I can't make so many decisions at one time. I'm not hardwired for it. Last night with Elle was amazing, *so* amazing I can't imagine it ever being better than that. But I got swept up. She was dancing and then the other guy… I acted completely on impulse.

And now, I am freaking the *fuck* out.

I can't do this. I can't commit to her when I don't even know what I'm doing with my life.

"Ow!" I look at my hand to see that I've pulled a cuticle off of my finger as I was sitting here. I didn't even realize I was doing it. A small line of blood drips down my thumb, and I grab a tissue and apply pressure to it, cursing myself. I am *unhinged*. Of course I can't do… whatever this is with Elle. A guy like me can't make her happy. Everything about my life is so unstable right now. What am I thinking?

Inhale, Oliver. Five, four, three, two, one.

Exhale. Five, four, three, two, one.

Inhale.

My pager buzzes on my waist. I pull it off of my scrubs and throw it across the room. It smashes against the far wall and the batteries roll across the floor. Good. That really helped the situation.

Inhale.

Exhale.

Inhale.

Exhale.

Not everything I think is true. Not everything I think is true.

When my own mind works against me, it's really hard to decide what is real and what isn't. Right now, everything feels out of control.

But nothing is going to be solved by me sitting in this windowless room.

I walk across the room and retrieve the broken pager, putting it back together with shaky hands. Then, I walk to the nurses' station and bandage my finger. I hide all these small signs that I'm slowly falling apart from the inside, put on my white coat, and go cure my fourth pneumonia patient of the day.

TWENTY-FIVE

Elle

I have no idea what the hell I am doing.

I am quite literally making it up with every minute of every day. All I know is that a moment spent with Oliver is better than any spent without him. And in that moment at the bar, I knew I *needed* Oliver more than I've *wanted* anyone in my life. Screw the consequences.

I'm not sure what this means, or if Oliver's feelings have changed about wanting a relationship. I'm too afraid to ask. Because whatever happened that night, it was *amazing*. And I don't want to ruin it. So for the first time in my life, I try not to get caught up in the *happily ever after* of it all. Even though my mind is filled with all the moments Oliver has shown me he does care about me: pulling me away from that sleazy guy, smiling when I got home from work, fixing up the couch so I always had exactly what I needed before he left for work for the night.

And then I think about how refreshing it was to be intimate with him and… *laugh*. To be comfortable. To not be worried about what he was thinking or feeling or trying to be sexy in the moment. I was able to just *be*. Never in my life have I ever felt so sure of myself, so *desired*, than I did that night with Oliver. And I'm afraid that after experiencing that, I'll never be able to settle for anything less.

And I really don't want to.

But the truth is, I have to be able to roll with whatever Oliver is willing to give me right now. Because Lucy was right. I shouldn't settle. And I deserve to give this thing with Oliver a chance, despite what he has said. I think Oliver is just so caught up in the past and all the pressure that's been put on him, that he's not used to being told how amazing he truly is. It's like he's needed Hype Girl Elle his whole life. And now I'm here, I want him to know how much I want him.

I can be with Oliver without a plan. Why not? I can roll with it. Go with the flow. Sure I can!

Screw. The. Consequences!

"You know you don't sound convincing at all, right?" Lucy asks after I've recited this speech to her one night after work. We're sitting on our respective couches on FaceTime. Both of our TVs are playing the same *Friends* episode and we're in our pajamas. Thor is curled up on the other end of my couch, and Blue is sprawled out next to Lucy. I haven't seen Oliver since Sunday, aside from picking up and dropping off Thor for the last two nights. Pick-ups and drop-offs which have included several make out sessions, but little else.

I ignore the thoughts in the back of my head that insist Oliver is avoiding having "the conversation" with me.

He's been quiet, more than usual, in the few moments that we've spent together. I can tell he wants to say something, but anytime I try to start talking to him, he kisses me, or rushes out the door for work. I'm trying not to overthink it. It's Oliver, he struggles to share things. We'll talk eventually. I'm know we will.

"Screw the consequences!" I add a fist into the air motion like I'm starting a revolution and not trying to convince my friend of something.

"Nope, not better."

"Eh, it's a work in progress, but I'm in it for the long haul," I say flippantly. I can be flippant. Sure I can. *Who can be flippant? Elle Thompson can!*

"Anyway, I can't wait to see this arrangement in action. Is Oliver coming on Saturday? Have you seen him since you hooked up?" Lucy asks, throwing a handful of popcorn in her mouth.

My cheeks heat when I think of how Oliver barely waited for me to open the door tonight when he dropped Thor off. I still had a grip on the door handle when he pushed his way in and wrapped me in his arms. He picked me up and devoured me into a kiss at the same time, his big hands squeezing my backside as he turned me around against the door. I couldn't catch my breath for several minutes after he left.

"I take your blushing as a yes," Lucy says, grinning. I stick my tongue out at her. "Elle, do you have any idea what you're doing?"

"Absolutely zero," I reply, making an "O" gesture with my hand.

"Great, let me know when you want to tackle that," she says knowingly.

"I did ask him to come on Saturday," I say, remembering the conversation from this morning. "He was a little weird about it though."

"Weird how?"

"Um..." My voice trails off as I remember Oliver swaying at my door this morning as I asked him to go to Lucy's book launch party with me.

"*Oh, I don't know*," he'd said initially.

"*You don't know? You like Lucy, don't you?*"

He'd curled his hand behind his neck, rubbing his shoulder. "*Yeah, yeah, of course—*"

"*Well, then it's settled.*" I reached up to kiss him on the cheek, and I felt his entire body tense.

I've tried to ignore the nagging feeling in my stomach since then.

"Anyway, I told my mom not to come. I think it will be too overstimulating for Nick," I add, trying to divert the conversation away from Oliver.

"Aw, really? I was looking forward to seeing them." Lucy pouts.

"Yeah, I think it is for the best," I say. Thor jumps off the couch and scratches his paw against the door. He turns and looks at me with his big black eyes. "I've got to take Thor out. I'll talk to you later."

"Okay, be careful," Lucy says, and I hang up.

I throw on a sweatshirt, relishing in the fact that I can finally put my heavy coats away for the season, and put on Thor's leash before we head out. I shake my head at the fact when I first met Oliver and Thor, it was March, and I had Thor dressed in sweaters to go outside, much to Oliver's dismay. Now we get to linger a bit longer on our walks, go a bit farther, soak up New York City in early May, when there's this short transitionary period between it being so cold your tears turn to ice and it being so hot that the entire city smells like a combination of B.O. and urine. It's a special time.

Thor and I head to the dog run, where I let him off the leash and take a seat at one of the benches around a tree. The park is fairly empty, with just a few other dogs for Thor to play with. I pick up one of the random tennis balls on the ground and throw it. Oliver would cringe if I did that. He only likes Thor to play with his own toys, not ones that people have left on the dirty mulch of the dog park. My lips quirk up into a smile thinking of Oliver and all his eccentricities. I notice every one of them, but I'm not sure he knows that I do. There's the fact that he would always rather get takeout than go to a restaurant—I think it's a combination of anxiety about being in a crowd and drinking out of a cup that isn't his. He hasn't verbalized this, but the more time we spend together, the better I get at reading him.

Then, there's his nighttime routine: brushing his teeth, placing his phone on the charger, checking that his alarm is set three times before finally placing the phone on the front right corner of the nightstand. His pillows: one behind his head and one on each side of him. The one behind his head is the light gray pillowcase and the two on the side are darker gray. I've seen him change his sheets and place them in that fashion every time. The light gray goes in the middle, always.

When we first met, he was the firmest, tightest closed book I'd ever met, but over time, I've been able to flip through his pages, appreciating every word they have to offer.

It's in that moment that I realize I've learned more about Oliver in a few months than anyone I've ever dated in the past. And the best part? It didn't feel like a job interview.

I didn't have to answer a dating survey to find someone compatible with my personality type. I simply found a friend. I got to know him—slowly and patiently. We had fun together. We laughed. We played. And now, I feel like everything truly led us here. Or rather, to where we ended up the other night. Didn't I always say I wanted to just be in a relationship without having to go through all the trouble? That's what happened with Oliver. We fell into it.

I'm just not sure that Oliver sees it the same way.

The sun has just set, so it's not completely dark out, but the sky is clear with the last sliver of light just peeking over the horizon. I look up at the sky, wishing I could see the stars. Most days, I'm happy with life in the city. Lucy hated it, but I love the convenience it offers. I love the walkability and the variety of cultures around every corner. But I miss the stars.

When we were kids, Nicky and I used to take Meatball out at night together. Nick was terribly afraid of the dark when he was little, and taking the dog out was one way I got him to face that fear. Meatball would roam around the yard—he wasn't very athletic, as his name suggested, so he wouldn't enjoy the intense game of fetch that I am currently playing with Thor—and Nick and I would name the constellations. His favorite was Orion, primarily because it was the only one he could ever find.

"*There he is, Well!*" he would say in his mumbled voice, his chubby finger pointing at the sky. He couldn't say Elle when he was little, so he's always called me *Wellie*. I'd look up and immediately find Orion's belt, and trace the line up to his arrow with Nick, so he could see the full picture.

I love the sky as it is now, at twilight. I think it is the time where it is most obvious that we live in a small world, on a small planet, in a system of many, in a universe of infinity. I think back to those nights standing on the lawn with my brother, feeling so insignificant with the endless sky above me.

Thor trots over to me and sits at my legs, his tongue hanging out the side of his mouth. I reach down and pet him, scratching behind his ears, an unsettling feeling in my stomach when he looks up at me. I've grown so attached to Thor. I love him, really. And yet, there's something in my gut that worries that he is temporary. He is Oliver's dog, and Oliver, as he has said himself, is not forever.

"I don't think that will be for me. Not anytime soon anyway."

It's those words that echo in my head long after I've gone to sleep that night, the same sense of worry staying with me the next day, thinking that this little life I've fallen into over the past few months is just a few words away from being taken from me.

TWENTY-SIX

Oliver

I do *not* want to go to this party.

Could I have told Elle that? Sure, I suppose I could have, but then I would have to provide a reason why I didn't want to go. And at the moment, I don't have an intelligible one.

Every time I've stood at Elle's door for the past week, I've knocked with the intention of talking to her. Telling her that I'm overwhelmed and I can't take on so much right now. I have sentence starters prepared in my head. But then she opens the door, and the memory of her beneath me comes rushing back, and I can barely remember my own name, let alone the conversation topics I had prepared. I then proceed to spend the next several minutes kissing the hell out of her instead of having the hard discussion I intended to. Not the most mature move on my part.

I couldn't exactly have the conversation now, before we're about to leave for Lucy's book party something or other, so I'm at a bit of a stalemate.

"Careful, you're drooling," I say confidently as Elle admires me in my outfit. I wasn't sure what one wears to a book party, so I opted for black dress slacks and a steel-colored shirt. I'm standing in her doorway, trying to suppress my stunned reaction at her appearance. She's wearing a satin dress that hugs every inch of her, with long puffy sleeves and a slit up her leg. Her hair is big and curly, with a clip on one side so it is not falling in her face. She's *glowing*. Or at least, she looks like it to me.

Her gaze runs up and down my body like she could *devour* me. The feeling is mutual. When her eyes meet mine, she bites her lip and I nearly jump her. She knows it drives me crazy when she does that. I raise my brows at her.

"How much time do we have before we have to leave?" I ask, taking a step into the apartment and wrapping a hand around her hip and squeezing, my eyes never leaving hers.

"Not enough to do what you're thinking of right now," she says with a small smirk.

I purse my lips. I kick the door closed behind me and press her up against it. "Enough for you to put new lipstick on?"

"What—?" I stop her words with my mouth. I'm not sure I'll ever get over the excitement of kissing Elle. It's intoxicating. *She's* intoxicating. Especially when she moans at something I do—like when I push her against the door and put my knee in between her legs.

She runs her hands up my torso and around the back of my head, her grip tight. She pushes her tongue in my mouth and I grip her hips harder, desperate for more. I start to pull the bottom of her dress up, and she stops me, pushing me away.

"No seriously, we have to go," she says, breathless. If I thought she was irresistible before, she's even more so now—her lips swollen, her hair slightly messy, her dress creased.

What did I need to talk to her about again?

"What I'm imagining won't take more than five minutes, tops," I reply, trying to take another step towards her.

She rolls her eyes and lets me pull her towards me. *Damn*, I love when she does that. "Yeah, right," she says, playfully pushing me away.

Elle moves herself to the tall mirror on her wall to reapply her deep red lipstick. I step behind her, pressing myself against the length of her body so she can feel how much I want her. I move her hair to the side and press kisses against her shoulder and up the back of her neck—where I'm quickly learning is one of her favorite spots.

Elle lets out a soft "hmmm," but turns around and sidesteps me. "Stop playing dirty, Cole." She puts her coat on and places a small bag on her shoulder. "Let's go."

I don't know much about what Elle does, other than she works with romance books. But the soirée that her company put together for Lucy is quite impressive. It's at a restaurant on the edge of the park, with a beautiful view of the lit-up skyline.

I try not to leave Elle's side as much as possible, but she does quite a bit of running around, trying to get Lucy everything she needs. We're in a private room in the restaurant, and the crowd isn't large—mostly friends and family, with some publishing people Elle introduces me to, whose names I forget immediately.

When Elle isn't with me, I stay on the periphery of the party, anxiety taking over as the number of people in the room increases. I keep the exit in my eyesight the entire time, and cringe anytime someone coughs. My OCD loves to shine when I'm anxious about big things in my life. And this is one of those moments.

Elle usually finds me and brings me back into the fold, which is how I find myself standing at a high-top table with a drink in hand, wishing I could rip my tie off my neck because of the chokehold it has on me.

I recognize Elle's boss from the night in the ER as she approaches us. Her hair is big, curly, and frizzy and her clear glasses take up most of her face. Her lipstick is red and all over her teeth. All of this seems pretty on brand for her, given the stories Elle's told me about her and her attitude when I first met her.

"Ah, so you're the boyfriend then, right? The doctor?" she says, reaching a hand out to shake mine. I drop my hand from Elle's waist as if I've been burned, and I feel a tightness in my throat.

"Anne, this is my *friend*, Oliver," Elle says, putting a hand on my chest, clearly unfazed by my panic. I straighten out my body to evade her grasp, instead holding my hand out for Anne to shake and immediately regretting it. Where was her hand before I shook it? I wonder if Elle has hand sanitizer in her purse.

"Yes, the hero who saved my life in the hospital," she says with a gummy smile. This lady is a bit of a quack, if I'm being honest.

"You weren't dying, Anne," Lucy says, joining the conversation and standing next to Elle. Lucy may be one of the coolest people I've ever met. She's dressed in a simple red dress with a bow on her waist, her hair tied back in a slick bun. I can see her cheeks flush from her drink, and she's definitely the most smiley I've ever seen her. I can tell why Elle loves her so much.

Everyone around me laughs. I try to let out a small chuckle to appear like I'm in the conversation, but it comes out as an awkward cough. Elle looks at me, her brows furrowed.

"Are you okay?" Elle asks when we have a moment in between conversations for just the two of us. "You're acting a little off." She squeezes my arm in a show of support and affection, and I cringe. The flash of confusion on her face makes something twist in my gut.

Elle doesn't deserve this. She deserves someone who doesn't question being her boyfriend. Who wants to stand beside her with the feeling of being *hers*. Not some chump whose mind is always elsewhere.

I hate that I can't tell if these are intrusive thoughts or just how I feel. That's what OCD does to you. It makes you doubt who you are and what you think.

"I think I need some air," I say, unwrapping myself from her and nodding to the other women around us. I practically jog out of the restaurant, taking in a huge gulp of air when I finally make it outside. The few people passing by on the street give me a wayward glance. I lean my hands on my knees in the middle of the sidewalk, trying to steady my breathing. Don't panic right now. *Please don't panic right now.*

Elle comes rushing out of the restaurant towards me. "Oliver? What's wrong?" She puts her hands on my back but I immediately move to avoid her.

The hurt is plain on her face, her lips parted as if she wants to say something, but she can't form the words. I think about a few hours ago, when I kissed the color off those lips, as if kissing them could breathe the life back into me that I've been missing for what seems like forever.

And now her eyes are dark, not warm and bright the way they usually are. The way I like them. They are shaded by furrowed brows, brows that make me question every step I've taken in the past week.

"Elle," I say, my voice weak.

"What's going on right now?" she demands, taking a stumbling step back in her heels.

I straighten up, running my hands down my face in frustration. Fuck, my hands are dirty. I wipe them against the side of my shirt, as if that will help me now. I scrunch my eyes closed, trying to physically push out the annoying thoughts.

Calm down. Please calm down.

"Oliver?"

Inhale. Exhale.

"I just need some space right now," I finally say, my voice tired.

"Space?" she says weakly. "From the party? Or from me?" I force myself to meet her eyes, and I know she knows which one I mean. "Oh." She takes another step backwards.

"Elle, I'm so sorry."

"For what, Oliver?" she asks, a coldness in her tone that I've never heard before.

"For… for—" I stutter.

"You don't even know!" she exclaims. "You're blowing things up, and you don't even know why."

"Elle, I just can't handle all of this right now. I can't—"

"Yes, you can, Oliver. It's just me. Look at me." She steps towards me, putting her hands on my cheeks. There are tears welling in the corners of her eyes, and something else inside me breaks, because I'm the one making Elle cry right now. And I can't even give her a good reason as to why. "Take a deep breath, Oliver. You're okay," she says, trying to calm my panic.

And I'm the asshole who's pushing her away.

"I can't do this, Elle. There's just too much going on, with my job and—"

I can see her brain working behind her eyes. The look she's giving me is the same one she gave me when she handed me an ice cube in my apartment and held my hands to my chest during yoga. She's trying to figure out how to make things better, like she always does. It's her default mode. But I can't be her project anymore. I just can't.

"Is this because Anne called you my boyfriend? Because if that's what you're freaking out about right now—" She trails off, and I don't respond. I take a step away from her and her hands fall from my face and hang by her sides. She shakes her head, disbelief written all over her face.

"God, I don't even know what I'm doing," she says, turning away from me to face the street. She runs her hand through her hair, frustrated. "You told me who you were right from the start, and for a minute, I guess I forgot." She presses her lips in a firm line, and I can tell she's trying to stop herself from crying. "My mistake."

"Elle, you don't want a relationship with me. You need someone who can be there and look after you, you deserve nothing less, but right now I'm a mess. I—"

"Yes, you warned me. And I fell for you anyway, like the idiot I am." I can tell she doesn't want to be angry with me. Maybe she's angry at herself that she wasn't able to fix me. That all her grounding techniques and new experiences weren't enough to get the wires straight in my head. I think she wishes she could go into problem-solving mode right now, because that is the way she thinks. But it's more than that now, and I think she's starting to realize that.

"Would you believe me if I said I was scared—"

"*No*," she says harshly, a tear rolling down her cheek. Her voice pierces through me, worse than any needle or knife I could ever imagine. I don't know how to come back from this.

"I'm not—I'm not normal, Elle," I say, hating the words I've chosen right away. "I mean *normal* is overrated and all, but the shit that goes on in my head… Everyone sees what it does to me and walks the other way. They make faces or comments and they can't handle it. I didn't want—"

"You know I never cared," she whispers, her voice cracking. "I never cared that the television remote had to be in the left corner of the nightstand before you went to sleep, or that Thor's leash had to be hung on the third hook by the door." She takes a step closer to me, her arms falling to her sides. "I never cared that you didn't take the subway or that you washed your hands twice before sitting down to eat. I knew you battled things in your head that you didn't tell me about. I hoped one day you would, because I understood you. You *knew* that."

Her words knock the breath out of me, and it takes all that I have not to fall to the ground in front of her. She saw everything. She saw everything and she never said anything. Never *did* anything.

"Elle, it's just... I wanted to do this right, and I can't right now. There's too much out of my control and—"

"Please don't say anything else, Oliver. I don't know who you're trying to convince, but you're just making stupid excuses." She shakes her head and wipes a tear from her cheek. "Why don't you just go home, Oliver? Please."

"Elle—"

"This is the biggest night of my best friend's life and I will *not* let this steal her thunder. *Go home.*" Her voice is barely raised, but the anger in her voice is palpable. She turns on her heels and walks back into the building, and my hands fall to my knees again, defeated.

TWENTY-SEVEN

Elle

I tell Lucy that Oliver wasn't feeling well and that he went home. I go to the bathroom and wipe my eyes and fix my makeup, because the show must go on. Tonight is not about me. It's about Lucy. That's who I'm here for.

Even so, the rest of the evening is a blur. Anne makes a speech that doesn't totally make sense. Liam makes a speech about the "love of his life" and tears fall down my cheeks as he speaks. I'm sure people think that it's because I'm happy for my friend. And I let them think that.

When I get home, I collapse into bed, but I barely sleep, thinking about Oliver sleeping above me. First thing in the morning, I'm standing at his door, with bleary eyes and knotty hair, demanding an explanation.

When he opens the door, I can see that he must feel the same way I do. His hair is disheveled and his eyes are dark. He's wearing a threadbare t-shirt that I recognize as one of the ones he always wears to bed, and long shorts. I'm sure he didn't sleep either, and I just don't understand. If we both feel this way, then why are we doing this? Where did the disconnect happen?

"Can I come in?" I ask, my voice quiet. Oliver takes one hand off of the doorframe and lets me walk past him. Thor greets me and I smile for the first time in what feels like forever. Oliver takes a seat at his bar top and I stand awkwardly in the hallway, waiting for the silence to break.

"I'm sorry about last night," he finally says, his voice gravelly. The stubble on his cheeks is darker than I've ever seen it, and he looks weary, more so than usual.

"What happened?"

"I panicked. I've been panicking ever since the night we..." He looks down and I feel something twist in my stomach.

"Why didn't you tell me? Why couldn't we talk about it?"

"Because that's not going to make a difference right now, Elle. I need to figure some stuff out, and I need to do it by myself."

He might as well have run me over with his car. Because that's what the blow of his words feel like. I feel squished, like the gravity in the room just got a thousand times stronger.

"I don't understand," I finally say, swallowing the sob in my throat.

He finally picks his head up and I see his lower lashes are wet. I have to resist the urge to reach for him, because I can't comfort him right now. Not about this.

"I know you don't. And I don't know how to explain it to you," he says.

How did we get here? I could have sworn I despised this man—with his loud music and aloof approach to dog ownership. I thought he was a jerk, a guy with an ego who didn't care what other people thought of him. But then the weeks went by, and I found out this rugged exterior hid a man who is afraid of bugs buzzing by his ear and can't stomach a gummy worm. I realized he cares deeply for the people he loves, and even though he appears grumpy, he wants to help people. He's experienced the weight of expectation and the fear of failure, and maybe doesn't think he's worthy of the kind of love I feel for him.

Because I do. I love him.

Somewhere in the midst of all of our wagers, our back and forth shenanigans, I fell in love with Oliver Cole. I fell in love with the person I became when I was with him. I finally found the man who could give me happily ever after—the thing I've been searching for since I read my first romance novel.

But he doesn't feel the same.

"I can't believe you're doing this, Oliver," I admit, shaking my head. I hate to look like I'm disappointed in him, but I am. I look at him like he's tearing out pieces of my heart, because that is what it feels like.

"I can," he mumbles.

I pick myself up off of the wall and start to head towards the door, but stop myself. I can feel my disappointment turning to anger, and I know I should walk out the door. I shouldn't turn around and say what I'm about to say. But part of me wants him to see. I want him to witness the impact of his sabotage.

"You *know* how hard it is for me to trust people." He watches me intently, surprised that I have more to say. "As much as I like to help people, I also isolate myself, which isn't necessarily a good thing, but I do. Because I realized that most people are never as good as books make them out to be. I always find myself *disappointed*." He winces at the last word.

"Things in my world can be so heavy, and I thought you felt the same way. I thought maybe when we were together, it was like there wasn't this fog around me that I couldn't shake." I scoff. "I guess I must have been imagining it."

I pause, waiting for him to interrupt me, to say he feels it too. But he doesn't. So I continue. "Sometimes, it feels like the stars are pressing down on my shoulders. Billions of them dragging the darkness down onto me." Oliver's gaze drops to the tattoo on my wrist. "These last few months, I felt lighter. When I was with you, the stars didn't crush me so much. I trusted you. You were my *friend*. And I can't believe that things are ending this way."

"I'm so sorry, Elle," he whispers, a tear falling down his cheek, but it's too late. I open the handle and turn around to look once more at the broken man sitting there.

"You should be."

"Wellie, your couch is *uncomfortable*," Nick says, his voice stumbling over the word. I reach over and ruffle his hair, and he lets out an adorable "*Hey*!" as he tries to fix it.

My brother is twenty-two, but the boyish smile on his face makes him look much younger. He's the only one in our family with red hair, and it looks like it has been freshly cut. He is wearing the new glasses that I took him to buy over Christmas, simple black rims that he thought made him look like Clark Kent. I even drew an "S" on his forehead in eyeliner when we got home from the store. I almost smile at the memory. Almost.

He and Mom surprised me by coming into the city for dinner and a sleepover. Even I can admit that when I video-called my mother yesterday, I looked and sounded like death. My eyes were swollen and my voice was hoarse. She tried to get me to explain what happened with Oliver, but I said I didn't want to talk about it.

Nick lays down on the couch, forming himself into the question mark shape that he sleeps in.

"Goodnight, Wellie," Nick says, pulling a blanket over him.

"Goodnight, Nicky," I say, kissing his cheek. When he closes his eyes, I stay on the couch for a moment and watch him, a knot forming in my throat.

When my brother was born, my life changed in so many ways. My parents divorced soon after, and my mom was so consumed by Nick's medical concerns that I'm not sure she ever got the chance to mourn her marriage. I don't think I did either. I was only six at the time, but I learned very quickly that my family can bounce back from challenging times, and when we bounce back, we bounce back hard. We jumped into Nick-mode. When I got home from school, I was whisked away to one doctor's appointment after another. I'd do my homework in waiting rooms and help my mom make grocery lists before I was even old enough to help with the cooking. I think at some point, I must have resented my brother for all the attention he took, but all he had to do was smile at me, or throw his head back with a loud giggle, and the feeling would dissipate. Because I loved my brother more than I thought I could ever love anything.

"Stop staring, Wellie. It's creepy," Nick mutters, his eyes closed. I tickle his side before getting up from the couch and joining my mom in my bed. She's a small woman, with burnt blonde hair that is always pulled back into a clip at the top of her head. The lines on her face show the strain she's been through in her life, but she tries not to complain. She's scrolling through her phone, but she stops when she feels me climb in next to her and opens her arms for a hug. I move over and place my head on her chest, tapping into the reassuring feeling of feeling her breath beneath me.

"Are we going to talk about it yet?" she asks, her voice reverberating in my ear.

"I don't know what to say," I admit, the lump in my throat getting bigger.

"Where did he come from?"

"It feels like he came from out of nowhere, and suddenly everything was different."

"Good different?"

"I guess I wasn't sure at first. He drove me crazy. But now—"

"Now you're sure," she finishes for me.

I nod against her chest. "But it's not the right time," I say, my voice barely above a whisper. I can't say my mother and I have conversations like this very frequently. Our heart-to-hearts are a little rusty.

"And why is that?" She squeezes her arms around me a little tighter.

"I thought we were on the same page, but I guess I was wrong. I'm not sure how things could move forward after this," I explain, tears welling up in my eyes for what feels like the hundredth time this week.

"I know everything seems confusing right now," she says. "But if this is something you really want, and any part of your heart tells you it's right, then don't give up on it. Maybe give it some time, but don't let it fade away. You have to chase—"

"The stars," Nick finishes from the couch.

"Go to sleep you weirdo," I say, throwing a pillow at him. He giggles from under his blanket. When I lay back down next to my mom, I look down at the tattoo on my wrist. "Do you know why I got this?" I ask her.

"I always thought it was because of all that astrology shit you believe in," she replies.

I snort. "I guess partly, yes, but it was also for you. To always remind me of how you believed in me. How you told me to chase the stars, like it was the easiest thing I could ever do."

"I never said it would be easy, but it's almost always worth it."

However hard our life was growing up, or however tough things got with Nick and his health conditions, my mother never held me back from doing anything I loved, including moving to New York.

"*Chase the stars, Chicken,*" she would always tell me. "*Your dreams are like the stars. They might be in the distance, but if you can see them, you can reach them.*"

Even after my mother has drifted off, I don't sleep at all. I lay in bed, staring at the ceiling, imagining Oliver above me, and the time I spent sleeping on his couch. There was a comfort in falling asleep with Thor beside me, knowing when I woke up Oliver would be in his bed, snoring away. But now that the floor separates us, I feel… hollow. Unsure.

I don't know what will happen when I wake up tomorrow, but I know I won't see Oliver. And those thoughts make me the most empty of all.

By Thursday, I admit to myself that I've been trapped in a cycle of negative self-talk since my mom and brother left on Tuesday. I've spent every waking hour trying to understand Oliver's reasoning for doing what he did. Up until last week, there was no possibility of us as a couple. I knew I was developing feelings for him—how could I not? But I know myself. When I meet a guy I like, I get my hopes up, picture the possibility of a future with him, a future of happiness, and then it never happens. It's the constant feeling of rejection that dating creates that really causes so much hurt for me.

I try to turn my attention to seeing Lucy next week and being present for her. I've thought so much about planning activities for her pre-wedding week just to drown out the reminder that I'm going to this wedding alone.

I sign myself up to teach as many yoga classes as possible, so that I don't spend my evenings in my apartment wondering if I'll hear Oliver or Thor upstairs. When I start the class on Thursday, I see some of the regulars who were at the class that Oliver took, and a wave of sadness rushes over me. I feel a tightness in my throat, my lower lip quivers, and I have to remind myself that I'm in front of a room full of people, people who are looking to me for guidance. I almost cackle out loud at the irony of that thought. I feel more lost inside my mind than I think I've ever been, and yet I'm supposed to teach a group of strangers about inner calm.

Well, here goes nothing.

"I want us to start in Hero's Pose," I tell the class, taking a seat on my shins. I look around at the small space, admiring the light from the sunset streaming through the glass windows at the top of the far wall. There's an orange hue outside tonight, and it's lighting up the studio and surrounding us in a heavenly glow. I smile at the simple things that nature can provide for us—light, peace, a sense of purpose.

"Let your hands lay gently in your lap," I say, demonstrating. "And close your eyes, if that feels safe for you today." I pause, giving everyone a moment to follow the instruction. "Today, I want to focus our practice on compassion and stillness. I recently reviewed some of the aphorisms from the yoga sutras, and one of them tells us that the aim of yoga is to settle the constant fluctuations of our mind. It encourages us to become a witness to our thoughts, so we can watch them, rather than be controlled by them."

I pause, looking around the room to make sure everyone is following. Then, I close my own eyes. "Imagine a sky during a storm," I say, trying to put on my best meditation voice.

"The wind blows the clouds at a rapid pace, maybe the clouds are varying sizes and shapes, some higher than others, some darker. Then, think about what it looks like once that storm has passed. The stillness in the clouds. Those high white clouds that appear in a thin layer in the sky. And then imagine the clear blue sky that finally emerges. Yoga helps us find that blue sky state of mind." I internally commend myself for that metaphor. "We know that the storms will always come, but if we can control our reaction to those scary skies, maybe we can weather the storm just a bit better."

I take a deep breath, encouraging the class to do so as well. I keep us there for a moment, inhaling and exhaling, finding a rhythm in our own bodies. My throat feels dry after my speech, and a knot forms in my throat, thinking about my own reactions to recent storms.

"Slowly flutter your eyes open, friends. Let's flow."

TWENTY-EIGHT

Oliver

I have a problem with the phrase "falling in love."

Falling happens fast. When you fall off your bike as a kid, it happens so fast, you're barely able to register what's happening before you hit the ground. When you turn thirty and suddenly tripping on a crack in the sidewalk turns into a weeklong back spasm, you don't remember the moment you fell. It happens too quickly.

I remember *every moment* of falling in love with Elle Thompson.

Which is why I won't say I fell. Of course, it doesn't sound as poetic, but I walked into it. Like an old lady crossing the street using a walker when you're sitting at a red light and have to pee. *That* level of slowness.

It wasn't like falling off of a bike or tripping on the pavement. I remember meeting Elle outside my apartment door at the ass crack of dawn. I remember the threadbare blue t-shirt she wore, and the disdainful look on her face when she saw me. I remember the first time I heard her laugh, and the smile that lit up her face every time she saw Thor. I remember the first time I kissed her, the first time I watched her sleep on the couch in my apartment.

Slowly, steadily, I walked into love with her. And there is no turning around.

"She was right to call you Grimace," Henry tells me one night at the gym, coming up behind me and startling me. I must have been staring into space again instead of actually lifting any weights.

"I'm sorry?"

"Elle. She told me she likes to call you Grimace, but not to your face. So on point," he says, sliding a weight onto a barbell.

"What is Grimace?"

"The mascot from McDonald's. Big purple guy with a grouchy face?"

I pull out my phone and Google this character. Once I see photos of it, I realize that it's the creepy purple guy that Elle would send me gifs of. Great. So glad it took me this long to figure that one out.

"I'm sorry I'm not a ray of fucking sunshine for everyone," I grumble, leaning against the cage. I miss Elle. I can't believe how much I miss her. She came barreling into my life at a time when I was so uncertain about what to do with myself. She gave me a kind of purpose, or a distraction.

No, distraction doesn't do her justice. Elle and I were so in tune with each other—trying to figure out what made the other tick. In a way, we were perfect for each other, the most unlikely friends. Elle wanted me to be her project, so she could be my "hype girl." But all the while, I just wanted to convince her that she is anything but the side character.

She's the main character of every room she walks into. I just wish she could see it.

"You have to snap out of this, man," Henry says, slapping me on the back. "Or you have to do something about it."

"Something like what?" I ask.

"Something that doesn't include moping around my gym," Henry says, his voice stern. "You made this girl think that being with her wasn't what you wanted. That you weren't the settling down type. Figure your shit out and show her that you are. Show her that you'll be here when she's ready to give you another chance."

I'm at the dog run with Thor early the next morning. I sit on the top of a wooden bench, watching Thor run around and have the time of his life. I shake my head as he rolls around in a puddle of water created by a sketchy-looking hose in the corner of the dirt park. This weekend is Memorial Day, and the weather is certainly warming up for it. I keep glancing at the entrance to the park, picturing Elle walking through the gate, smiling when she sees me. Wishful thinking.

Central Park on a slow morning has become one of my favorite things about the city. Maybe *the* favorite. I never thought I could accept living here, let alone loving this city so much that I think of it as home. So much has changed since Elle took me on our first outing to the Highline. *I've* changed. A part of me always felt like being in New York was somehow giving in to my father, letting him win. These last few months with Elle, Henry, and even Thor have shown me that I've made a life for myself here. New York is not the enemy anymore.

Henry's words echo in my head for most of the day. I know he's right. I need to do something. I guess part of me has been procrastinating, letting myself live in limbo for a while. I think the truth is I've been second-guessing myself. Is being a doctor really something I can see myself doing for the rest of my life? Do I want to be where my dad is in thirty years?

With that thought, my phone rings in my pocket, and I'm disappointed to see my sister's name flashing on the screen. I've only spoken to my sister a few times over the last few months, so I sigh as I answer the call.

"Hey Soph," I say, my voice low.

"Hey, I'm FaceTiming you, why didn't you turn your video on?"

"I'm at the dog park with *your* dog. I'm not going to be one of those idiots who FaceTimes in public," I say loud enough for the person on the bench opposite me to hear. The person who is very much on a FaceTime call. I eye the person next to me knowingly. She nods.

Sophia ignores my snide comment. "How is my little buddy?"

"I think he's officially mine at this point." *And Elle's*, I finish in my head. My stomach drops at the thought.

"Um, I'm not sure if that's true," Sophia responds, drawing out her words.

"You adopted a dog and moved away from it for a year, Sophia. I don't know what kind of monster has inhabited my sister, but I wouldn't give this dog back to you even if you—"

I stop, because on the other end of the phone, my sister is laughing.

Hysterical laughing.

What the fuck?

"What the fuck is wrong with you?" I say, again too loudly, so much so that other dog park inhabitants give me a wary look.

"It's nothing, I'm just so happy when I'm proven right," she says, suppressing a snort.

"*What?*"

"Oliver, you've known me for twenty-four years, you really think I'm the kind of person to abandon a dog?"

"I don't really know you that well, I guess," I admit.

"*Ugh*," I can practically hear the roll in her eyes. "I got the dog for *you*, you dumbass."

I open my mouth to speak, but hesitate. "*Huh?*"

"Oliver, maybe you don't know me well—maybe because you don't pay attention or you're too busy being grumpy all the time, or maybe because you're a *man*—but *I* know *you*. You were miserable in New York. You left to get away from Dad—from all of us. Maybe it's a little selfish of me, but I wanted you to see that you could have some happiness at home, and maybe convince you to stay."

I rub the fingers of my free hand against my temple. "Sophia, you are literally making no sense right now."

She groans. "Oliver, I learned I was going to Italy the same time I found out you were moving back home. I knew I wouldn't be there to try to convince you to stay, so I needed a representative."

"And you chose a dog that could pass for a giant rabbit and named it Thor?" Thor stops running after a fluffy white poodle thing when he hears his name, and I swear he side-eyes me.

"I sure did," Sophia replies confidently.

"W-why—" I stutter. "Why would you do this? Do you know how hard it has been having a dog and working twelve-hour shifts?"

"Because you're my big brother, Ollie, and I love you. I don't want you to live on the other side of the country anymore." She pauses, and I'm glad I'm not on video at this moment, because I'm not sure what my face would say. A mix of shock and disbelief, probably. "I know Dad is hard on you. I know you were pushed into this life. I know you resent me for how Mom and Dad treat me—"

"I don't resent you," I interrupt her, a crack in my voice.

"Yes, you do, and that's okay. Because I resent you too," she says matter-of-factly.

Um, ouch.

"For what exactly? Seems like you got the better end of the deal here. Not sure what you have to be resentful about."

"You're Oliver Cole, the next great *Dr. Cole*. How could I ever live up to that?" Sophia reasons. "Sure, Dad was a jerk to you, but you were his golden boy. He bragged about you to everyone—"

"That was just his own ego trip," I interject, disdain in my voice.

"It doesn't matter, it is all I heard growing up!" she counters, her voice going up an octave. "I wanted to be the center of attention. I wanted *your* attention. I wanted everything that *you* had."

"That's a bit ironic, I guess."

"Why?"

"Because I've always wanted the freedom that you have," I admit. I rest my elbows on my knees and hang my head.

Everything that Sophia is saying is striking a nerve. And I have too many nerves that are sensitive to striking right now.

"You have freedom, Oliver, you've just always been afraid to use it."

"That's not true. I never had a choice—"

"Of course you had a choice, you idiot! What, did Dad physically force you into medical school? You never stood up to him, that's on you."

"Okay, can we dial down the tough love here, Soph? I'm in the middle of a dog park," I respond, trying to take down the emotional level of this conversation.

"So yeah, I wanted my brother to be happy," she continues, ignoring my comment. "I wanted him to be home. Because I missed him. So I got a dog and dumped it on you. How did my plan work out? Do you want to stay in New York?"

Aw, fuck.

She *Miyagi'd* me.

My little sister *Miyagi'd* me. How the hell am I going to explain this?

"Oliver? Did I lose you?"

"No, I'm here..." I say, my voice fading. "I guess I just never knew you felt all of that. And I'm sorry I left. I missed you too while I was away."

"No, you didn't, but it's fine."

I take a deep breath. "You're right, I never stood up to Dad. Because as much as I hated him forcing me into a life that I never said I wanted, I do actually kind of want this life. Or some form of it. My own version of it. Maybe not one where I'm on call every week. But maybe still medicine. I guess I never wanted to deal with his reaction. Being mad at him was easier."

"So is there a version of it where you stay in New York?"

"I hope so, but it's not the dog that is going to keep me here," I say, just as Thor jumps up on the bench beside me. "Alright, it's the dog and something else."

When I get back to my apartment, I'm exhausted from the verbal beating I just got from my sister. I plop on the couch as Thor takes a drink and rubs himself all over the carpet, trying to dry his face. In the process, he kicks something from under the couch. I bend down to retrieve it, and realize it must be a book that Elle left here from one of her ginormous canvas bags. I flip it over in my hands and fan the pages, then read the back of it. It's about a princess of a small country who falls in love with her American bodyguard. They can't be together because she has to marry someone of nobility.

I flip through the book and stop at the Acknowledgements when I see Elle's name. The author thanked her for supporting her on her writing journey. A sense of pride blooms in my chest. Supporting someone on their journey—sounds completely accurate, knowing Elle.

That's how I find myself laying on my couch, on the pillow that still smells like Elle, reading a romance novel. It makes me feel closer to Elle than I have in weeks. Knowing that she helped create this, that it's something she's passionate about, makes me want to absorb every word.

It's not as cheesy as I thought it would be. I thought it would be like the Hallmark movie Henry tried to summarize for me, but really, it's about a girl who is trying to figure out who she is and where she fits in the world. It's about a couple who are told they can't be together, but realize the alternative is unacceptable.

By the end of the book, the princess makes the government repeal the law that says she has to marry someone royal, and she marries the bodyguard. She basically says, "*This is what I'm doing. If you have a problem with it, suck it.*" That was my favorite part.

I read the entire thing in one sitting. It's supposed to be an uplifting story, but really all it does is make me miss Elle more. But it also gives me a sense of hope, because even though the princess gets to marry the guy she loves, they don't know what their future is going to look like. The princess makes a whole speech saying that she doesn't have everything figured out about how their relationship will work, but she loves him, so the rest of it doesn't matter.

I snap the book closed and toss it to the other side of the couch.

I hate how Sophia was right. Since I've been home, not only did I get to meet someone as amazing as Elle, but I also feel more content in the state I grew up in than I have in a long time. When you're young, and dreaming of changing the world, maybe it doesn't always occur to you that being away from the world you know can be so demoralizing. Over the last few months, I have made connections that make me feel like a human again. I've fallen in love.

Maybe I don't need to have every part of my life plan ironed out at once. Maybe I don't have to figure it out by myself. And maybe now I can admit to myself that I don't want to. Elle has seen me struggle and supported me the entire time. I don't know what's next, but I know I want to figure it out with Elle by my side.

Henry is right. I need to make a plan.

I'm going to show Elle that I'm permanent. I'm here to stay.

The next day, I email my supervisor at the hospital and ask for a meeting at his earliest convenience. I send it before I can change my mind. I feel like I might throw up once I do, but it's done. I need to make some changes. Radical ones. I need to take control of my life, because I don't want my father's.

The next thing I do is Instagram-stalk the *shit* out of Lucy.

I don't want to call or text Elle and I know she hasn't been home for the last few days. Is the wedding this weekend? Should I not bother Lucy the week of her wedding?

Screw it. She'll understand.

I find Lucy's "bookstagram" account (didn't know that was a thing) and message her. She replies within a few minutes.

Lucy
THANK GOD

Lucy
She is the most miserable maid of honor I could ever have. (I still love her tho.) If you can make her happy, get up here and do something about it.

Lucy
Hudson Hollow, New York. Haul ass, lover boy.

TWENTY-NINE

Elle

I think Lucy might be the most chill bride in the history of weddings.

I've been at her house for almost a week now—helping her run errands, pitching tents (never thought I'd say that), setting up tables, and on and on. And through it all, Lucy has laughed, made jokes, and eyed her future hubby like she just wants to squeeze him all the time.

But me and my heart can't catch a damn break.

I'm not sure where to go from here. When Lucy first told me she loved Liam, I basically pushed her onto a bus upstate. I don't think I can do that for myself. I don't know that I can stand in front of Oliver and ask him to give us a chance. To bet on *me*.

So here I am, the night before my best friend's wedding, which I will be attending *alone*, jumping on a bouncy castle in my pajamas.

Naturally.

I would love to be able to text Oliver right now and

tell him that I got a bouncy castle for Lucy's bachelorette party. I wish I could tell him that such a place as *AdultBouncyCastleRentals.com* exists. But I'm not ready. I don't know how to make the grand gesture like Lucy did. I'm good at pushing people past their limits, but I can rarely see past my own. Maybe that will be my undoing.

I kicked Liam out of his own house about four hours ago, before any of the festivities began. I sent Lucy to the next town over, Catskill, in search of a specific margarita mix that I know doesn't exist, and I created the most epic bachelorette party in the history of womankind. Liam's sister Jill and her friend Nora were a huge help. But really I should get all the credit. Because this is *awesome*.

"Elle, is that an ice cream truck?" Lucy calls, bouncing down so she is seated at the edge of the mesh. Liam and Lucy's backyard is on a bit of a slope, so the party is mostly happening on the front lawn. The bouncy castle is to the right of the front door, so we can see the truck coming down the block. I invited the old couple across the street, Al and Mella, because we're literally partying right in their face. They're the first ones to the ice cream truck.

"You bet your ass it's an ice cream truck. All soft serve, babe," I say, joining her in sliding out of the castle.

"You seriously get me. I couldn't have asked for anything better than this." She pauses for a moment, taking in the scene around her. "I can't wait to rub this in Liam's face."

"Rude," a deep voice says behind her. I smirk at the sight of Liam coming around the corner of the bouncy castle with a devilish grin. He runs a hand through his hair, scuffing it up in a way that makes him look "deliciously disheveled" as Lucy once described him.

"What are you doing here?" Lucy squeals, pushing his chest.

"It's a small town. You think I wouldn't find out you had a bouncy castle? We heard the ice cream truck all the way down Main Street!" he explains excitedly. "You think I was going to drink beers on a boat when you have ice cream? We're crashing this shit, *Mamma Mia* style!"

A hoard of men whose names I don't know except for Max, the owner of the town's grocery store, and Liam's friend Brett, come hurtling up the beach like a pack of children descending on a playground.

"Elle, can you believe this?" Lucy wraps her arms around me and squeezes.

"That I threw a better party than Brett? 100 percent."

By the end of the night, Lucy tells me that she doesn't need a wedding after that. "That was the time of my life, Elle. Surrounded by people I love, being silly. I would say I felt like a kid, but I don't know that I remember having that much fun when I was a kid."

"Me neither," I sigh, jumping into bed with her. Liam has once again been kicked out of his house, but he took it like the champ—or beta hero—that he is. Lucy's wedding will be small, mostly consisting of relatives from the town. Most of her family is staying at a hotel in Catskill, because the one bed and breakfast in town only had two rooms. It's just Lucy and me in her house tonight. I'm her only bridesmaid. Brett is Liam's best man. It will be small and fun, just like tonight. Very Lucy.

"Are you excited?" I ask her when we're both lying down in bed, staring at the ceiling.

"At the idea of being a bride? I don't know if I'd say *excited*." She turns over and faces me, curling her arms around a pillow. "I made this wedding as small as humanly possible. You know I don't like to be the center of attention."

"But this is the day girls—"

"Girls dream of, I know, I know," she finishes for me. "I don't buy into that. I didn't dream of a wedding growing up. Sure, I love romance novels, but that was never the part of the story I focused on. I wanted the *life*—the person who would make me breakfast on Saturdays, know my order at our favorite restaurant, who would be my permanent plus one, run to the pharmacy at 2 a.m. when I'm sick, or always offer me his elbow when I get old and *crotchety*." I giggle at the way she says the word. "I want more than just this one day. I'm excited for all the days that follow it. That's what I always dreamed about."

I let out a quiet exhale, trying to hide the sniffle in my nose. I didn't realize that tears had pooled in my eyes until she finished speaking. I swallow hard, but a single tear manages to escape down the cheek facing away from Lucy. I quickly wipe it away with the sleeve of my sweatshirt.

"Do you know what I mean?" she asks eagerly when I don't respond right away.

"Yeah," I say, my voice barely above a whisper. "I dream of that too."

"I know I used to give you a hard time about all of your *happily ever after* talk, but I guess deep down, I was hiding the fact that I wanted the same thing. I was just scared that I was never going to get it. You know?"

I nod, swallowing again. "I know. I think everyone is scared when it comes to being happy."

I'm so grateful that she doesn't say anything else, because I don't think I could hold my breath any longer. I make an excuse about needing the bathroom, and quietly sob on the toilet bowl. It's the kind of cry that makes my ribs hurt—my *heart* hurt.

When I go back to bed, Lucy is asleep, her head tipped to one side on the pillow. I lay beside her, facing her, thinking about how jealous I am that she had someone like me to push her toward her dreams. I wish I had someone who would force happiness on me, someone who would make a grand gesture, show me how much I mean to them, and take care of me, like I take care of everyone else.

That's my main character energy. That's what I want.

I don't sleep much that night, but when I do, I dream of Oliver.

We're up way too early the next morning.

Lucy's one major request for her wedding day was that she had nice hair and makeup, and a beautiful dress of course.

"*I'll sit in my room all day in the whole getup. I don't care. As long as I get to be all done up*," she'd said.

So from the hours of 9 a.m. to 2 p.m., we are pampered from head to toe. Lucy's mom comes over and makes us breakfast. We found two girls from Catskill to come to the house and do our hair and makeup. My hair ends up in a half-up/half-down situation, with ringlets falling down my back. Lucy's hair is up in a ponytail, her long brown hair curled behind her. My mind is so busy, thinking of everything Lucy might need before she even asks for it that before I realize, it's time to go.

The ceremony and reception are in the same spot where the town holds literally any event. Hudson Hollow sits on a lake, lined shore-to-shore with beautiful homes. In the middle of the lake is a small peninsula with a beach, a large grassy area, and a concession stand of sorts. We've spent the last week making the area wedding-ready. A large tent now sits on the grass, where tables adorned in white cloth and pink roses sit underneath. The ceremony will be on the beach, where the altar and chairs are placed strategically to align with the sunset behind the mountains. Liam and his dad built the altar, which has vines of white and pink roses cascading down over the arch.

We arrive by car and park at the back of the grassy area, where the town's boss-lady-in-charge, May, has created a triangle with three SUVs, so Lucy can get ready with no one seeing her. May called it a "truck blockade." Sometimes I want to be May when I grow up. Unless it's the day of a town function and she has a megaphone—I'm a little scared on those days.

"You ready for this, Luce?" I say, stepping out of the car. I look down at my dress—it's a simple, blush pink number, with wide straps and a tufted neckline. It falls to my ankles and is actually very comfortable. Leave it to Lucy to give me full control over my bridesmaid apparel.

"Are *you* ready for this?" she replies, and I look at her, confused. She has an odd smile on her face. She presses her lips in a line and smiles brighter, as if she's trying to hold in her excitement.

I follow her gaze as she nods her head behind me. When I turn around, I gasp and say "Holy shit," way too loudly.

At the end of the reception tent stands Oliver, in a black suit, his hair pushed back off of his face, hands in his pockets, an anxious smile pulling at his lips. Next to him, Thor sits at attention, his tail wagging furiously when he sees me. He has a bandanna around his neck that falls in front of him. It has a suit design on it, complete with a bow tie.

Oh my God.

He's here. In Hudson Hollow. At Lucy's wedding.

My brain can't process it. How—How did he know where I was? How did he get here? How did he manage to wrestle Thor into wearing that bow-tie?

"Let's get a move on this, people. We have a wedding to get to," May says behind me. I turn around and see May linking arms with Lucy, whose smile looks like it might break her face. I can't imagine what my face looks like right now. I can feel a sob in my throat, and no one has even spoken a word yet. But it doesn't matter.

Oliver is here.

I turn back to face Oliver, who takes a few steps towards me. My instinct is to back away, but I'm frozen in place. That is, until Thor barrels towards me. I bend down to pet him before he gets near my dress, and then he makes his way to Lucy.

I don't take my eyes off of Oliver for a second.

I want to throw myself at him. I've missed him so much. I can't believe he's here. I think he can read my thoughts—so much is said between us in the few silent seconds it takes for him to come within a foot of me. When he is finally close enough that all I would have to do to touch him would be to reach out my arm, I let out a shaky exhale. This is real. He's here. I can't reassure myself of that enough.

"Hey," he says, and his voice is enough to lodge a knot in my throat. He looks down for a moment, and I resist the urge to bend down to catch his gaze again. I'm magnetized by his eyes. He quickly looks back up and I see him swallow hard.

"So, I have recently come into possession of a romance novel," he starts, a laugh in his voice. I inhale at the prospect of where this is going. "And from what I've read, and from what Lucy's told me, this is the time for a grand moment—"

"Grand *gesture*," Lucy calls from behind me. I turn around and glare at her. Thor is sitting at May's feet, loving every second of this adventure.

"Did you do this?" I whisper, barely holding in the tears that are threatening to break free.

"Be quiet, he's in the middle of a speech," Lucy scolds, pointing for me to turn around. When I do, I'm greeted with one of Oliver's smiles, and my knees start to feel a bit like the turrets of the bouncy castle being deflated last night.

"Elle, I would like to formally apologize for being an absolute ass," he says. I can tell he's fidgeting with his hands in his pockets. "I'm so sorry it took me so long to figure my shit out, but I just… got stuck."

I inhale shakily when he reaches for my hand, lacing our fingers together.

"I love you, Elle," Oliver says, and I let out a whimper at his words. I can feel my lip quivering. There's a part of my brain, the one part that is not currently functioning on solely heart-eye emojis—that can't believe this is happening. Not only did this man come find me to tell me that he loves me, but I am the sappy heroine crying during the grand gesture. I never would have predicted this for myself.

"I'm here for your happily ever after. Whatever it looks like, whatever it takes, I'm here for it. Because I love you so much, and I promise I will never knowingly hurt you again."

He takes a breath, still looking down at our hands. "I'm sorry that I ever did it in the first place. It's up there in one of the dumbest things I've ever done. My—you know, the way I'm... *me*—" I squeeze his hand, as he takes a breath. "It has always scared women away, and I was so tired of it. So, from the first time you scolded me in the hallway, I had myself convinced it would happen again. Then the more I got to know you, the more terrified I became, because everything around me felt like it was hanging in the air. I thought I couldn't give you the stability of a relationship that you wanted. But I should have believed in us. I'm sorry."

"That was a pretty good speech," I hear May mutter behind me.

"I think mine was better," Lucy whispers back.

"Also, I should tell you that I quit my job—"

"What?" I say, my voice breathless.

"It's a long story, but you were right. I guess I needed to find my—what do you call it? My main character energy?" I smile. "I want my own life. Not the one my father forced on me. I don't know what that life looks like, but I don't want to figure it out alone. I want you by my side, and we'll work out the rest together."

I don't know what to say. I don't know what I *can* say. All my life, I've been chasing the perfect ending of a book—the carriage riding away from the castle, the final musical number, the crowd cheering as the heroine won her final battle. I became convinced that I would only ever find that ending in the form of ink on a page. As hard as I tried, I couldn't shake the feeling that I was an observer, a reader in the book of life, never a starring character.

I look at Oliver, who squeezes my hand a little tighter when our eyes meet, and I take a deep breath. I love my life, I love my family, but I don't think I've ever felt as much a part of a bigger story as I have these last few months with Oliver. Life with him was another star I was afraid to chase, but I reached for it anyway. And I got it.

"You didn't need the speech," I say. Oliver furrows his brows at me. "You being here, in Hudson Hollow, today of all days—that was the grandest of grand gestures. Plus, you brought a dog in a bow tie," I add with a laugh.

Oliver seems to sigh with relief, his shoulders relaxing as he chuckles softly. In one smooth step, he cups my cheeks in his hands and presses his mouth against mine, his soft lips devouring me. Kissing him feels like a release of weeks, months, years of bated breath, all culminating in this moment. The moment that someone stood up for me. The moment this main character got her happily ever after.

THIRTY

Oliver

I have said it to her about a thousand times tonight, but my girlfriend looks *stunning*.

I may have only met Lucy a few times, but she is quickly becoming one of my favorite people. Her wedding matches her personality perfectly, as well as the personality of this quirky little town I now find myself in. After I kissed Elle for what was not nearly enough time, she was whisked away from me, and I was shooed into a seat by some pushy lady named May. She put us—me and Thor—on the aisle in the back, I'm assuming because one of us is a canine.

Thor wasn't the only furry friend in attendance. Liam's dog—whose name I now know is Blue—was the ring bearer. He is an impressive-looking German Shepherd. Impressive in that I think he could eat Thor for breakfast, but the two have been getting along since their introduction at the reception.

The setting was beautiful. I can understand what Lucy loves about this place, and why she picked it over the city.

The ceremony started right before sunset, so when Elle walked down the aisle with a bouquet of white and pink flowers, her dress matched the hue of the sky. She was still crying, but the smile on her face was infectious. Mine grew even wider at the knowledge that I was the one who put it there.

Liam looked like the happiest guy I've ever seen, but secretly I think I was happiest person at the wedding. Elle watched me throughout the entire ceremony, and I was filled with a sense of pride as I stared right back at her. Everyone in the audience may have been watching the bride and groom, but it was impossible not to notice the knockout of a maid of honor. And she was mine. *Mine.*

As the night winds down, I can tell that Thor is getting restless, or just plain fed up with being the plaything of a bunch of five-year-olds. Elle returns from tending to Lucy with the same exhausted smile on her face that I see on Thor. Her hair is starting to look disheveled after it took a hit from all the bouncing during Cotton-Eyed-Joe. She lost her high heels hours ago—I think she took them off right after the "I do" actually. She falls into my lap with a contented sigh, and I wrap my arms around her, squeezing her hips to make sure she is real.

"Are you real?" she says, laying her arm on my shoulder and propping her head on her hand.

"Can you read my mind?" I ask, taking a curl in between my fingers and wrapping it behind her ear. She lets her head fall into my hand.

"Probably," she says with a small smile. "Right now you're thinking about how much you want to take me home."

"That thought hasn't left my mind since the second I saw you, babe," I say, kissing her quickly. I can taste champagne and something fruity on her lips, and I can't wait to get her alone.

"Liam and Lucy will be leaving for the airport soon," she says, brushing my hair off of my forehead. "I was going to stay the night at their house anyway, and bring Blue to Liam's sister's place in the morning."

"Are you propositioning me, Elle Thompson?" I joke, squeezing her side until she squirms. When she giggles, I kiss her again, eager to taste every inch of her.

"See, you can read my mind too," she says, pressing her lips against mine, holding me for long enough that the idea of not taking her to bed this instant becomes intolerable.

Elle and I take our positions as the dog handlers—her with Blue and me with Thor—as the last leg of the farewell line. Liam's white Jeep is decked out in "Just Married" decorations, which seems to mostly consist of stickers and streamers with dogs on them, like something you might find at a child's birthday party.

Elle must see the look on my face as I evaluate the truck, because she leans over and whispers in my ear, "It's all the party store in the next town had. I may have forgotten this last part of my maid of honor duties."

"I think it's pretty spot on," I say with a small chuckle.

When Liam and Lucy finally reach us, Elle and Lucy embrace for a long time. Lucy has changed into a white sweat suit with *Mrs. Miller* bedazzled on the back of the shirt. Lucy's eyes start to fill with tears, and Elle holds her friend's face in her hands, the two exchanging conversation that only they can hear. Liam gives his dog a goodbye that

I thoroughly approve of and shakes my hand. He places a hand on Lucy's back and Elle swats it away, hugging Lucy once more.

When they finally drive away, Elle and I walk back to Lucy's house, in no hurry to be anywhere. We let the dogs meander on the pebbly path, holding each other's hands, awkwardly bumping hips as we steady ourselves on tired legs. We stop at my rental car for my bag, which is parked somewhere near the wedding venue. Lucy wasn't exactly specific with her directions to the town. I pretty much put Hudson Hollow into my GPS, followed the caravan of people, and ended up at the right place.

I'm not sure what I was expecting from Liam and Lucy's house, but I am astonished when I walk through the door. I can see straight to the lake through floor-to-ceiling windows from the front door. The house has a log cabin meets hotel-chic type of feel that I could definitely get used to.

Elle gets Blue settled for the night, leading him to his bed in the master suite. Thor makes himself at home on the couch, thoroughly enjoying the view. When I see Elle again, she appears from the hallway with her hair undone, waves upon waves falling down her shoulders. She leans up against the wall and runs her fingers through her hair, a sleepy smile on her face.

"Did you ever think we'd end up here?" she asks, her voice hoarse. I think the last verse of "Paradise By the Dashboard Light" really got to her.

"You mean when I was first accosted by a half-dressed blonde in the hallway of my building—" Elle feigns a gasp. "Did I ever think I'd end up in love with her?"

Elle nods, a cute smile on her face.

"I would have *bet* on it," I say, smirking.

The smile grows wider, a sense of relief and satisfaction washing over her face.

I stand up and shrug my jacket off, stepping towards her with newfound urgency. She reaches for my hand and I let her lead me into the guest room. She sits down on the bed slowly, her eyes making their way up my body. I release her hand so I can cup her head in both of my palms, and lean down to kiss her.

I take my time, pressing against her full lips with a gentle tenderness. She matches my pace, each of us seeming to want to savor every second of this moment. She nudges her tongue into my mouth, her teeth scraping my bottom lip. We stay like that—hands wandering across each other's torsos, lips grazing every inch of flesh we can find—until Elle finally stands. She turns around and pulls her hair into a bunch in front of her, urging me to unzip her dress. I kiss the back of her neck, feeling excitement flow through me in response to her small whimpers. I kiss her shoulders and down her spine with every inch that I unzip.

I spend a few moments on the back of her neck, a soft "mmhmm" escaping her as my tongue runs up and down the top of her back. I run my hands down the front of her as the dress falls off of her, finding nothing covering her chest. I press myself against her and she leans her head against my back, fluttering her eyes closed. I take my time spreading my hands all over her, squeezing her breasts, tracing her nipples with my fingers, until I finally reach down far enough that I can feel the wetness between her thighs.

She gasps when I crawl my way into her panties, pressing my whole hand against the warmth of her. I let her slickness coat my fingers, pushing them in and out of her until her hips start to move in tandem with my hand.

When she turns around, the dress falls to her feet, pooling around her ankles, revealing a bare, beautiful body, covered only by a thin pair of underwear.

"Beautiful," I whisper, gently grazing my fingers down her soft skin. She shudders at my gentle touch. She slowly unbuttons my shirt, spreading her hands across my chest once she finishes, pushing the fabric off of me. She places gentle kisses across my chest, nibbling at the skin leading to my waist. I help her with my belt, letting her pull my pants off before I gently push her onto the bed. Her hair falls onto the blanket and sprawls out in every direction. I climb on top of her and press my face into her hair, breathing in her salty sweetness, her usual berry scent mixed with hairspray and moisture from the lake air.

I lean my body to the side, placing my head on my elbow. I trail my finger down her body and I see her start to tense up at my touch. I look her in the eyes, telling her to relax with my mind. She lets out a small breath and I see her shoulder and legs release with a shrug.

"You know every guy in the place was looking at you tonight," I say in a low voice. Elle shakes her head.

"It was a wedding. Most people were focused on the bride," she says with an eye-roll.

I shake my head, placing my knee in between her legs, loving the way she squirms from the contact.

"Not me. I could see eyes wandering to you. But I knew you were mine. I knew only I would be the one doing this tonight." I pull her panties down her legs and fling them to the floor. I thread my arm behind her and pull her further up the bed, turning so I'm above her.

I take a moment to admire her—from her red lips to her perfect breasts. She admires me right back, her eyes heavy. I run a finger down her chest, sliding my hand down her thighs. I lay on my stomach, leaning my head down to nibble the sensitive flesh on the inside of her legs.

"I'm the only one who gets to do this," I say, practically growling, as I let my lips meet her most sensitive part. Elle cries out, clutching the bedsheet next to my head. I cup her bottom in my palms, massaging the delicious flesh and she writhes beneath me. I feel myself moving against the bed, anxious to be inside of her.

I lick my way up her center, letting my lips settle on her clit. I push two fingers into her as my tongue circles her. Her moans ignite something in me, and I crave the taste of her release. She starts to tighten around my fingers and I move my tongue faster, her hips grinding against my mouth. One moan leads to a satisfied scream as she comes around my fingers. I lick her up and down, pressing kisses to the inside of her thighs and letting her ride out her orgasm with my fingers still inside of her.

"Oliver, *please*," she moans. I waste no time grabbing a condom from my bag, slipping it on, and resting myself above her. I push some hair out of her face, and she rests her head in my hand, still panting. I kiss her swollen lips hard as I push into her, groaning as she moans into my mouth.

"*Holy shit*," I mutter, the feeling of being inside her even more vibrant and exhilarating than I remembered.

Elle grips my shoulders as I pump into her, her whines getting louder with every motion. I slow my movements to lean down and kiss her, our tongues connecting in a way that makes me want to thrust into her harder. But she gently pushes me back so that I'm laying towards the end of the bed. She climbs over me, settling her hips on top of mine. I sit up and take one of her breasts in my mouth. At the same time, she reaches down, lining my cock up with her entrance, and sits on top of me. She drags out a moan and I bite her nipple harder.

"*Oh my God*!" she screams, wrapping her arms around my neck. I curse into her chest. She starts to move, pressing her hips against me as she rides me, the friction of it all-consuming. My hands splay against her back and I play with her nipple in my mouth, licking and teasing until her movements take my breath away.

She slows and flips her hair over her shoulders, so I can see a beautiful smile spread across her face. I chuckle as I kiss her, feeling her smile against my lips.

"I love you," I whisper, moving so I can place a kiss below her ear. Her hips move faster again, so she can only manage to mouth the words back to me. I grip her tighter, as if that could make this moment last longer.

Elle cries out as I feel her tighten around me, making me explode at the same time that she screams. I feel her vibrate against me, and I hold her clenching ass as she rides out her release, her hips moving over me as she moans into my ear.

We ride the waves together, shivering and embracing each other, kissing and whispering until we regain our breaths.

We lay there for hours, touching, kissing, talking, one or both of us falling asleep before the other wakes up with a hunger that can only be satisfied by the other. At some point, a little before dawn, Elle rests her head on my chest and squeezes her arms around me, a firmness in her grip. I nod my head towards her, curious at the change in her position.

"I want you to know something," she whispers. I can feel her lips move against the skin of my stomach.

"Mmm?"

"I'm not going to get scared away." She turns her head to look up at me, her chin resting on my ribs. I fold a blonde curl behind her ear. "You were so afraid that I wouldn't be able to handle all your crazy. But I have crazy of my own. And maybe that's why this is different from anyone else before. Because your crazy matches my crazy."

The corner of my mouth lifts up. I pull her up to me, until our foreheads are touching, and she is laying over me completely. She kisses me gently, her lips moving over mine like she can't get enough of the taste. Lucky for me, neither can I.

EPILOGUE

Oliver

"This seems like some touristy shit to me," I tell Elle as she drags me down 57th Street.

"Just because you like to call yourself a New Yorker now doesn't mean I can't show you touristy shit sometimes," she says, pulling me by the hand through a crowd of people.

It's the middle of July in Manhattan, which means it is hot and smelly and disgusting. But of course, none of that bothers Elle, because she has a plan in her head, and I'm just the guy who knows that I'm going to go along with it, whether I want to or not.

The street is absolutely packed with people—some with tripods, some with selfie sticks, but all with their phones out, which is both depressing and really fucking annoying. Elle made us leave our phones at home for this reason. We wouldn't be the gawkers recording this moment. We would be the observers watching it.

Again, I just work here.

She finally finds an acceptable spot on 57th and 8th, which wasn't her ideal spot, but we couldn't make it further East in time. I personally don't think the exact location makes that much of a difference, but when it comes to Elle's plans, my opinions don't really matter. Which I'm fine with. I love when she takes the lead. She calls them her main character moments.

She likes to tell me that we're the main characters of our own stories. I tell her that I don't care about any story that isn't hers. But in truth, she has changed my story. For the better. In every way possible.

After quitting residency, I started working as a paramedic for the FDNY while applying to Physician Assistant programs in the Northeast. I haven't told my father about becoming a P.A. because I don't want him to have anything to do with it. We haven't even spoken since I left my residency at Mount Sinai, but my mom has come to the city to meet Elle. She claims that my father needs time to get past things. I argue that he needs time to recover from the blow to his ego, that he will not have a legacy of Dr. Coles to follow him. I'm sure we'll find a new version of normal, I'm just not sure when, or what that will look like. Elle would love to make that a project of her own, but I refuse to let her. She doesn't have to solve the world's problems. And she's starting to learn that.

One thing Elle has taught me is that it is okay to accept help. She wants me to try speaking to someone about my panic and OCD again, and I think one day soon I will. In the meantime, I have found a medication that is helping with my obsessive thoughts. I've resisted it for so long, but Elle has a way of changing my perspective on things. And I want to feel better. I want to be in control of my own mind. Not just for her, but for me.

Elle stops in the middle of a crowd of people and turns to face the street. She's wearing a tank top with one of her silly sayings on it. Today's is: *"If I can't bring my dog, I'm not coming."* Which is very true in most instances, including this one. I look down at Thor who is pitter-pattering his feet next to Elle. He has no idea what is going on, but he is excited about it nonetheless.

"Ready?" Elle asks, looking up at me. Her long curls are in a ponytail that reaches down to her back, and it sways when she turns her head.

"Ready for what?"

She looks down at her watch and grins. That can't be good. I follow her gaze to the streetlight in front of us. When it turns red, Elle throws herself on my back, wraps her legs around my waist and her arms around my neck.

"Hurry up! Run to the middle of the crosswalk!" she yells, hitting my shoulder. Thor jumps up on my leg, excited by what Elle is doing.

"What? Why?" I say, putting my hands under her thighs so she doesn't slide off of my back.

"Just do it! *Go*!"

I run to the middle of the bustling two-way street with a woman on my back and dog at my side. I stop in the middle where a crowd of people with phones and selfie sticks surround me.

"Now what?" I ask, looking around.

"Look West, dummy!" she says, pointing down the street. I turn and see the sun setting through the towering buildings, casting a bright hue of orange and yellow down

57th Street. I squeeze Elle's legs a little tighter and shake my head.

"Welcome to your first Manhattanhenge," she says, kissing my cheek, then resting her chin on my shoulder.

"Why didn't you just tell me what we were doing?" I ask, turning my head.

"Because it was more fun to surprise you," she says, kissing my neck. Thor is still trying to climb up on me because apparently I look like a human jungle gym right now. "And here's the most fun part," she adds.

"What?"

"CARS! RUN!" Elle screams, her voice full of laughter.

I see the streetlight turn green above me and I race back to the sidewalk, Thor in tow, Elle cackling in my ear, and the rest of the crowd running alongside me. When I get back to the corner, I look down the street and see crowds of people doing the same thing at each crosswalk for as far as I can see. I set Elle down and put my hands on my knees, out of breath.

"You're a weirdo, you know that?" I say, turning to Elle, but I can't help the smile that spreads across my face.

"But I'm your weirdo," she says, smiling right back. I stand up and kiss her because yes, she is.

Her eyes go back to the street. "Red light. Let's go!"

She takes off into the crosswalk again, and I'm pulled into the street with her and the miniature dog that started it all.

ELLE AND OLIVER'S PLAYLIST

Boat / Ed Sheeran

Dark Side / Bishop Briggs

Human / Rag' n' Bone Man

Maybe I'm Afraid / lovelytheband

Surface Pressure / Jessica Dallow

Numb Little Bug / Em Beihold

Curtains / Ed Sheeran

Skin / Rag' n' Bone Man

Lose Control / Teddy Swims

Happy / NF

I Wanna Get Better / Bleachers

ACKNOWLEDGEMENTS

My first thank you will always be to you, the person holding this book. You are making my dream come true. To romance readers everywhere, thank you for welcoming me into the community. Elle and Oliver's story is really special to me, and I hope you love them as much as I do.

Thank you to my agent, Sian Ellis-Martin, for being my emotional support publishing person and fielder of all of my crazy emails and WhatsApp messages. I wouldn't be here without you.

Thank you to Aubrie, Sophie, Holly, and the team at Aria and Head of Zeus for taking a chance on Lucy and Elle. Thank you Sophie for editing the *shit* out of this draft and turning it into the book it is now. And thank you to Holly for getting us to the finish line! Thank you Anna for finding all of my timeline issues and doing an awesome copyedit. Also, thank you to Debs and the art team at HoZ for another gorgeous cover.

Thank you to my friend, Camerin, for brainstorming NYC locations with me. I used them all I think! Also, the word "agape" was for you. I hope you caught it.

Thank you to the booksellers and stores that were so

supportive of my debut. This industry thrives on your love of books and extraordinary support of authors like me. Thank you!

Thank you to my street team (aka Cristina's Wolfpack). These ladies read my first book and volunteered to support me in any way they could. Forever grateful for Erin, Jennifer, Dawn, Tiffani, Mandy, Ashley N., Lizz, Em, Bee, Ashley W., Makenna, Tricia, Kelley, Kayleigh, Katie, and Kathy.

Finally, thank you to my friends and family for your unrelenting support on this journey. From book launch parties, traveling to bookstores and conventions, hosting book clubs, proofreading manuscripts, and being my biggest cheerleaders—thank you.

ABOUT THE AUTHOR

CRISTINA WOLF wrote her first book in the third grade. It was an adventure book about her beagle, Abby, complete with hand-drawn illustrations and top-notch handwriting. Needless to say, writing and reading has been a passion of Cristina's from the beginning. After graduating from Marist College with a double major in Business and English, Cristina pursued a career in the publishing industry while earning her Master of Science in Publishing from New York University. Cristina has experience working at literary agencies and as an editorial assistant at a publishing house. Finding life in NYC a bit different than she expected, Cristina returned to her native New Jersey where she earned her Master in Teaching from Monmouth University. She now shares her love of books with her students as a middle school English teacher.

Other than working or writing, Cristina loves spending time with her dogs, Zoey, Winnie, and Mabel, exercising on her Peloton, laying on her hammock with a good book, and planning her next trip to Disney World. Follow her on Instagram @cwolfbooks.

Stories to fall in love with.

Aria

THANKS FOR READING!

Want to receive exclusive author content, news on the latest Aria books and updates on offers and giveaways?

Follow us on X @AriaFiction and on Facebook and Instagram @HeadofZeus, and join our mailing list.